CARYL PHILLIPS

Caryl Phillips is the author of numerous acclaimed works of fiction and non-fiction, including the novels *Crossing the River* (shortlisted for the Booker Prize 1993) and *A Distant Shore* (winner of the Commonwealth Writers' Prize 2004). Phillips has won the Martin Luther King Memorial Prize, a Guggenheim Fellowship, the PEN Open Book Award and the James Tait Black Memorial Prize, as well as being named the *Sunday Times* Young Writer of the Year 1992 and one of the *Granta* Best of Young British Writers 1993. He has also written for television, radio, theatre and film.

CARYL PHILLIPS

A View of the
Empire at Sunset

VINTAGE

1 3 5 7 9 10 8 6 4 2

Vintage
20 Vauxhall Bridge Road,
London SW1V 2SA

Vintage is part of the Penguin Random House group of companies
whose addresses can be found at global.penguinrandomhouse.com

Penguin
Random House
UK

First published in Vintage in 2018

First published in the United States of America by Farrar, Straus and
Giroux in 2018

penguin.co.uk/vintage

A CIP catalogue record for this book is available from the British Library

ISBN 9781784709013

Printed and bound by Clays Ltd, St Ives Plc

Penguin Random House is committed to a sustainable future for
our business, our readers and our planet. This book is made
from Forest Stewardship Council® certified paper.

For Lucien and Andre

Contents

I

Going Home

1

Going Home

The bleak afternoon had been made all the more dispiriting by having to overhear Leslie on the telephone busying himself with his attempts to make arrangements for their potential sea voyage. Finally, her husband sat down heavily in the armchair and began to annoy her by continually seeking reassurance that the recent misunderstanding between them was now resolved. After sharing a life together for nearly eight years, her husband still seems incapable of admitting that things between them have never been quite right. He has, as he promised her he would, attempted to provide her with a stable financial environment that might compensate for her difficult down-at-heel years on the Continent, but his efforts in this department have been an unquestionable failure. Keen to please her in other respects, he has tried to demand little of her in the way of an explanation of both her past and her present, and she has certainly never pressed him about his own history, but as a consequence, she often feels as though they barely know each other and she wonders if the decent thing to do would be to release this man from what he once referred to as "occasionally boorish behaviour."

She is standing in deep shadow to the side of the bay window in their lacklustre Bloomsbury living room and staring out at the leafless oak trees that decorate the iron-gated square. Then, recognizing that she has temporarily forsaken her husband, she turns towards him and smiles weakly, and Leslie's nervous face lights up with relief.

Eventually her tired husband empties his pipe and slowly rises from the armchair. He slips on his jacket and overcoat and cheerily announces that he is stepping out for a twilight stroll. She hears the front door rattle shut and then looks down into the lamplit street and watches him striding away from the house, and this is her prompt to pick up the small stool and carry it through into the bedroom. Having carefully eased the shabby suitcase from its hiding place on top of the narrow wardrobe, she places it lengthwise on the bed and opens it in a manner that causes the dusty object to unexpectedly resemble a book. Only now (as she tries to ignore the freckles of age that are beginning to pepper the backs of her hands) does it occur to her that there are two problems. First, she is unsure of just how long Leslie imagines they might tarry in the West Indies; second, she doesn't own anything that will be even vaguely suitable once they reach their tropical destination. In England she has come to understand that a nice bright shawl and a decent pair of shoes will typically suffice to fool most people, but back home eyes are more discerning and she will be held to higher standards. Once she returns to the West Indies, she has no desire to make an exhibition of herself.

She sits wearily on the edge of the bed and tries hard to reconcile herself to the fact that a woman who has journeyed even a short distance beyond the age of forty no longer has any right to expect admiring glances, but she continues to find it difficult to abandon all hope. Of course, money would help to ease the embarrassment of the spectacle she presents, but any mention of the thorny subject tends to plunge Leslie into a monosyllabic mood. Last night, however, her husband surprised her with talk of an unforeseen windfall and the possibility of a voyage to the West Indies. She stands and opens both the top and the bottom drawers of the dresser and confronts the reality of her situation; it is true, there is not a single article of clothing that merits serious consideration for the upcoming journey, for, having been washed and ironed too frequently, all of her clothes are shiny and hideous in appearance. Having closed the drawers to the dresser, she shuts the empty suitcase and turns the key in the tiny lock. Leslie's frustrating telephone calls have led her to believe that it might well be weeks before her husband secures confirmation of their passage, for apparently winter is the most popular season in which to set sail for the region. This being the case, there is still time for her to broach the idea of a shopping expedition, but not quite yet, for betraying either enthusiasm or anxiety has never played any part in the detached manner in which she generally likes to conduct herself with her overly sensitive husband.

Last Saturday night there was no need for Leslie to burst into The Rose and Crown and embarrass her in front of everyone. He took her firmly by the arm and ordered her to be quiet, and then topped his performance by apologizing to the stupid landlord for *her* behaviour. ("I'm so sorry, but I'm afraid there's a little bit of a drink problem.") But what she was saying was correct: unless somebody woke up and took notice, this new chancellor, Herr Hitler, would soon be tramping his muddy boots all over the map of Europe. It wasn't as though anybody in the pub disagreed with her, but at some point the landlord must have telephoned her husband, for suddenly Leslie made his entrance and began to coax her towards the door, all the while urging her, with an impatient sharpness, to please moderate her behaviour. When she started to shout, he barked at her in a firm whisper, telling her to either hold her tongue or keep it down. "You seem to be unaware of the ill nature of the emotions you arouse." She snatched her arm away and smartened up her dress with the palm of her hands, then she reminded him that the only reason she had come out for a quiet drink to begin with was to get away from his miserable presence, which was creating a foul atmosphere in their rooms. Once they were out on the pavement, and safely beyond the hearing of those in the pub, Leslie stared at her with a strangely distracted look on his face before raising his tone and beginning to affect a modulation that the poor man clearly hoped might come across as authoritative. "Why, Gwen, do you insist on leaving your good sense in glass after glass of wine? I'm afraid I simply don't understand you."

All day Sunday she refused to talk to him, although he tried desperately to be pleasant. He asked her to please try and understand why he had been forced to remove her from the pub. "Dearest, it was a bad business. You were talking loudly to yourself, and the patrons were simply ignoring you." But what rot, they were not ignoring her, they were asking if she was actually in sympathy with this Herr Hitler, which they must have known was a stupid question. "Of course I'm not," she said. "I speak French, not German. Why would I want to begin the process of acquiring another bloody language?" By late Monday afternoon she had decided to allow things between herself and Leslie to thaw a little, for she could sense that her demure husband was troubled by a letter he had received in the morning's post. She tied on a headscarf and, without a trace of bitterness, asked if there was anything he would like her to pick up, as she intended to venture out to the shops. A newspaper, perhaps? Her husband smiled and shook his head. "No, thank you, Gwendolen. I'll just listen to the evening news on the wireless." When she returned, he poured them both a glass of sherry and then looked up and wondered if she might consider discontinuing her two-night exile on the sofa. Before she had time to frame a response, he pressed on and shared with her today's surprising revelation regarding an unexpected legacy from his late father, the Reverend Tilden Smith. He held the solicitor's embossed stationery in both hands as though it were some kind of offering and suggested that now that he appeared to be "in funds" it might make sense to think about renting a nicer place, perhaps in Chelsea. Meanwhile, he wondered if she would be amenable to his treating them both to a voyage to the West Indies, for he understood how desperately she wished once again to see her birthplace. He paused, his brow wrinkled in perplexity as though unsure how his suggestion might be received, but she said nothing and so he felt obliged to continue. He informed her that he had some inkling of how much it might mean to her to reacquaint herself with her island. Was a West Indian sea voyage something she might consider?

2

The Letter

The short note had evidently been typed on an old machine with keys that were misaligned, and then folded into an envelope and addressed with a painstakingly precise hand. It was difficult to read all of the words, for the imprint of some of the letters created only an indistinct smudge and the number of brief handwritten emendations suggested that her brother was most likely mortified by the limitations of the instrument, whose ribbon was also in need of replacement. Owen had written to her "in the hope that she might find it in her heart to forgive his recent silence," and he explained that he had been suffering some difficulties with his health. He had, however, been pleased to receive her communication with the exciting news of her impending voyage, and he now wished to broach a matter of some delicacy. Straightaway, he wanted to stress that it was not his intention to press for repayment of the five-pound note he had sent to her earlier in the year, but he once again asked that she never mention the offering in the presence of his wife. Clearly her sister-in-law's sentiment that she was little more than a pretentious dilettante remained unchanged, and she fully understood her brother's dread. After all, he was unemployed and struggling to support Dorothy and their six-year-old son, so the revelation that he had given money to his self-indulgent sister would most likely strike a body blow to his marriage.

The letter had arrived with the second post, and she had sat huddled in the armchair and read the three concise paragraphs by the light of the dim bulb in the metal standard lamp. She then placed the single sheet of paper on the low table in front of her and made her way across the room, where she filled the kettle and proceeded to boil some water for tea. Having made a particularly strong cup, she returned to the armchair and reread the letter, once again noting the perturbed but scrupulously polite tone in which it was written. And then she read it once more. Her brother had recently returned from Australia with yet another failed business venture to his name, and she worried greatly about his state of mind. In fact, her childhood memories of the free-spirited older brother she so admired were now in danger of being permanently obscured by the words of this frightened, guilt-stricken man who was writing to her from some unfashionable suburb south of London.

That evening her husband returned from having spent the greater part of the day visiting various West End travel agencies. He sat and threaded his hands together before informing her that because most vessels were already overbooked and the shipping lines were operating a sparse midwinter schedule, it was now clear that they would have to wait until February to undertake their voyage. The good news was, however, that he had gone ahead and purchased their tickets. In the meantime, he wondered if they might perhaps seize the opportunity provided by the delay and take advantage of the unseasonably mild weather by embarking upon a weekend-long excursion to the Sussex coast. Doing so, they would be able to temporarily escape London and take in some of the English countryside, but he spoke to her as though he were tendering the glories of pastoral England as some kind of gift. All those cows lolling around, she thought, and idle sheep, and silly little bushy fences. A gift would be the chance to see her thirteen-year-old daughter in Holland and once again try to forge some kind of relationship with the girl. Or perhaps Maryvonne could come and visit with them in London? Why spend this sudden influx of money on Sussex when she longed to see her somewhat truculent child? She looked across at Leslie, his eyes now closed and his head thrown back onto the antimacassar as though listening to his favourite Brahms or Handel on the wireless, and she wanted to tell him that his beloved English countryside held no interest for her, but she decided to be generous and leave the exhausted man in peace.

Later that evening, after the regular whine of his breathing suggested that he had finally succumbed to sleep, she eased out of her narrow bed and made her way into the living room, where she poured a large glass of red wine. She sat back on the dimpled leather sofa and cradled the wine in both hands. No doubt her husband had convinced himself that after a relaxing trip to the Sussex coast he might look forward to a marked improvement in her behaviour. This was precisely the kind of phrase that Leslie loved to use. "Marked improvement." The truth is, Leslie should have been a prep school master or a man of the cloth like his father. She took another sip of wine and then slipped the letter out of its envelope and began to reread it. To her mind, as a young man her brother had carried on with an admirable streak of rebelliousness, although there were those who expected better from the privileged child of a colonial doctor. Sadly, his subsequent career failures in Canada, and more recently in Australia, had evidently left him a reduced man. Having received the surprising news from his sister that she intended to return home for a short visit, he was now asking her to help him repair some of the damage he had caused in his youth, but he was framing his request as though he bore little real responsibility for his earlier actions. She took yet another sip of red wine and replaced Owen's letter in its envelope.

3

Rivers and Mountains

Last night, after she had finished the red wine and then discovered where Leslie had hidden the bottle of whisky, she clumsily knocked over an empty glass and watched as it spiraled to the floor and smashed. Almost immediately her glum-looking husband appeared in the doorway in his belted dressing gown, and as she knelt and began to gather up the pieces, he gazed down at her with a strange combination of poorly disguised exasperation and forgiveness. His intrinsic kindness annoyed her, and she rose unsteadily to her feet and told him that when they returned from the West Indies he should forget about the idea of using what remained of his father's money and moving into a more spacious Chelsea flat. Going their separate ways might well be a better option. Leslie said nothing and stared blankly at her before slowly turning and trudging back in the direction of the bedroom. She was actually offering her husband a chance to unshackle himself from the past eight years, but the stubborn man seemed incapable of accepting the fact that his wife was, and always would be, beyond his control. Over the years she often asked herself what on earth would have happened to him if she had not entered his life. Has he ever considered this? They both know that he has neither the resources, nor is he cut from the right cloth, to have ever contemplated joining a gentlemen's club where he might while away the hours and pretend to prefer the civilized company of other men as a substitute for his failure to establish a satisfactory relationship with the opposite sex. Without her he would, she imagines, most likely have already drifted into a single room somewhere on the Pentonville Road and be attempting to ckc out a bachelor existence on the fringes of so-called literary London. Instead, the poor man has a wife whose looks have long since fled the scene, and who no longer merits a second glance. It is clear that she is a woman who is utterly incapable of helping her husband achieve any form of social or professional elevation, so why on earth can't he accept how things are? After all, he is still handsome enough to attract another woman, but sadly, timid Leslie will most likely never find anybody else, for it is simply not in his nature to extend himself when confronted with the tyranny of female charm. He did so with her, but she can see in his sometimes dejected eyes that he now understands this to have been a mistake, for, as was the case with his first wife, he has absolutely no notion of how to bring a woman to heel.

It is now late afternoon and she is curled up on the sofa drinking tea and watching her husband, who sits sullenly at the small dining table with a plate of bread and cheese before him. He is indulging his habit of stuffing oversized portions of bread into his mouth which take an eternity for him to swallow. He occasionally glances in her direction in the hope that some contact might force her to speak, but she says nothing, and so he breaks the gloomy silence and addresses her with resignation. "You're slipping away from me, aren't you?" The weak light filtering through the bay window is picking out the lines on his face and causing the grey strands in his hair to periodically sparkle. She looks at a visibly distressed Leslie and thinks back to their original appointment at his cramped office. Initially she had hoped she might encounter a mature man whose confidence was born of years of experience, and who possessed a deep rumbling laugh and exuded a leathery smell of cologne on salty skin, but when she took up a seat on the other side of this man's desk she looked closely into his eyes and searched in vain for any sign of authority. Unfortunately, long before the end of their first meeting it was clear that this prudent man was certainly not the savior she was hoping for, but what choice did she have?

He pushes the plate away and leans back in the chair. "Are you truly determined to leave me, Gwen?" She smiles, but says nothing, and then reminds herself that it has always been so much easier for them to talk about plans as opposed to feelings. My dear Leslie, you have now purchased the tickets for our transatlantic voyage, so let us just go to the West Indies. I will show you the public gardens by the library where I used to sit as a girl and stare out at the sea and try to imagine the world beyond my island. But, of course, I had no real conception of what lay beyond the horizon. I will show you rays of sunlight filtering through clouds, and ribbons of water falling from palm fronds and grooving trenches into the earth. We two can lie in a hollow and witness the shimmer of late-afternoon heat making corrugated iron of the air, and listen to a nearby stream trickling noisily over smooth stones, and watch a puff of wind grow hurriedly into a sudden squall and begin to playfully bend the trees. I will show you the rivers and the mountains, and come evening, as the New World day convulses towards dusk, I will share with you a spectacular elevated view of the empire at sunset. Perhaps, my husband, if I show you the West Indies, then you will finally come to understand that I am not of your world, and maybe then you will appreciate the indignity I feel at not only having to live among you people but possibly die among you, too. I am so sorry. Truly I am, for I have no yearning to cause you hurt. Her husband continues to look at her and he waits patiently for an answer to his question, and so she offers him one that she knows will be received with skepticism. "No, Leslie, I am not determined to leave you." She pauses and tries to discover a second, and more comforting, half to the sentence, but words elude her.

II

Home

4

Sister Mary

Sister Mary's voice and mannerisms were gentle and pleasant, while those of the other nuns were harsh and unforgiving. If a girl arrived late, Sister Mary would encourage her to take a seat and ask for an explanation only at break, after everyone had left the schoolroom. Should a child find herself the object of teasing or laughter, the young nun would rescue the situation by turning on one of the persecutors and quietly asking her a question designed to still her tongue. At Christmas the class presented Sister Mary with a floral bouquet, which was a mishmash of individual flowers collected by each pupil and clumsily tied together with a purple ribbon. Sister Mary picked up the limp bunch from her desk and cradled it in her arms as one might a newborn child. The young nun then buried her face in the scent, but she could see that her teacher did so only in order that her tears would not be visible to the girls. After Christmas, Sister Mary let them down by not returning to the school. Initially, it was unclear why a rather fierce replacement was teaching their class, but being the daughter of the medical officer she knew that their teacher was ill. However, after three weeks—during which time they were not offered any explanation—she took it upon herself to raise her hand and ask after Sister Mary. In a firm and clearly irritated voice, the new nun announced that Sister Mary was not well, and it was unlikely that she would be resuming her duties at the school, and a collective sigh of disappointment filled the small classroom.

The following Sunday afternoon she and her friend Gussie de Freitas set out on a short, private adventure up into the hills behind Roseau. A month ago on New Year's Day, her father had travelled up to the Flambeau Plantation to visit Sister Mary, but when her father returned, he failed to mention the young nun, although he had plenty to say about the unhygienic condition of the Great House. Apparently the old widow who lived on the now-neglected estate still maintained the ground floor of the property and Sister Mary had taken a room there. She overheard her father telling her mother that he had recommended to the young nun that she urgently find alternative accommodation, but the stubborn girl claimed to be content where she was. On a sweltering Sunday afternoon that was particularly heavy with the unapologetic lassitude of the Sabbath, she watched transfixed as Gussie laboured up the three stone steps and knocked loudly at the door to the dilapidated Great House, whose once proud fluted pillars were now rotten with age, while what little paint remained upon them was blistered and peeling. It was the old lady herself who opened up, and she appeared before the pair of them squinting painfully into the bright light. Gussie made polite inquiry after Sister Mary, but having carefully scrutinized her unexpected visitors, the old lady motioned with her heavily veined hand that they should remain where they stood, and she then disappeared into the house.

On their way back into Roseau the two girls stopped by the river and sat together on a steep grassy bank that was fenced in by wild clusters of ridged bamboo that flared skywards. She looked on as Gussie tossed small stones into the water, and it was her friend who found the first words.

"Sister Mary didn't look like Sister Mary."

The old lady had escorted them across the full breadth of a large room that was full of sheeted furniture, and she was terrified, for she was sure that cockroaches and centipedes were most likely hiding beneath these flimsy shrouds. Thereafter, they were ushered into a bedroom where Sister Mary lay propped up among a collection of pillows, but the heat was suffocatingly intense and felt as though it had been trapped in the room for many days and nights. The young nun's eyes appeared to have sunk into her head, and her two arms—which lay lifeless on top of the sheets—were smooth and twisted like thin willow branches. The old lady dabbed gently at Sister Mary's lips with a moist cloth, but this didn't appear to help relieve the young woman's distress. Sister Mary could no longer make any words with her mouth.

Climbing to her feet, she turned her back to the river and addressed Gussie.

"Let's not tell anybody about Sister Mary. We should forget that we ever went there."

Gussie continued to pitch small stones into the river, but eventually she looked up.

"Alright," she said. "We never went there."

She continued to stand, but a vast distance suddenly seemed to have opened up between herself and Gussie, and she didn't possess the words to explain the strange sadness of the feelings that were now coursing through her small body. For the remainder of the afternoon, the two friends lingered by the riverbank and listened to the unhappy repetition of birds plaintively calling out to each other.

Towards the end of the Easter holidays she sat with her father on the veranda and watched as he closed his newspaper. When her mother came out to say "Good night," her father announced that the Irish nun that he had been treating for the past year had just left this world at the tender age of twenty-four. He began to shake his head, but refused to face his daughter, and then he muttered that for some time now it had been clear to him that nothing could be done for the poor nun. He sighed and returned to his newspaper. She understood that as a nine-year-old girl she was too young for a full explanation, but if only her father could have found a way to extend himself a little further in her direction and share with her what he was truly thinking, this would have helped. Poor Sister Mary. They had brought her flowers and shown her loyalty. Devotion, even. But her father chose not to offer any explanation to his daughter as to why the young nun had decided to forsake them in this way, and for what remained of the Easter holidays she felt betrayed by both Sister Mary and her father.

5

Francine

Every Sunday morning she would stand by the window and watch as the Negro made his slow way up the street towards the house with his young daughter in tow. Francine would be clutching her father's hand, but as they moved closer, the girl would suddenly break free and run expectantly in the direction of the iron gate that led into the yard and shout for her friend, "Gwennie!" Her mother was usually in the kitchen instructing Josephine the cook, who would be busily preparing Sunday lunch. Drying her hands on a towel, her mother would step out into the yard, where her daughter would now be waiting. Her mother would cast her ten-year-old child a quick knowing glance, while trying to disguise the fact that her mind was once again contracting into judgment and disapproval.

Francine was generally out of breath, and her eager eyes betrayed her excitement as she shifted her weight from one foot to the other. Her sturdy father would come up behind her in his sober church clothes and, sporting a black hat with a particularly wide brim and placing a gentle hand on his child's shoulder, the Negro would remind his daughter to work hard in the kitchen and not cause Mrs. Williams any bother, but her mother would always assure the man that Francine was never any trouble whatsoever. Satisfied that everything was in order, the Negro would touch his hat and then set about his yard work. Francine had an uncomplicated roster of tasks to perform in the kitchen, but as soon as they were done, she frequently seemed to have an idea of what the two of them ought to do, be it a quick sprint down to the river to pick a batch of wildflowers or a fierce determination that they should engage in a search for a particular bird or lizard that had recently captured her imagination. Everything with Francine was an adventure, and although she occasionally felt obliged to throw up an objection to her friend's suggestions based on either the weather or the sheer impracticality of the plan, she would invariably have nothing to offer in its place, and so she inevitably capitulated to Francine's schemes.

One week they might amuse themselves by crawling around the empty marketplace on all fours playing "zoo"; the following week Francine might suggest a sandy spot by the bayfront that would be perfect for them to once again play castaway and native, with Francine always assuming the role of the tragically helpless castaway. She sang songs with Francine, the words of which she seldom fully understood, and her friend taught her how to dance with a freedom below her waist that she intuitively understood to be unseemly. However, all of this took place beyond her mother's eyes, and although the two girls were often tired and dirty by the time they returned to the house, her mother always greeted them with two glasses of juice and allowed them to sit together on the veranda and eat sandwiches, while Francine's father squatted near the gate and ate from a small package that he normally carried tucked beneath his arm. Once the girls had finished, it was her mother who took it upon herself to come and clear their things, and it was understood that this was the signal for Francine to get to her feet and rejoin her father. Mother and daughter watched as the Negro girl made her reluctant way to the gate, and then, together with her father, her friend began to slowly amble her way back down the street.

During the hottest weeks of the summer her mother decided to pack her off to be with her great-aunt at the family's Geneva estate, but she missed Francine. On the Sunday after she returned from the cool of the mountains she saw her friend cantering up the street with a scrap of mongrel on a long piece of string and the girl's father making no attempt to keep pace with his child. She began to laugh gleefully at Francine's latest gesture of willful eccentricity, and then she glanced up and noticed the look of antipathy on her mother's face. She already knew that her mother was filled with hostility towards Negroes, and clearly disapproved of any extended period of exposure to their presence, but she was now beginning to realize that her mother's irrational fear of Negroes was yet another example of the increasingly unbridgeable gap of understanding that was opening up between them. Luckily, her friend appeared to be oblivious to her mother's discomfort, and by the time Francine had shown her how to feed the puppy pieces of jackfruit, and let her cradle the whelp in her arms, she was convinced that she too wanted one. Her memories of the few weeks that she had spent at the family estate, and the books that she had read, and the long solitary walks that she had taken in the rainforest wondering when her breasts might appear and if anybody might be interested in them, all quickly disappeared from her mind. Later that same day, after Francine and her father had departed, she announced to her mother that she too would like a puppy on a long piece of string, but her mother avoided her gaze and pretended that she hadn't heard her daughter's voice.

The following week Francine slipped her hand from that of her father and ran up the street and knocked at the iron gate to the yard. Her mother rose imperiously to her feet and instructed her embittered daughter to remain where she was in the tranquility of the living room with her book spread open on her knees. Sunlight slanted through the jalousies and cast an oddly striped pattern across the floor, and she listened as her mother stepped out into the yard. Before the Negro girl could ask for her friend, Mrs. Williams's sugar-coated voice made it clear that Gwendolen was resting. Furthermore, it was simply too hot for her daughter to be out in the sun. Her mother suggested that on such a particularly scorching morning it might well be more comfortable for Francine if she went straight to work in the kitchen, thereby securing some shelter from the heat. Francine's father arrived at his daughter's side and immediately detected a new register in his employer's voice, one which his child was not yet attuned to. He took hold of his girl's arm and thanked Mrs. Williams for her thoughtfulness. Francine would spend her last day as an employee working in the relative coolness of the kitchen with the other household servants.

6

The Mango Tree

She peers down at the washerwoman standing in the yard beneath the huge mango tree and decides that if necessary she will stay up in the branches all night. Miss Ann points at her. "You think I can't see you up there, hiding like a damn monkey." The woman puts both hands on her hips and continues to look up at the raggedy head of the great tree, which casts a heavy shadow across the whole yard. "Child, you can play big woman with your mother, but you don't fool any of we. Why you can't behave your backside and come down? You too damn willful." Eventually Miss Ann gives up and sits on a stool next to Josephine the cook, and the two servants begin to laugh.

Whenever people suggested to her mother that girls were more trouble than boys, her mother always expressed surprise. After all, her first child, Edward, had gone off to study medicine and seemed disinclined to communicate with anybody, while Owen's waywardness continued to embarrass the family. It was Owen who kept her mother awake at nights, for the second son seemed determined to do whatever he pleased without any regard for the consequences. He was habitually absent without explanation, and when he did show his face, one could be sure that complications, almost invariably connected to local Negresses, would soon follow him in through the door. The girls were easier; the eldest, Minna, had been sent to live with relatives in the Bahamas, which left just herself and her younger sister, Brenda, who besported herself as an obedient angel. These days, however, it was her own stubborn eleven-year-old behaviour that was making her mother fretful and causing her to wonder if perhaps there *was*, in fact, some truth to the belief that girls were more trouble than boys.

On the day the island learned that the Empress had died, her mother decided that she would hold a small tea party on the veranda for her group of ladies. The men had hurried off to Government House to mingle on the manicured lawn and raise their glasses and begin to make plans for a more official event, but it seemed important to her mother that the formally gloved ladies of the island mark the passing of Queen Victoria with an impromptu gathering of their own. To this end, her mother had asked Miss Ann, the washerwoman, to lay out Sunday-best dresses for Gwendolen and Brenda on their beds, and she instructed the woman to thereafter join Josephine in the kitchen and set about preparing tea and cakes for no more than a dozen guests. As she sat on the edge of her bed and watched a skittish Brenda eagerly changing into her dress, she decided there was no reason for her to take part in this ridiculous afternoon tea. She tossed her clean dress to one side, and then marched purposefully downstairs and out into the yard, where she saw the rangy cook scraping yams while crouched unsteadily on her three-legged stool.

"Child, why you looking so vex?"

The question surprised her, for she was trying hard to appear as though she didn't have a care in the world. Josephine scratched her squat nose and then hitched up her shapeless sackcloth dress and laughed at her.

"I already tell you if you want to survive in this world you mustn't let people read what you thinking. Now change your face."

She looked at the barefoot woman, who she feared was some kind of obeah woman, and then she began to scurry away, for Josephine had from time to time tormented her with cockroaches and spiders and centipedes, all of which she knew terrified the young mistress.

"You just wait a minute."

Josephine put her provisions down on the ground and stood up. "Look at me and straighten up your mouth." She stopped and turned to face the cook. "Good, now your mouth is fixed I want you to look yonder with your eyes, and don't blink. That is how your face must be when you talk with people, you hear? Make your eyes dead like so."

She did as Josephine suggested.

"Good. That is good. Everything is in the eyes."

Her frustrated mother stood in the doorway to the bedroom and shouted at Brenda and demanded that she go and bring her sister inside, but Brenda began to cry. Feeling as though she might at any moment burst with anger, her mother passed quickly downstairs and out into the yard and approached the cook, who, having repositioned herself on her stool, spoke without looking up.

"Mistress, I believe the child just gone up in the mango tree."

Knowing that her ladies would be arriving imminently, her mother strode across the yard to the foot of the tree, flapping a garden hat to fan herself.

"Gwendolen, I insist you come down here this instant."

Miss Ann returned from the bakery with a basketful of goods, and she entered the yard and began to talk rapidly with the cook, but her mother had no idea what the two Negresses were saying. Then a still-sobbing Brenda appeared, and conscientiously holding the hem of her dress clear of the dirt, she joined her mother, and together they craned back their necks and squinted up into the bushy underbelly of the tree.

"For heaven's sake," continued her mother, "the Empress has died. Show some respect."

She ignored her mother and looked at the red rust on the roofs which, from this height, she could see leafing their way downhill towards Mr. Bell's pier, where an old launch had been moored for the greater part of the day. As she stared out towards the horizon, she knew that soon she would be able to witness the final defiant ignition of the sun as it slid into the sea and flashed its farewell for the day. This was her town, and from her perch in the mango tree she could see the full extent of the capital and she couldn't understand why anybody would want to board a ship and leave such a place. Then, confident that nobody could see her, she rubbed a hand across her chest and once again made sure she was finally budding.

It wouldn't be too long now, and she imagined that her mother's anxieties about her would only increase once she began to secure the attention of men. Suddenly a fruit plummeted with a heavy thud from an overladen branch into the yard below. She looked directly down through the branches and could see that her mother was beginning to appear foolish, for her eleven-year-old daughter was hidden away out of sight, and to any onlooker it would appear as though her mother had taken leave of her senses and was addressing a mango tree.

"Please, you must come down here where I can talk properly with you, or your father shall hear about this." Brenda gently touched her mother's arm. "Young lady, do you hear me?"

Dusk fell at the same time each evening, and it did so swiftly, as though an expert finger and thumb were snuffing out a candle. Thereafter, a theatre of noise established itself as the air was filled with a discordant fracas of cicadas and frogs. She listened attentively, while, to both sides of her, bats began to swoop and whistle around the mango tree. She could hear the low hum and clatter of the ladies taking tea on the veranda, and she could see the agitated shadow of her mother fluttering about and trying to steer the evening along a course that might be considered both solemn and convivial. She knew her mother would be assuring them all that although they had suffered a great loss, there would indeed be a new beginning. Her father, on the other hand, would be standing under one of the great saman trees in the garden of Government House and accepting yet another glass of whisky from a silver tray borne by one of the liveried Negroes who had been trained to serve. Her father's mind would be unruffled by what he would regard as sentimental tosh about the passing of Queen Victoria. After all, death was a physical fact, and even though in the case of this particular individual it marked a moment of incontestable historical significance, it remained an occurrence that was a familiar part of his professional routine. She slapped a mosquito off her arm, and then inhaled the sickly sweet aroma of the night lilies, which drifted up in her direction. Immediately beneath her she could hear Miss Ann and Josephine talking as they sat together in the yard waiting for the tea party to conclude.

"The child something, eh?"

Miss Ann shook her head. "It look to me like Miss Gwendolen catch somewhere between coloured and white."

"Maybe so, maybe so."

They were silent for a moment, and then the cook reached down and rubbed a foot whose skin was as calloused as that of a horned toad before lighting a small clay pipe.

"Mind you, if a child of mine ever speak to me like the girl speak to the mother, then the child going feel my hand."

Miss Ann nodded in agreement and then used the front of her apron to wipe the perspiration from her brow. The washerwoman stood and stared up into the tree. Then she pointed.

"You think I can't see you up there, hiding like a damn monkey."

7

The Day Trip

For the past hour, she has sat anxiously on the edge of the pier with her legs dangling over the side, studiously ignoring the end-of-the-day bustle along the bayfront. Instead, her eyes have been firmly fixed on the horizon, hoping to catch sight of the boat in which her father is journeying home. At the height of the afternoon, when the sun is at its most cruel, the young girl from across the street shouted and disturbed her as she sat reading on the covered veranda. The girl suggested they play a game of hopscotch, and so she put down her book and let the Negress into the yard, but after a few minutes the stubborn girl abruptly lost patience with being told what to do and turned on her and called her a "white cockroach." Without hesitation she dispatched a stone in the direction of the girl, but it missed and clattered against the iron gate, whereupon Josephine appeared. The forbidding woman looked from one child to the other before targeting her with a cold stare and promising to put an obeah spell on her. "You little white devil, maybe it's only this will fix you for good." She was familiar with the cook's idle threats, but this time there was something unnerving about the way in which Josephine glowered at her. She darted past both the cook and the Negro girl, and ran into the house and bound up the stairs where she shut the door to her bedroom and sat trembling on her bed. She sat in silence and waited until late afternoon before hurrying downstairs and passing straight out onto the street. When she heard her mother call to her from inside the house, she hitched up her skirt and began to scamper in the direction of the bayfront.

Finally, she sees her father's vessel, which to her squinting eyes appears to be a distant black smudge mournfully steaming its sluggish way north towards Roseau. As it moves closer, the ship achieves only an indistinct outline, for by now the sun has already slipped into the sea and above her head the tired pelicans are little more than gliding silhouettes. As the men begin to step from the bobbing steamer, the twenty or so members of the Executive Council seem relieved to have survived the squally passage, and they chatter excitedly now that they are home. However, she is surprised to detect any gaiety in the air, for after all, the purpose of their day trip has been a sombre one. The steamer had left Roseau at dawn, and together with the other men, her father had undertaken a journey to inspect the site of the tragedy that had occurred some six weeks earlier when Morne Pelée had erupted on the neighbouring island of Martinique, killing all the inhabitants of the capital, Saint-Pierre. She makes a visor with her hand and can see that her father is one of the last to step ashore. Like the other council members, he seems reassured to have once again returned to Dominica, although he is clearly taken aback to see his daughter waiting for him on the pier. As he moves towards her, he offers his child a hesitant wave.

"My dear, is everything alright?"

She nods her head and then smiles weakly, unsure if her presence is displeasing to him.

"I take it your mother knows where you are?"

She ignores the question and surveys the stooped greyish apparition that is her father. His clothes and boots are coated with a thin layer of ash that the channel crossing has evidently failed to blow off. Noticing her quizzical scrutiny of his condition, her father apologizes for his appearance and then turns and slowly points a finger in the general direction of Martinique.

"Let me tell you, the southernmost portion of the island is burned grey and hideously disfigured, as though a mantle of green skin has been peeled back from the body." He pauses as though embarrassed to have resorted to such a gruesome medical image, but his daughter stares at her father and silently encourages him to continue. "And the city itself, which I remember as a decidedly pretty and civilized place, is reduced to a smouldering heap of black stones and mud, above which there hovers a ghastly stench of rotting flesh. But, my dear Gwennie, let us please talk no more of this. The whole day has been too much."

He looks down at her and smiles, and then it becomes clear to her that her father has been drinking. As ever, he lacks companionship, and had she not made the effort to meet him coming off the steamer at the completion of this most distressing of days, the poor man would have been abandoned to walk home by himself. She studies her glassy-eyed father and decides to wait until tomorrow to tell him about the young

Negress calling her a "white cockroach" and Josephine's sub-sequent threats. Her father brushes some ash from his jacket before the pair of them begin to move off, and for the initial part of their journey they are accompanied by a visibly ribbed dog who walks jauntily beside them with the devil-may-care air of a nomad.

As the evening gloom inks the final streaks of light from the sky, they leave behind the bayfront and enter Roseau proper. They pass by neat houses which she knows boast tiny bougainvillea-choked gardens, and every second or third property proudly displays a chained basket or two of orchids hanging below the elaborate gable fretwork. When they reach the elbow where Old Street crosses Cork Street, her unsteady father suddenly stops and produces a pair of small gnarled brass candlesticks from beneath his jacket.

"I pulled them from the ruins of a church. You may hold them if you wish."

He passes the partially melted objects to his daughter, who takes one in each hand.

"The heat must have been passionate to cause such dis-figuration, don't you think? Apparently, in just forty-five seconds, and with little in the way of an announcement, the Paris of the Antilles was rendered a total ruin. Can you be-lieve that thirty thousand people were stifled by just one deadly cloud? Furthermore, in the avalanche of sliding earth I tell you not a building has been left standing. We have all, every last man jack of us, spent a whole day scrambling about in mud, but to what purpose?"

Her father realizes he is talking too much and gently touches the crown of her head with an open palm. He then turns to move off, but as he does so, he stumbles and she throws out a reed of an arm to prevent him from falling, but he quickly rights himself and then retrieves the candlesticks from her.

"I thought your mother might like them. As a souvenir of the day."

But they are both fully aware that her mother will look upon her father's gift with derision. Should she be pressed to take the candlesticks, her mother will undoubtedly push them to the back of a cupboard and immediately forget about their existence, and so perhaps the reality is that her father has brought the candlesticks for her. Is this possible?

When they arrive at the door to the house, her weary father experiences some difficulty placing the key in the lock. He shouts for his wife (*"Minna!"*), but his voice echoes weakly in the night air and his halfhearted plea-cum-announcement remains unanswered. She surreptitiously glances up and down the street, for her father appears to be oblivious of the fact that he is in danger of making a spectacle of himself. Fortunately, the key turns on her father's second attempt, and she ushers him into the tomb-like silence of the house and closes the door behind them. Miss Ann, the washerwoman, would have long ago gone home for the evening, and her mother and sister have evidently retired to their respective bedrooms. Once again her father passes his daughter the twisted candlesticks.

"Take them and set them where your mother might see them in the morning."

She waits until her bleary father has slumped down into a wicker chair on the veranda, and then she passes into the living room, where she gently sets the candlesticks down on the table and then turns up the flame of a small kerosene-oil lamp. Glancing over her shoulder at her father, she realizes that she has made the correct decision; this is not the time to complain to him about Josephine or the girl. After all, the tiresome cook has intimidated her before, and she will do so again, and her father is mindful of the woman's bizarre disposition. Last month, when news reached them of the tragedy on Martinique, the strange woman fell to her knees in the yard and proclaimed the volcanic eruption to be an act of divine punishment. "Everybody know the town is a wicked place and the women don't have no shame. Lord have mercy, Judgment Day reach." As the fine grey ash continued to fall from the sky and coat Roseau in a chalky layer, Josephine's doleful lament was taken up in other yards, so that by dusk everybody in town was subject to a mournful outpouring of biblically inspired grief that echoed across the full breadth of the small capital.

She steps back onto the veranda and realizes that her father's snoring has suddenly achieved a deep, sonorous regularity, which means that it will be extremely difficult for her to rouse him. When he breathes out, the thick bristles of his heavy moustache ripple as though being moved by a light breeze. She stares at her father and notices that a few shadowy bars, created by the moonlight slanting through the jalousies, appear to be imprisoning him in his chair. She decides she will take the candlesticks with her when she goes upstairs to her bedroom, but before doing so she kneels before her father and begins to unlace his ashy boots, which are tightly strapped on his feet. Having eased them off, she places the boots neatly to one side and then covers her father in a blanket. Miss Ann will find him at dawn when she comes to work. It will be Miss Ann who will help him to stand up, and then Miss Ann will point her father in the direction of the staircase so that he can shamble upstairs and join his wife, who will no doubt still be sleeping. In truth, this vigilance over his well-being is something that *she* would happily undertake if only her father would ask. She knows that in the morning, once her father is safely upstairs, Miss Ann will compose herself and thereafter take charge of all household matters. Miss Ann will do her best to make sure the day unfolds for the master and his family both smoothly and with a minimum of fuss.

8

Civilization

She sits stiff and upright on a chair to the side of her parents' bed, above which a canopy of mosquito netting has been delicately twisted and knotted so that it hovers in a discreet manner. She looks at the jumble of ornately framed photographs that decorate her mother's dressing table and fights back tears. Her parents' bedroom is heavy with the scent of freshly cut flowers, and an opulent floor lamp with a white gauze shade gives off the gentlest glow. A few months ago her father had announced to his wife and children that civilization in the form of electricity was about to reach their island, and between the hours of six and ten in the evening the hospital and some select residences in Roseau would be receiving the benefits of this new development.

Downstairs her mother is hosting a party because, according to the informal roster that the ladies of the island appear to have committed to memory, it is her turn to do so. Her mother has always maintained that accepting an invitation to join a couple *At Home* obliges one to reciprocate; in fact, in her mother's world, society can function only if one has the good manners to intuit when one's name has once again risen to the top of the list and thereafter respond by forthwith dispatching invitations. For the past few hours, the two dozen or so guests have continued to circulate downstairs with glasses in hand, having earlier listened to her father address them on his latest topic of complaint. After almost a year, her father has finally given up berating the government for having the temerity to construct the Roseau waterworks without consulting a medical man. He never seems to tire of reminding people that he is, after all, the chief medical officer of the region, and the subsequent epidemic of dysentery, with its accompanying high mortality rate, might well have been avoided had somebody from Government House exercised some simple common sense. Mercifully, the outbreak now appears to be under control, and so of late the doctor's ire has been directed towards the new settlers from the colonies of Ceylon and Malaya.

As her father began to address the assembled company, she stood silently to one side with a glass of lime juice. Her father scoffed at the arrogance of the newcomers, who claimed that having successfully tamed nature in their faraway corners of the empire, they intended now to take advantage of the construction of the island's new interior road and buy up accessible acreage in order to "try out" the West Indies. Her father paused and theatrically made his captive audience wait. He took his time relighting his Cuban cigar, and then he continued. "These people have the opportunity to be somebody here, but some of them appear to be interested in little more than the social cachet of writing their names in the visitor's book at Government House in the hope of an invitation to the fortnightly receptions and the opportunity to display their ignorance of our ways. Has it not occurred to them that they must leave behind their old attitudes and adopt our own? We drink cocktails, not 'sundowners.' Our people are not coolies or punkah wallahs. Negroes are not open to being treated with disdain. You mark my words, unless these infernal interlopers change their tune, then both the flora and the Negroes shall carry the day."

Spindly, grey-bearded Mr. Howard was paying little attention to her father's speech and continued to stare intently in her direction. Clad in an elegant white linen suit, Mr. Howard had reluctantly broken off his whispered conversation with her when her father began to lecture his guests on the subject of the newcomers. A temporary visitor to the region, Mr. Howard had made it his business to befriend her parents shortly after his arrival. Within a month he was declaring to anybody who would listen that he had become so enchanted with the island that he had decided to extend his stay through the winter. As her father began to speak, she watched Mr. Howard's painfully thin wife extricate herself from the company of the Catholic priest and take up a position next to her husband. As her father continued to expound on the idiocy of this new wave of migrants, Mr. Howard attempted to once again establish a hushed intimacy with her. "I must say, the good doctor makes a fine case." She heard Mrs. Howard tactfully cough, letting her husband know that he ought to immediately cease talking, but she knew that there was no guarantee that Mr. Howard would take his wife's hint. She closed her eyes, for the thought of having to endure more words from this man made her feel nauseated. Without bothering to excuse herself, she turned and set down her lime juice on a side table and then slipped out of the living room and quietly made her way upstairs. Her sister had retired early, so in order to find some solitude she tiptoed her way along the corridor and opened the door to her parents' bedroom and cautiously closed it behind her.

She sits now on the stool in front of the dressing-table and picks up a sepia-coloured photograph of her mother in a petite straw hat. Her mother is poised awkwardly on the steps that lead up to her family's house at their Geneva estate in the south of the island. Strangely, there is no evidence of joy in her mother's features despite the fact that she is surrounded by her five children. She recognizes herself standing slightly apart on the lowest step; she is a five-year-old girl with boredom clearly imprinted on her face. Why, she wonders, has her mother chosen to dress her in a dreadful, overly pleated skirt that is far too large for her? It is a hot day, that much is clear, and she and her siblings are costumed with comical formality, but why line them up for this contrived photograph when surely her mother must have realized that their greatest desire was to race off and bathe in a river pool and thereafter run wild for what remained of the day? And where was her father? Presumably visiting patients in the surrounding villages, or maybe on duty at the hospital in Roseau. Was her lonely mother having further doubts about her marriage to the loquacious Welsh doctor? Was she chastising herself for having chosen a colonial arrivant from outside her family's Creole world? She stares at her poor mother and wonders: After the photograph was taken, did her mother find it in herself to unpin her straw hat and release her children to roam free and go play in a rock-strewn gully through which ran a lazy stream that when replenished with rain from the mountains quickly became a dangerous thundering river? Or were the children instructed to file one after the other up and into the shade of the dining room and sit politely at the table while the servants served lunch? Has her mother, she speculates, ever known pleasure?

The evidence of her mother's despondency is again clear in the largest of the photographs on the dressing table. In the formal portrait her mother's hair is drawn back from her heavily powdered face and secured tightly in a severe bun, although her lipstick appears to be far too dark. Is it possible that her mother has overly decorated her face so as to discourage interest of any kind? She holds the photograph up to the light and can see just how well her mother has hidden herself away behind the mask. As yet she doesn't possess the evasive skills of her stern-faced mother, for this Mr. Howard clearly regards her as one who might be easily duped. Before her father began to hold forth, Mr. Howard ran his hand down her arm as though it was a familiar landscape and murmured that he very much enjoyed looking at her, but she already knew that men of all stations liked to steal furtive glances at girls. Mr. Howard continued and whispered that she was truly beautiful. "My dear, you have a haunting sensuality that very few young ladies ever achieve. But trust me, you're not yet the finished article. You're like a flower opening up, but for whom, may I ask?" It was then, as her father began to speak, that she saw Mr. Howard's wife offer the Catholic priest a hasty excuse and begin to nudge her way across the room. Evidently she had finally noticed that her husband appeared to have developed an interest in the fifteen-year-old daughter of their hosts. As her father settled into his oratorical stride, Mr. Howard endeavoured to extend their blundering conversation. "I must say, the good doctor makes a fine case." Mrs. Howard coughed. Ignoring both the grey-bearded man and his thin wife, she resolved now to hurry upstairs, where she would remain until each and every one of her parents' guests had departed from their home. Only then would she quietly make her way back downstairs and then go out onto the veranda, where she would join her father. Once there, the two of them would sit quietly, their tranquility interrupted only by the intermittent flash of fireflies, and together they would wait in silence until the island's electricity supply was switched off for the evening.

9

That Williams Girl

She knocked timidly on Mother Mount Calvary's door, but there was no answer. She was about to raise her hand to try again when she heard the nun call out "Enter," and her heart sank, for there was no longer any possibility of avoiding this audience. At lunchtime, Mother Sacred Heart had wandered over to her and whispered that once classes were finished for the day she was to report to Mother Mount Calvary's office, but the strict-looking nun with pursed lips gave her no indication as to why she was being summoned. However, they both knew that something must be amiss, for the Mother Superior seldom spoke directly with individual pupils.

"Well sit down, then."

She took up a seat on the other side of the imposing mahogany desk and waited for the senior nun to lift her head from the papers she was scrutinizing. The shutters were open, but in this part of the Convent School little light seemed to find its way into the building, for a large two-story brick residence that stood behind the school meant that beyond a certain point in the afternoon it was impossible for sunlight to penetrate.

Eventually Mother Mount Calvary put aside her pen, drew her hands together in a prayerlike clasp, and then looked at the girl seated across from her. The white band and black veil that framed the nun's face were in stark contrast to the woman's otherwise soothing countenance.

"Well, do you know why I have asked to see you?"

She shook her head, but instantly knew that this was rude. However, it seemed to her too late to rectify the situation, so she remained silent and simply studied the nun's mottled hands.

"Really, you have no idea?"

"No, Mother Mount Calvary."

"I see." The nun paused, and then sat back in her chair. "Well, this morning your mother visited the school and asked to speak with me. I take it you know what it was she came to tell me?"

She nodded slowly and stared out through the window, where in the distance she could discern the feathered head of a royal palm swaying gently in the wind. She waited for Mother Mount Calvary to continue.

Last week her mother had opened the door to the living room and stood before her in a pink dress that she had chosen to complement with a matching pink hat. The Colonial Administrator, Mr. Bell, was hosting a late-afternoon cocktail party for the ladies of the island before moving on to his new posting in the African territory of Uganda. Her mother had assumed that the eldest of her remaining daughters would be accompanying her to the event, but when her mother saw that she was not yet dressed for the occasion, and was in fact curled up on the sofa reading another one of the oversized novels that increasingly seemed to command her attention, the older woman struggled to control her irritation. Her mother swallowed deeply and ordered her daughter to go upstairs and prepare herself.

"Come along, we don't have much time."

She looked quizzically at her mother and furrowed her brow.

"No," she said as she puzzled over the absurdity of her mother's directive. "I don't want to go to Mr. Bell's."

"Gwendolen, I'm serious. We mustn't be late."

For a few moments, she continued to look at her embarrassingly overdressed mother, and then she simply returned to her book. When she glanced up again, her mother was angrily stripping the pink hat from her head, and the woman now declared that she would wait until her husband had returned from his duties at the hospital in order that she might urgently inform him of how appallingly his daughter had behaved. Her mother's hands were trembling and she looked as though she might at any moment explode with fury, but the now bareheaded woman managed to compose herself. She watched with some bemusement as her mother retreated noisily from the living room and went to sit by herself on the veranda, where she struck a silent and sullen pose, although it seemed clear to her that her mother continued to smoulder with rage.

She was upstairs in her bedroom when she heard her father return from the hospital. Thereafter, she listened to his leaden footsteps as he painstakingly made his way up the staircase, and then she heard him tap gently on the bedroom door. Her drowsy father came in and kissed her on the forehead, and then sat opposite her on a flimsy cane chair that was too small for his heft. They were both aware of her sister Brenda, who was already asleep in the bed beneath the window, and in a half-whisper her father asked if he might speak with her downstairs. She closed her book and nodded, and then watched as her father smiled and stood up and eased his way out of the bedroom, leaving the door ajar so she might follow.

She sat calmly on the living room sofa and faced her father, who blinked his tired eyes as though attempting to clear them before beginning to choose his words carefully.

"I gather you are experiencing some difficulty with your mother." She listened, but decided that she should remain quiet and allow her father time to discover the right words. "You see, your mother has told me what happened this evening." He paused and scrutinized his daughter's face as though anticipating some form of a response, but she said nothing. "To tell you the truth, for some time now I have thought that it might well be beneficial for you to travel to England for a year or so of schooling, what do you think? Such a course of action will also enable you to see something of the world beyond our island." She felt momentarily stunned, as though she had been struck an unpleasant blow. "Your mother said you screamed at her, is this true?"

"No, of course not."

Her father nodded and closed his eyes in exasperation. She could see that he had already anticipated the answer and he clearly regretted having posed the question.

"I'm sorry, but I had to ask." He paused. "You see, Gwen,

your mother feels that you are obstinate and growing beyond her reach and influence. However, your mother is not altogether well, and she is fearful of many things. I do think it best that you perhaps accompany your Aunt Clarice on her Atlantic passage, and I feel sure that things will be easier on your return." She stared at her poor father, who was finding it difficult to return her gaze. She understood that he no longer wanted her to suffer under the same roof as her mother, but the thought of leaving the island was impossible for her to grasp. And for England? She bit down hard on her lip and tried to think of how she might respectfully respond to her father's hurtful suggestion.

She looked on as Mother Mount Calvary lit a small candle on her desk. Dusk was closing in and the flame began to dance, which suggested that from some hidden corner a small draught was blowing through the musty office.

"My child, you're a misfit, that's what we'd call you in England."

"I'm sorry, Mother Mount Calvary."

"I'm sorry, Mother Mount Calvary." She heard the nun mimic her voice. "Tell me, are you trying deliberately to sound like a Negress?"

"No, Mother Mount Calvary."

The English nun perused her closely.

"People are forever talking to me about 'that Williams girl,' and I hope you understand that a bad reputation can't be washed away with soap and water. But you're not a bad girl, are you?"

Without taking her eyes from the Mother Superior, she

shook her head and whispered, "No." And then she continued.

"I don't want to go to England."

"No, of course not. For heaven's sake, why would you? To the English, women from the colonies can be very aggravating, droning on at length about the virtues of their climate and the lushness of their vegetation. I imagine that's how they'll perceive you. At least to begin with."

She stared keenly at the nun, and then she self-consciously introduced a remoteness into her eyes and looked down at the dusty floorboards. God employed this woman, and it was clear that Mother Mount Calvary revered Him and wished to do a good job, but she was beginning to wonder if the Good Mother had had experience of employment out in the world before assuming this present role.

"Your father is only trying to do what he thinks is best for your family, so try not to be angry with him. However, at some point you *will* have to choose whether to accept or reject your own stubborn nature. After all, it is extremely exhausting to live life without compromise. You do understand, my dear, that you run the risk of simply wearing yourself out if you persist with your war against social decorum."

She continued to stare at the floor, and then she heard the hiss of the sputtering candle, and when the flame settled, the room seemed to some degree brighter, although her own mood remained despondent. She pictured her mother marching triumphantly up the hill to visit the Convent School in order that she might announce her daughter's imminent departure, which she no doubt did with some enthusiasm. Her mother knew instinctively that this particular daughter was never going to live a quiet life behind the jalousies, and she presumed that her mother, having successfully lobbied her father, was delighted that she would soon be rid of her. She sensed that Mother Mount Calvary was most likely still looking in her direction with her lips divulging the most delicate of smiles, and she decided to avoid any further eye contact. But could the nun please help her? Could she not do something to alter her fate? Please. They sat together in silence, and they both listened to the sound of a solitary dog barking as it ambled its way along the alleyway to the back of the school.

10

Mr. Carnegie's Gift

Mr. Wilkinson stamped the book and handed it back to her. He then peered over the top of his spectacles and offered her a smile before sharing with her the hearsay that a lady novelist would soon be visiting the island, but he admitted that he knew little more than this. Mr. Bell had informed him of the writer's impending arrival, but the Colonial Administrator had now departed for his new posting in Africa, so the librarian had no way of acquiring more information, nor did he have the time to make inquiries. At present he was working in the midst of turmoil, for the complete inventory of books was being carried from the small Reading Room across the compact and neatly manicured public garden to the newly constructed library, a gift from the American philanthropist Mr. Andrew Carnegie. From dawn until dusk, the enterprising librarian with his tweedy English clothes harried his team, which included a gaggle of short-trousered schoolboy volunteers, for he was determined that every book would be in its proper place in time for the ribbon-cutting formalities.

A week or so after the Carnegie Library finally opened its doors, she decided that at the end of the school day she would make the brief walk down the hill and visit the new building. As she entered the spacious premises, she noticed a small handwritten poster pinned to an otherwise empty display board that hung above a cabinet of small wooden trays. Apparently, a Mrs. Evelyn Richardson would be reading from her work on the following Monday afternoon and all were welcome. Mr. Wilkinson observed her studying the announcement and he stood up from behind his desk and scurried over to greet his most avid young reader. He explained that the wooden trays held the new index cards, which would allow readers to more efficiently search for books, and then he gestured in the direction of the poster. Mr. Wilkinson lowered his voice and disclosed that the lady's husband had recently purchased a good deal of acreage in the hope of introducing rubber trees to the island, and while Mr. Richardson was engaged with his agricultural project, he had been led to believe that Mrs. Richardson would be actively seeking new topics upon which she might exercise her literary imagination. The clearly preoccupied librarian seemed excited at the prospect of a real writer sharing her stories with them, but having delivered his news, he encouraged her to explore the rest of the building and excused himself. She watched as he hurried back to his desk, and then she looked again at the handwritten poster. That evening, as she grated a little nutmeg over her father's rum and lime juice, she told him about Mrs. Evelyn Richardson. Her father took the drink from his daughter and stirred it before handing the spoon back to her and taking a sip. "This is splendid, Gwennie." She placed the spoon on a small cork mat next to the flask of iced water, and then she sat opposite her father. "You know, my dear," he began, "you mustn't count on too much from this Mrs. Richardson. I expect she's just another one of these haughty types who think they can simply arrive here and write us up as they please."

On the afternoon in question, Mrs. Richardson rose warily from the front row in an uncommonly tight dress that was beaded with sequins. As she turned to face her audience, she nodded a superior greeting and then with a stately carriage walked the few steps towards the podium, upon which she placed a sheaf of papers. A robust-looking lady in her forties, Mrs. Richardson wore her horn-rimmed spectacles uncomfortably high on her nose, as though they had been grafted permanently into place, and around her neck she exhibited an ostentatious gold locket. She stared at Mrs. Richardson and tried to imagine the author as either a mother or a wife, but she failed to see her occupying either role, for this would require the clearly self-absorbed woman to extend herself in somebody else's direction. She listened as the lady novelist cleared her throat by quietly coughing into a handkerchief, and then the woman poured herself a glass of water from the pitcher on the table to her left and raised her head and smiled, bestowing the full weight of her constructed glamour upon those present. As she looked at Mrs. Richardson, she wondered how on earth her father had managed to so quickly understand the truth about this woman without ever setting eyes upon her.

She was sitting out in the garden under the shade of the large ficus tree when the reading concluded and the question-and-answer session commenced. Having positioned herself on a forlorn-looking bench with her back to both the decorative fountain and the solid grey stone one-story building across the street that was Government House, she now found herself staring out to sea in the direction of Scotts Head. Her reverie was interrupted by a smattering of applause as Mrs. Richardson dealt successfully with the first question, but she felt entirely indifferent to events in the library. Having sat patiently through a half-dozen lengthy poems in the hope of a short story or an extract from a novel, she eventually understood that Mrs. Richardson was, in fact, more poet than prose writer, and the poetess was determined to do nothing more than serve up old work warmed over for this humid occasion. Therefore, when a suitable break between poems presented itself, she slipped out of her chair and stepped discreetly onto the library veranda and then down into the garden, where she took her seat.

Out at sea she could distinguish a solitary fishing boat slinking its slow way back to shore, the fishermen no doubt hoping to reach Roseau before darkness swallowed the day. It pained her to realize that this time next week she would be on board a ship bound for England and leaving behind her island. She envisioned herself leaning against the rails and staring at the surrounding flatness of the ocean and trying hard not to grieve for her loss. As she continued to look out to sea, a bat blundered towards her face and then flapped violently upwards and into the thick, shaggy heart of the tree. She knew that in the days that remained, her task was to secure the island in her mind so that whatever transpired on the far side of the Atlantic Ocean, she would always be able to immediately conjure a picture of home. She closed her eyes and attempted to fix a sequence of images that might appeal to all of her senses: the distinctive sharp smell of dark velvet nights, the musical beat of rain on tin roofs, pipe water thundering into metal pails, the sun flaming against the sea before it disappears, the excessive, burdensome fertility of the island's fruit trees, the vast electrical bravura of a sudden thunderstorm, the irritating flailing of a dead frond against the trunk of a palm when visiting her mother's family estate and attempting to find sleep. She thought of the cacophony of cicadas and frogs that would soon be shrieking behind the cloak of night, knowing full well that nobody was listening to them. She thought of her mother, who of late could barely bring herself to look in her daughter's direction, let alone address her; and she thought of her father, who two decades ago had arrived on the island as a twenty-eight-year-old junior doctor from a place called Wales, and who now spoke openly of this island as his home. As Mrs. Richardson answered her final question, there was a salvo of hand-clapping from the direction of the library, and then the audience began to file out onto the veranda. A few adventurous souls spilled down the steps and into the public garden, which was her cue to rise quickly from her bench. She was ready. It was time to leave before an undoubtedly concerned Mr. Wilkinson made his way over towards her to ask if everything was alright. Everything was not alright. It was almost time to leave. Everything was not alright.

11

The Passage

She stood on the deck of the ship as it inched its way towards the coastline. The wind continued to whip through her hair, and one hand now held down her new boater while the other clung to the iron railing. Her misgivings about this journey continued to give her sleepless nights, and she remained unsure of what kind of people she might discover in the grey country she could now see sitting confidently on top of a cliff. Her father had insisted on travelling with her from Dominica to Barbados on the small mail packet that regularly tripped its way through the islands. In her mind, she held a picture of him standing somewhat nervously at the stern of the steamship as they pulled away from their island at dusk. Although a fair number of houses now had electricity, the majority remained illuminated by kerosene lamps, which from the vantage point of the sea flickered like huge fireflies. Her eyes drifted upwards to the shield of the moon, whose glow reflected off the surface of the water, and she wondered just when she might see her home again. Her father turned towards her and urged her to go below and try to find some sleep, for, according to the captain, it was likely they were going to encounter some turbulent water and it was recommended that ladies and children should remain in their rudimentary cabins. *"Good night, my child."* As she edged her way towards the staircase, she wondered what her father would do now. Most likely remain on deck and converse, for after all there were five men on board and she had already witnessed them jabbering as though they had been acquainted for years; she understood that three were from Antigua, where the steamship had originated; another boarded in Guadeloupe. Now there would be no more loading of cargo, human or otherwise, for the small vessel would bypass Martinique and St. Lucia and make directly for Barbados. She imagined that her father would at some point join her below so that he might sleep off the brandy-induced headache that she knew would soon be establishing itself, but in the meantime she resigned herself to spending the evening alone and reading a book while stretched out on her bunk.

Having entered the narrow cabin, she closed the door behind her and lay down. She worried about the fact that she was not able to draw the bolt across, for this would prevent her father from entering. The next thing she was conscious of was bright sunlight streaming through the upper porthole and burning her face. She took breakfast by herself in the cramped dining room, and then up above on deck she heard the sound of raised voices and scampering feet and understood that the ship was about to dock at Bridgetown. Her bleary-eyed father made a belated appearance at her table, but his dishevelled demeanour led her to conclude that he had most likely spent the whole night drinking and smoking cigars with his compatriots. He asked his daughter if she had slept well, and she assured him she had, and he then suggested that they spend the day undertaking a carriage tour of the west coast of Barbados, with a break for lunch, before sometime in the early evening returning to town so she might rendezvous with her Aunt Clarice and board the ship to England. She understood that her father would eventually make the return journey to Dominica, but he had already shared with her the news that he had business matters to attend to and so would most likely remain in Barbados for a day or two.

Bridgetown presented a spectacle unlike any she had ever seen. People appeared to rush neglectfully in all directions, voices were permanently raised, and such a press of humankind she had never before encountered. The day was oppressively hot, and she discovered that down by the harbour it was impossible to find any shade. Her father quickly secured the assistance of an elderly Negro who possessed a serviceable carriage, and they soon left behind the hullabaloo of the capital and found themselves bowling along the narrow coastal road and being cooled by a stiff breeze. The carriage wheels turned noisily against the tarmacadam, but once the road degenerated to dust, they revolved with less clamour; the further they moved away from Bridgetown the bumpier their passage became, until the dust finally gave way to dirt and she realized that they were moving along little more than a crude track. She looked across at her delicate father and resolved that she would attempt to enjoy what time remained with him before she would have to embark upon the ominous journey to England. After all, ever since he had made the decision to send her to England, her father seemed to have fallen into a depression that she understood was most likely connected to their impending separation, but his decision to not speak with her about his conflicted heart had only served to widen the melancholy distance that seemed to have opened between them. The waiter at the seafront restaurant her father selected for lunch seemed familiar with him, and perhaps because of the man's solicitous attitude her father was overly polite and, having eschewed breakfast, ordered both callaloo soup and grilled fish. Her own nerves had been so distressed by the upheaval of the carriage journey she knew that she would be able to manage only the soup, and as they waited in silence, both father and daughter were held captive by the sight of the pelicans diving in harmony as though linked together by an invisible thread.

After the obsequious waiter had cleared the plates and left them alone to decide whether they wished to order ice cream, her father stopped playing nervously with his moustache and reached across the table and took both of her hands in his own. He was unkempt, for he had not bothered to shave, and the skin around his nose and beneath his eyes was rough and blotchy where certain blood vessels had established a permanent presence near the surface. "I shall speak plainly, for it pains me to think of you disappearing over the horizon without our having had the opportunity to confer." She smiled weakly at him and wondered just what it was he expected his sixteen-year-old daughter to say in response to such a statement. The waiter reappeared with his notepad, but her now-impatient father firmly dismissed the dark apparition so that once again it was just the two of them, and the sound of the sea lapping up the shallow incline of the beach, and the silent pelicans describing their graceful turns, although neither father nor daughter felt moved to continue to witness the performance.

"I believe that in the midst of some heated exchange your brother Owen once called you 'a replacement child.' Her father paused and she waited for him to resume. "We were unfortunate to lose a daughter, but as you know, you came along within a year of our loss. Your brother's words were thoughtless, but I presume he apologized." She looked beyond this sweating, hesitant man and fixed her attention on the fishermen hauling their boats high up onto the sand and unloading the silver flashes of fish into a huge tarpaulin, which they then proceeded to drag into the shade. People gathered around under the trees and to the side of the guava bushes, where the fishing nets were now spread, and they pointed at various fishes which were immediately lifted clear of the cloth and tossed into proffered buckets. It was clear to her that if trade continued at this lively pace, then there would be no need to take any of the day's catch to the market.

"You do understand that Owen's behaviour has made life difficult for us all, and the visit of your challenging aunt has done little to help us reestablish any sense of domestic harmony." She turned and stared incredulously at her father, for this was the same fiend into whose custody she would soon be delivered. Aunt Clarice had travelled ahead, ostensibly to visit a friend in Barbados, but she suspected that her aunt's early departure from their household had been hastily organized. "My sister has less than positive feelings about our world, and she appears to enjoy badgering your poor mother with her observations of our West Indian shortcomings. You no doubt overheard some of this unpleasantness?"

Her father smiled and squeezed her hands, and as he did so it was clear to her that her father had not formed a coherent idea in his throbbing head of what exactly it was that he wished to share with his daughter. Her mind turned to her sour mother, whose fierce assessment of people was rapid and unambiguous. Unpolished shoes or filthy fingernails were impossible to recover from, as were ill manners at the dining table. Peas were to be pushed up onto the back of a fork, food was to be chewed thirty-two times, elbows must never be placed on the tabletop, the soup bowl must be tipped away from oneself and napkins returned to the table at the end of the meal. Her confused father continued to smile, and she once again hoped that he would put aside his caution and make the decision that tonight he would board the ship and escort her to England and in this manner save himself.

Her father took her back to Bridgetown by way of an inland route which, despite the tedious flatness of the island, enabled them to achieve a slightly elevated view across the top of the swaying sugarcanes which dominated the landscape in every direction. Occasionally she glimpsed an avenue of ramrod-straight, evenly spaced palm trees that led towards an estate house, but there was little else to disrupt the spectacle of nodding tropical produce. As they re-entered the outskirts of the capital, her father commanded the driver to come to a halt outside a dilapidated house whose appearance suggested that it might at any moment fall to the ground. She followed her father into the building and up two flights of well-worn creaking stairs to the top floor, where he knocked quietly on a door and then pushed it open. Together they entered a shuttered, queer-smelling room with a single inadequate rug that attempted to cover the bare boards. In a cot in the far corner lay a prematurely aged Negress who looked as though she had lain there for many months and, having embraced degradation, would clearly never again rise from this place. Her father asked his daughter to remain where she stood, and she watched him cross the room and take the thin bony hand of the woman and whisper some words before touching his patient lightly on the forehead and attempting to reassure her, but the scrawny woman was serene, for it was clear that Jesus had long been the only man in her life. Her father calmly opened his doctor's bag. On the wall above the cot she saw two nails, which she assumed must have at one time supported pictures or paintings. The walls were marked with rectangles of darker paint, and while her father was occupied with the ailing woman, she tried hard to imagine what exactly might have hung in these now empty spaces.

Once they reached the harbour, her father paid off the elderly Negro, whose local vernacular remained impossible for her to penetrate. The two of them then stood together and waited for the return of the rowboat that would take her out to the ship that was festooned in lights and anchored a short distance offshore. The rowboat was ferrying out a handful of passengers at a time, and it was apparent that her aunt must have already decided to go on board, but she had expected this desertion. Together with her father, she listened to the futile washing noise of the sea as it lapped up against the quayside, and then, as it was getting chilly, she snatched her shawl tight around herself. She didn't pull away when her father draped a heavy and lifeless arm across her shoulders, for, having left the bedside of the mysterious woman, he had insisted on pausing for a beaker of rum at practically every shop they passed en route to the harbour. He slurred a little as he spoke. "My darling daughter, shall I tell you about England? Would that interest you?" She didn't trouble herself to peer into his face, for she had no desire for her final image of her father to be that of a man whose eyes were damp with emotion and whose tongue was heavy with alcohol. "In the small country of England it is not uncommon for a man to look you in the eye and say one thing while meaning another thing altogether, and thereafter abandon you to bridge together for yourself the gap of reason which clearly exists between the two positions." He paused as though allowing her time to absorb the import of what he had said, but in truth she had heard him express this and other far harsher sentiments over a good many years. His caustic observations about England were generally aimed at his wife, or any casual visitor, including his sister Aunt Clarice, which, she assumed, partly accounted for the existence of bad blood between them. "As you know, I am content to live out the remainder of my days among these West Indians. I have studied the English newspapers, and savagely suppressing uprisings in various quarters of the globe has only encouraged the English to think of themselves as all-conquering heroes. But you tell me, what glory is there in defeating a horde of barefoot primitives with spears for weapons and no experience of rifles and cannons?" By now people were glaring ungenerously in her father's direction, and as the two of them shuffled their way along the pier, she longed for this ordeal to be over. Her father slipped his arm from her and stepped around to gaze at her. With one solitary finger he reached down and raised up her whole face. "Don't forget your family, Gwennie. I for one am looking forward to your letters. Write often, but not at the first shock. You won't disappoint, will you?" She now looked into her father's eyes and tried hard to dispel her fears, for she had no understanding of how he might pass the night or if he had even booked lodgings. Her father swayed a little and then pulled her to, and as he hugged her she could feel him crushing her coral brooch.

Each week, on thin sheets of poor quality newsprint, the island newspaper, *The Guardian*, both recorded and reported the highlights of the events of the previous week in bothersome, smudged print. She could already picture her father with a drink to hand on their veranda, carefully dropping his eyes past the narrow births, marriages, and deaths column, and the lists of those who had attended various social functions, to the succinct paragraph which announced the arrivals and departures from their small island. It was there that he would find her name in tiny print, with the details of her vessel and its date of departure and the intended destination and antici-pated date of arrival. Slowly, all the while fixing his eyes on the pertinent paragraph, her father would rise and pour more rum over the melting ice in his glass and then, profoundly shaken by a grief he was too proud to share, he would grope behind his back and ease himself back down and into his chair. His daughter was gone. His dear Gwendolen was on her way to England.

She held on to her boater and stared at England, but it re-mained impossible for her to empty her mind of the sadness of her final hours in Barbados. During her first few days at sea, life was busy, as they dropped anchor at various islands to pick up produce and passengers. Eventually they left Trin-idad and the steamer set out across the broad anonymity of the ocean, and the officers changed from their equatorial whites into heavy dark uniforms, but her mind continued to be flooded with wistful thoughts of her father. She was old enough to know what their community said about the doctor once he was out of earshot; about how he was habitually late, and how he would sometimes attempt to perform his routine procedures with quivering hands, but these people had no notion whatsoever of the difficulties of her father's home life. After a week or so on the ship, it became abundantly clear that the rhythmic heaving of the ocean did not agree with her, and the motion of the vessel caused an upsurge of vomiting which abated only after her aunt pressed some pills upon her. Soon after, she was able to eat and even walk about the deck, but she spoke only to those who bade her "Good day" or asked if her queasiness had subsided. At the most forward position on the top deck she noticed an elderly Negress dressed only in black who sat alone each day swathed in blankets and who appeared eager to turn her heavily lined face towards even the smallest sliver of sunshine. On the days when the light gusts evolved into a contemptuous gale, the woman tied an incongruously bright red scarf around her head to hold her battered bonnet in place, but even this gay scarf could not lift the gloom that enveloped this wretched figure who seemed beyond the help of any passengers, and who was therefore ignored by all. And then, after three weeks, her father's world came into view. It seemed to her that the cliffs of Dover were more grey than white, and she turned her face into the wind and clung to the iron railing. Perhaps when she saw her father again she might have stories of a now joyful country to counterbalance his unhappy memories. Perhaps she would be able to help him.

III

Aunt Clarice

12

Aunt Clarice

Having identified her trunk, she saw the plump, busy hand of Aunt Clarice impatiently beckoning her as though signaling to a dumb animal. Her aunt had insisted on going ahead in order that she might secure help, and having rejoined the agitated woman, she listened as her aunt ordered the bewildered porter to fetch both of their trunks and be quick about it. She then followed the waddling woman as they passed together through a set of imposing tall gates, and as they did so, she decided that she would ignore her aunt's curt instruction to fasten her coat, thus extending the antagonism that had bedeviled their passage across the Atlantic. They sat in silence on the train to London, but she avoided looking at her aunt, for whenever their eyes met she felt the temperature drop. She watched as her father's fussy sister opened her purse and took out a handkerchief, which she then used to wipe first one hand and then the other, before pushing it back into her purse, which she shut with a businesslike snap. Eventually her aunt submitted to drowsiness and closed her eyes, and the other occupant of the compartment, an older lady dressed in dowdy brown serge, spread a large map over her knees, then smiled at her before returning to her struggle with the over-sized sheet of paper. Meanwhile, she remained alert and stared through the window at mist-shrouded farmland where solemn-looking cattle appeared to rove silently in treeless, hedgerow-bounded fields. Later, as the train slowly crept its way into what she imagined must be London, her aunt stirred and promptly began a short whispered lecture about the places she considered to be the principal sites of interest—St. Paul's Cathedral, the Houses of Parliament, and the Tower of London. As her aunt pulled on her sensible animal-skin gloves, she informed her niece that at the Tower of London visitors were able to view dungeons and instruments of torture, but it puzzled her why anybody would wish to see items that caused misery. She continued to look through the window of the train, but to her eyes London appeared to be comprised of little more than endless rows of houses boxed tightly together so that it would be logical for any newcomer such as herself to assume that English people lived like yard fowl in small coops.

13

England

On her first night in England she discovered that she would be sharing both a room and a bed with her aunt in a disheartening small hotel in the central London district of Bloomsbury. As she stood with her aunt at the reception desk and waited for the elderly female employee to present her aunt with the key to their room, it struck her again that she would have to listen closely to English people, for she found it difficult to understand what they were saying. She had mentioned this problem to her Aunt Clarice as they had journeyed across London in a motorized taxicab, but the woman simply turned towards her and asked if she didn't suppose that English people might experience some frustration comprehending her. That night, unable to find sleep, she spent several hours trying to discover a place of comfort on the sagging mattress and avoid rolling in the direction of her aunt. She shivered under the scratchy blanket, which she pulled up to her neck, and she listened to the strange snatches of conversation and occasional bursts of laughter that rose up from the street. She tried hard to avoid touching Aunt Clarice, which meant moving ever closer to the edge of the bed, but her aunt appeared to take her niece's restlessness as encouragement to spread out even further, and she soon feared that she was in danger of toppling onto the floor. After a long, restless night she eventually opened her eyes and saw the first light of day beginning to stripe the corners of the curtains and decided that it was time to flee the imprisonment of the shared bed. She stepped down onto a small square of rug and quietly pulled on multiple layers of clothing before cautiously opening the bedroom door and silently making her way along the corridor.

Out on the streets London appeared to have suddenly burst into life and people were walking in all directions without bothering to greet one another or even look into the person's face. She watched an old man slowly pedalling a bicycle, his head bent low over the handlebars and his face contorted with effort, and then a carriage raced by and splashed water, which caused her to rapidly step back to avoid the spray. A filthy wisp of a boy selling newspapers began to roar with laughter and point in her direction. He said something unintelligible to her ears, and she stared in fascination at his lack of teeth. As she moved off, she wondered what had happened to cause this boy such disfigurement. On this first morning she idly followed street after street, and listened as the tumult of sound grew all about her. When she finally came to her senses, she discovered herself marooned at a junction with the world rushing by on all sides, and nothing appeared to be familiar.

She remembered the address of their hotel and the fact that it was near a place called the British Museum, and so she asked a passing woman if she might point her in the right direction. The stranger was kind enough to give her instructions, but the concerned woman touched her arm and asked if she was alright. She nodded and attempted to compose herself, but the woman continued to appear worried. "Are you sure, my dear?" Again she nodded, but as she moved off, she could feel the woman's eyes upon her and she sensed that her would-be rescuer would most likely continue to watch her until she was swallowed up by the crowd.

Back at the hotel, the elderly receptionist rushed nervously from behind the desk and quickly escorted her to Aunt Clarice's table in the breakfast room. She understood that she must be a fairly ludicrous sight, decked out as she was in mismatched articles of clothing, and she began to sniffle, for her nose was blocked up with the beginnings of a cold. "Well," said her aunt, barely bothering to look up from her bowl of porridge. "Would you care to explain this morning's attempt to flee?" She had to suppress her desire to laugh, for surely her aunt didn't imagine that her intention had been to run away? After all, she had just made a great effort to find her way *back* to the hotel. "Do you intend to continue to insult me with your mute insolence?" By now she could see that other guests were gaping at them. "Well?" Her aunt now raised her head and stared directly at her before carefully placing her spoon on a side plate and gently pushing her bowl an inch or two away from herself. She realized that her lack of sleep and her cold, plus the stressful adventures of her early-morning walk, had left her feeling lightheaded and hungry and in need of some food on her stomach. "Well?" asked her aunt. "Are you pretending to be ignorant of the fact that you owe me an explanation? Clearly your parents have failed to inspire you with the prevailing ideas and responsibilities of your class."

14

Dear West Indies

During the late spring term she was called before the head-mistress to explain her disconsolate demeanour, and so she confessed to Miss Kennett about Myrtle's hostility and she was thereafter directed to go and sit by herself in the chapel. An hour later, Miss Kennett came in and first sat, then knelt, in the uncomfortable, overvarnished pew, and without turning her head, she asked if Myrtle truly was the reason behind her unhappiness, or was there something else that was troubling her? She chose not to kneel beside the slender woman whose hair was hooked artlessly behind her ears, for she sensed that Miss Kennett wished to avoid any familiarity and speak with her in this odd manner, which forced her to address the back of the headmistress's head. "No, Miss Kennett, nothing else is disturbing me." Miss Kennett suppressed a cough. "You have done well at the Perse School, and in your short time here I have watched your self-esteem grow, despite the fact that you don't appear to have been the recipient of a murmur of tolerance from some quarters. But really, you cannot allow one silly girl to ruin your life."

At the beginning of the school year her exasperated aunt had conveyed her recalcitrant niece to Cambridge, where her father had apparently decided that she should attend the Perse School. From the moment that she saw the building she knew she could never be happy in such a place, for behind the neatly trimmed shrubbery the school loomed ominously like a small brick castle. Whether this school truly *was* her father's scheme, or something that her Aunt Clarice had suggested to him, she couldn't be sure, but once they passed inside the building their footsteps echoed eerily in the cold corridors as they made their way to the headmistress's office. She sat and listened to her Aunt Clarice making polite conversation with the vigilant Englishwoman, and then her aunt turned to face her and pressed a piece of paper upon her with both her aunt's name and home address written neatly upon it. Aunt Clarice stood abruptly and then bent forward in order that her niece might peck her on the cheek.

After her aunt's departure, the headmistress smiled and opened a folder on her desk. She explained that a girl had already been assigned to show her the school and introduce her to both where she would sleep and the location of her classroom. The girl would also help her to understand how everything functioned at the school, and the headmistress assured her that she shouldn't worry, for she would be in safe hands. "Myrtle is one of our star pupils." Then, as though pre-arranged, there was a knock on the door, and when it opened she saw a small, confident-looking, black-haired girl who seemed bored at the prospect of helping anybody.

During the course of the next few weeks this Myrtle would

one day pretend to be her friend and the following day openly conspire against her with the other girls. "We don't understand what you are saying." "Do you speak English?" "Why do you wear such old-fashioned clothes?" "Have you no other shoes, you heathen?" "What do you mean you have never ridden a bicycle?" "Snow is white, stupid, and it falls from the sky. Like rain." "Do you have monkeys in your family? I mean as relatives, not pets?" "Why would you think anybody might be interested in seeing you, of all people, upon a stage?" "Truly you have no singing voice. You screech like one of your parrots." Myrtle, she suspected, was part foreign, and perhaps that was why the headmistress had chosen the girl, but although Myrtle herself was not much to consider, with her flat chest and funny little screwed-up eyes, the spiteful girl's habitual taunting made her feel as though somebody was pinching her skin. "What boy will want to walk out with you, Gwen Williams?" "When I leave school I shall travel with my mother to Switzerland to join my father at his business." "Tell me honestly, do you even have a mother or were you hatched from an egg?"

After Miss Kennett left the pew, she sat by herself and looked up at the stained-glass windows through which she could see daylight falling and coming to rest in long blue and red streaks on the stone pavement which led up to the altar. She had now spent over a year in England, with only the occasional brief letter from her father giving news from home. On her birthday she received a card signed by everybody, her mother included, but it troubled her that her father had never suggested that she might return home, nor did he raise the possibility of his journeying out to keep her company in England. At Christmas her Aunt Clarice had claimed to be ill, and so she had remained in Cambridge with the other "orphans," and they had all pretended they were somehow superior to those who had to endure the onerous rituals of family. However, privately it pained her to be cut off from her father in this way, even though she knew she bore some of the responsibility for the rupture as she had not stirred herself to write with any regularity. As an elderly servant sauntered her way into the chapel to light the candles, it occurred to her that the two Christmas weeks she had spent at the school without Myrtle sniping away at her had been the time she had most enjoyed at Perse. Once the candles were lit, the servant paused and then turned in her direction, and she wondered what the poor woman imagined she was staring at. A devout girl perhaps, who had spent the greater part of the afternoon praying and asking to be absolved for her sins? It was then she realized that the servant was waiting patiently, and so she clambered to her feet and followed the old woman out of the candlelit splendour and into the heavily shadowed courtyard.

The beginning of her second year at the school proved a little easier, for Myrtle seemed preoccupied with establishing herself with an older set of girls, all of whom wore brassieres. Myrtle's indifference enabled her to begin to forget her so-called friend's campaign of vindictiveness, and the slightly discomforting spring afternoon in the chapel with Miss Kennett, and direct some energy towards exploring what the school might have to offer. To this end she volunteered to play the part of Tony Lumpkin in the school production of *She Stoops to Conquer*, and much to everyone's surprise, she turned out to be a great success. After this her mind was made up. In a somewhat dramatic telephone call, Miss Kennett told her Aunt Clarice that she had "run off" to London to audition at a stage school, and despite the fact that she had returned safely at the end of the day, the school demanded corroboration from her aunt that there had been no inappropriate liaison whilst in London. It was only after her aunt visited the school and spoke with the headmistress that the headmistress calmed down. Miss Kennett informed her aunt that although she still regarded her absconding in this way to be a serious breach of the rules, she saw no reason not to accept her explanation that she went to London for the sole purpose of auditioning for admission to Mr. Tree's Academy of Dramatic Art. Less than a month later, and much to the school's delight, she received a brief letter informing her that she had won a place at Mr. Tree's school. She had already discovered that when she pretended to be somebody else there was nobody available for Myrtle, or any of the other girls, to mock. A week or so after she received the acceptance letter, she was advised that she should visit the headmistress's office, where Miss Kennett warned the aspiring actress that she must be mindful, for London could be a treacherous place for a young girl. In particular, she should take care not to dress in a manner that might appear flirtatious. She nodded, but she would not look up and meet the woman's eyes. The headmistress continued and promised her that despite her aunt's strenuous objections she would once again write to her Aunt Clarice and suggest that she should cease pressing her niece to go back to the West Indies and give her the chance to discover herself on the London stage, for, of course, such opportunities would be impossible when she returned to the colonies.

At Christmas she was happy once again to remain at the

school with the "orphans," her aunt having written and suggested that she might find it more convenient to be among those of her own age. Myrtle went off to Switzerland, having announced that her mother was in the process of securing a divorce, and her former adversary wrote to her from Geneva. "Dear West Indies," she began. It transpired that Myrtle not only wished to apologize, she appeared eager to let her know that her performances on the stage had impressed them all. Did she know, asked Myrtle, that she might now be considered to be one of the more popular girls? She diligently folded the letter and replaced it in the envelope. Unfortunately, when Myrtle returned to the Perse School in January she would very quickly discover that there was no longer any possibility of her developing a friendship with the now popular "West Indies." The immigrant girl would already be in residence in London at a boardinghouse near Mr. Tree's school that a frustrated Aunt Clarice had selected for her.

15

In the Name of Love

Aunt Clarice asked the woman on the other end of the line to please wait a moment. She put down the telephone and quickly threw open the door that led from the hallway to the dining room. The flustered maid appeared to be dusting the teak cabinet, but the young girl wouldn't meet her eyes. "You may begin upstairs now, Gertrude." The young girl speedily gathered up her feathered contraptions and muttered, "Yes, ma'am," but she continued to avoid looking at her employer. It was clear that the maid had been loitering near the door and eavesdropping, and unless she changed her ways, the girl would soon have to seek new employment. She would speak with her later. If Miss Kennett was irritated by this break in their telephone conversation, she showed no sign of it. The headmistress continued and explained that after the audition at the Academy of Dramatic Art, her seventeen-year-old niece claimed to have spent the remainder of her time in London wandering the streets, but admitted to doing so without a chaperone of any description. The girl adamantly insisted that there had been no secret congress with anybody, and Miss Kennett said that she saw no reason to disbelieve her, but she remained irked. "Gwendolen caught the very last train back to Cambridge." She paused. "It would, I think, be fair to conclude that the excitement of her adventure affected her judgment in a most unfortunate manner."

She listened carefully to the woman and tried to understand the implication of her words. Was Miss Kennett really suggesting that her gawky niece might have attracted the interest of a suitor? The girl dawdled and occasionally dragged her feet, and she had noted that the child seemed to take pleasure in deliberately scuffing the toes of her shoes. When a person addressed her, the queer fish stared at a point six inches above their heads and any fool could see that there was something simple and impossibly willful about her.

"I take it you'll be coming up to the school to speak with her? I would rather not bring this matter before the governors until you are perfectly satisfied with Gwendolen's side of the story."

"I see." She was startled, for it had not occurred to her that the episode under discussion might merit any further investigation. "And so the matter is not closed?"

"Well, hardly. The child is refusing to explain herself beyond these vague claims of meandering aimlessly in the theatre district after her appointment at Mr. Tree's establishment. Her word alone will not suffice. We require some confirmation from a parent or guardian. Otherwise the school's reputation might well be at stake. I take it you do see the dilemma?"

"I understand."

Having closed down the conversation with a pledge that tomorrow she would call back and announce her intentions, Aunt Clarice returned the telephone to its cradle and peered abstractedly through the diamond-shaped leaded-glass panel in the front door. She blamed her brother, who, since establishing a life in the colonies, had never troubled himself to maintain the correct standards of decency that might serve as an example for his children. The rumours of his own increasingly slipshod behaviour had, during her last visit to Dominica, begun to assume the authority of fact as she witnessed for herself his excessive drinking and prolonged and unexplained absences from the family home. She was sure that his unhappy choice of a wife had most likely contributed to her brother's decline, and it was now irrefutably clear that his renunciation of decorum and restraint had most likely influenced the behaviour of this wayward child. That said, try as she might, she still could not picture Gwendolen skulking about London in the company of a strange young man, let alone secreting herself away with such a person for a few hours of shabby communion. It was a preposterous hypothesis to think that Gwendolen might stir the interests of the opposite sex. As far as she was aware, the child knew nobody in London, and the kind of men who massed near the train stations of the capital looking for girls to prey upon would most likely never display any interest in a cautious thing like her niece. They were on the lookout for bright-eyed girls from the provinces with fresh faces and a spring in their steps; girls who were relieved and exhilarated to be beyond the choke hold of their hometowns, and eager to please any Jack-the-Lad who promised to introduce them to the bright lights. Timid maidens who didn't know how to groom themselves properly would surely be overlooked.

A year or so ago, on that first morning in London, she had tried to speak with her niece when she returned to the hotel. She sat opposite the unrepentant runaway as the girl poked at her haddock and poached eggs. "If you wish to wear your hair like a golliwog, then I can't stop you, but in England it is customary for a young lady to spend some time preparing herself before she enters the world each morning." The discovery that her niece had stolen away from the hotel without any announcement had frayed her nerves, but as she watched the vacant child nonchalantly push her eggs from one side of her plate to the other and then back again, she realized that with this young madam her words would most likely always fall upon deaf ears. On the train journey to Cambridge the obstinate child showed no desire to put aside her bag of sweets, and her warnings about the inevitable effect of such indulgence on one's figure were rudely ignored. Her private hopes that a well-regulated school might produce improved strength of character had now been thoroughly dashed. Clearly the girl had inherited the stubbornness of her father, but the truth was, she had already noticed these distasteful traits on her first winter in the tropics, when the child could have been no more than seven or eight years of age. The atrocious table manners, and the strange guttural tongue, had now blossomed into a delinquency which made her short time with the girl, travelling across the Atlantic Ocean, and then chaperoning her from the ship to London and then on to the Perse School in Cambridge, among the most trying interludes of her life.

Harold arrived at seven o'clock precisely. He placed his

umbrella in the stand, hung his hat on a peg, and only then did he begin to unbutton his heavy coat and hand it to her. As she slipped it onto a hanger, he positioned himself in front of the hallway mirror and adjusted his bowtie and then thoughtfully finger-combed the bristles of his moustache. He had told his wife that on Monday evenings he had to spend the night at the university hospital supervising junior members of staff and so his wife had come to understand that she should not expect him until sometime on Tuesday. As a result, over the course of the past decade he and Clarice had established the rhythm of their Monday evenings, with the only interruptions being those to accommodate Harold's annual summer fortnight in Dorset with his wife and two children, and her own occasional winters in the West Indies with her brother and his family. They used to meet at one of the two acceptable restaurants that lay on the main square in the shadow of the Methodist church, but after the first year Harold decided that in a small town it was not worth risking the possibility of falling victim to prying eyes and loose tongues, and so it was she who made the necessary arrangements that would enable them to dine at her house. Once he took up a seat in the living room, Harold generally complained about the patients he had seen during the day, and although he was judicious enough not to malign anybody by name, it was clear that he had now reached the stage in his career where he had little to offer beyond reciting an entirely predictable list of woes concerning what he and other physicians were expected to do for the lower orders, who invested little time or energy in taking the trouble to keep themselves in the pink of physical condition.

Because she lived off a small independent income and had

no children, and did little more than intermittently involve herself in the affairs of the Women's Institute, Harold felt it unnecessary to ask Clarice about her week or to playact any interest in her life in general. He enjoyed the spice of secrecy that surrounded their arrangement, and he revelled in the guilt-free pleasure of being the centre of attention and she, understanding his need to be indulged, played along and made sure that their conversation remained as uncluttered as possible with the detritus of her own existence. As usual dinner was prepared by Gertrude and left in the oven for her to serve once Harold had finished washing. The meal always involved some form of meat, usually beef, infrequently chicken, with a fruit tart of some variety for dessert. As he shovelled up the food, he spoke and chewed at the same time. He told her about the new Scottish nurse who possessed the most exquisite hands—the hands of a surgeon—although of course the poor thing could never become a surgeon. It soon became clear that it wasn't only her hands that Harold was interested in, and as he continued to speak, she looked attentively at him and smiled, knowing that this was his way of testing her. Only by continuing to smile would it be possible for her to pass this particular examination.

After their dinner she cleared away the plates, and then they both made their way to the living room, where Harold mixed himself a brandy and soda, but he remained puzzled. "Would it really be so awful if the girl *had* spent the afternoon with a man in a hotel room?" She poured milk into her coffee and waited for him to continue. "You know, get the blasted thing over and done with. Isn't that what you did?" She almost let go of the milk jug and was forced to carefully regrip it. She had shared with him the problem of her niece only in the hope that he might have some opinion as to how best to deal with Miss Kennett when she spoke with the woman in the morning.

"Oh come along now. Don't look at me like that. Girls have needs and worries, and a decent and diplomatic young gent might prove to be quite an asset. Tell me, wasn't there such a fellow for you?"

Later that same evening, they lay together in bed with their feet touching and the fingers of their hands linked together.

"You know," she began, her eyes fixed firmly upon the ceiling, "I was extremely fond of a boy who one day went away and took up some kind of low-level administrative appointment overseas. He attended the school across the fields from our own, and we would often meet covertly at the end of the day. Of course, nothing untoward transpired. We were young, sixteen or seventeen, a little younger than Gwendolen, but the boy was very keen and insisted that we should run away together. I knew full well that my parents would never survive such unpleasantness and so I broke it off, but the girls at school were merciless and referred to me as 'knickerless.' The boy's name was Nicholas. They thought it very funny. Actually, I still see some of them from time to time, although by now they've most likely forgotten all about the episode."

Harold unlaced their fingers and then propped himself up on an elbow. "You little minx, you." She glanced over at him and could see that he seemed quite pleased. She looked now at her moderately fleshy hands and very gently brought them together.

"After some time in India they moved Nicholas on."

"Oh really, to where?"

"He wrote on occasion, and then I stopped hearing from him. And then some time later I got the news that he had been killed in South Africa in a terrible mining accident and I cut off all my hair. Not all of it, of course, but it no longer fell towards my waist. My mother cried for a week, but I never explained to her why I'd done this damage to myself. Once I realized that Nicholas wasn't coming home, I knew that in all probability I had already enjoyed my hotheaded moment in the sun."

She felt a small crease of consternation begin to spread across her brow. "I'm sorry, Harold, I have no right to bore you." She offered the doctor a resigned smile, but decided not to tell him anything further. He winked.

"What do you think the girls would call you if they could see you now?"

IV

Performance

16

The Island Simply Doesn't Exist

She watched as the Turkish girl continued to stare into the hand glass, the loose tumble of her semi-pinned hair obscuring half her face. The girl had made no effort to apply any makeup, or even take off her coat, and the call was in ten minutes' time. "She telephoned last night. He's disappeared again with a new woman, and you know the type. One of those who when she crosses her legs shows her stockings, and it's no accident. Mummy's too ashamed to go out and face the servants, and so she's locked herself in her room." The girl wiped away her silent tears with the back of a gloved hand. "After Daddy died I told her that she should leave Paris and come and stay with me in London, but she refused. She said she didn't want to interfere with my life, and then because she was lonely she married this stupid Count."

Mr. Tree's stage manager knocked and threw open the door. The Turkish girl raised her voice in protest, but the man ignored her and continued to make his way down the corridor knocking and pushing at doors as he went. She looked over as the distressed girl now quickly removed her gloves and then slipped off her rings and dropped them into a lacquered jar that stood behind the cluster of creams and ointments that the girl no longer had time to apply. She already understood that after the curtain fell the girl's gentleman would come to the dressing room and the two of them would leave without saying a word to her, but in the meantime it now appeared that the girl had suddenly discovered a sense of urgency. The animated young actress threw off her coat and then yanked the pink satin blouse over her head and turned pleadingly towards her and asked if she would please help. Of course she would, but it irritated her that her dressing-room partner would once again be stepping out onstage with her mind not on the performance, relying on others to cover for her when she forgot her lines. She fastened the last snap on the girl's waistcoat before standing up, and with a flat hand she straightened out the wrinkles in her own costume. She thought about Harry, whom she still hadn't heard from. "I admit I worry too much about Mummy," said the girl, who had now stationed herself in front of the full-length looking glass, "but I'd worry more if it wasn't for Mummy's poodle. Ten years in dog years makes Lucky something of an old man, but she had him before she met this Count, and I'm hoping that he'll be with her when she finally leaves the fool. I suppose Lucky's her real consort." Again there was a rapid knocking at the door, but this time the stage manager didn't bother to poke his head inside, and then a bell began to screech and they both heard feet scampering down the corridor. "My gentleman says I ought to get a dog of some kind, but I don't know. He'd have to walk it, and what are the chances of him agreeing to do such a thing?"

She had initially set eyes on Harry six months ago on the cold January morning that she registered at Mr. Tree's school. Her Aunt Clarice had reluctantly agreed to follow her father's wishes and help her remain in England, although her aunt would have clearly much preferred her nuisance of a niece to have taken a passage back to the West Indies. Having settled into a respectable boardinghouse for young ladies which her aunt had recommended, she realized she had nearly a whole week in London by herself before Mr. Tree's school was open for registration, and so she fell into the habit of taking daily walks in Regent's Park, where she learned to bend into the blustery wind as she made her way up and down Primrose Hill. One afternoon she happened upon a bandstand where a musical concert was already under way, but the audience seemed to be mainly comprised of the elderly and the deaf, who were sitting as closely as possible to the musicians. She lingered for a brief period, but felt gauche standing hesitantly behind the rows of deckchairs and intruding upon what appeared to be a private recital. She soon came to understand that sitting on a bench by herself was not a good idea, and so when the weather was unkind, and the pale January sun refused to appear in the sky for even an hour or two, she grew accustomed to spending most of her time in her small room at the boardinghouse, with its divan bed, and rickety wooden chair and table, and a washstand with an enamel jug and bowl, idly leafing her way through her well-stocked pile of fashion magazines.

On her first morning at the Academy of Dramatic Art, she stood anxiously in the school secretary's office and answered the fearsome woman's questions regarding her name, current address, and age. She noticed that hovering to the side of her was a confident-looking young man clutching an envelope. He appeared to be rather shorter than average, and carrying a little excess weight, but his round face seemed considerate. His clothes were smart, but the cut of his jacket around the shoulders was a little too broad and the garment hung uneasily, while his unfortunate blue shirt and yellow tie gave him the air of a dandy. It was his eyes that attracted her curiosity, however, for they shone with a brightness which suggested genuine, unfettered enthusiasm. The secretary turned from her and addressed the young man brusquely. "May I be of some assistance?" He stepped forward and held out the envelope with both hands. "My fees. Twelve guineas." The secretary accepted the envelope and then turned her mind back to the odd new girl. The woman reached into a drawer and took out a single sheet of paper which she passed to her. "A list of what you should buy if you are to study here." Once again she heard the young man's strangely modulated tenor voice, but this time he was addressing her and offering to help her decide what to buy. "Young man," said the secretary as she folded her hands together and placed them squarely on the desk in front of her, "do you enjoy making a nuisance of yourself?" The student took this as his cue to step forward. He ignored the secretary's question and introduced himself to her. "Harry Bewes." He held out his hand. "I'm honoured to make your acquaintance."

While the secretary busily collated all of her forms, this Harry—having declared himself so dramatically—took a step back and quietly waited his turn. She glimpsed at her reflection in the window and could see that she appeared to be sallow and tired, although her clothes pleased her. The lavender dress hugged her slim figure, and the recently purchased red shawl made her feel theatrical. However, her makeup couldn't transform her pallid countenance into the rosy, beaming visage she craved, and of course there was nothing to be done about the angular shape of her head beyond styling and restyling her hair to draw attention away from this flaw. What, she wondered, did this young man see when he grinned at her? And then the secretary rose from her desk and left the small office by a back door, which she deliberately left ajar. "They say it might rain later." Harry's accent made it difficult for her to be sure she had heard him correctly, so she just smiled and waited for him to continue, but he appeared to have nothing further to say. The secretary hustled her way back into the office and once again slid behind the desk. The woman looked up at her and held out yet another piece of paper, which she took. "Your receipt, Miss Williams. Welcome to Mr. Tree's school. Tomorrow at nine o'clock sharp."

As she made her way down the corridor, she heard the scuffling of footsteps behind her and then a breathless rush of words. "Do you mind if I walk with you? I can always register later today." Without breaking stride, she turned to face this Harry. When he smiled he revealed somewhat crooked teeth, which made her wonder why this young man, who had barely passed the stage of pimples and blotches, imagined he was in any way suited to a theatrical career. His strange appearance, his awkward gait, his peculiar accent, and now his teeth all marked him as an unlikely future star of the stage, and yet the man seemed imbued with self-belief. He touched her lightly on the arm, and she took this as a signal to stop walking and turned to face him. "I must apologize," he began, "for I have a sweetheart. I really don't know why, but I feel obliged to tell you this, Miss Williams. You don't mind if I call you Miss Williams?"

Most mornings of the week, Harry took the trouble to slide his politely composed notes into the gap between the door and the frame of her locker, but he was always careful to never leave a part of the envelope visible. Her days began with elocution, followed by movement, and in the afternoon acting and speech, but she always had the sense that she was never alone, not only because of Harry's physical presence in these same classes, but because in his messages Harry continually sought to reintroduce himself and explain just who he was. Harry was from Devon, and when he first spoke to her about his home, he did so with such a sense of pride that she was convinced this "Devon" must be an extremely important place. She soon came to understand that he had grown up with a solicitor for a father, but he insisted that it was his mother who had taken the greater part of the responsibility for his development. Harry claimed to be different from other children. He frequently used the word "different," as though he wished to remind himself of the peculiar course of his life's journey. His hardworking mother was different, his emotionally detached father was different, his lonely childhood was different, but here he was now, one step away from the place that he had always dreamed of—the London stage. He told her that he admired her for having had the courage to come to England by herself, but he admitted that despite consulting two maps he had failed to locate her place of birth. The first map confused him, for her island seemed to be divided into two kingdoms, one part French, the other Spanish, yet there was nothing about her that suggested she might be Continental. On the second map it appeared that her island simply didn't exist.

Having endured a month of Harry's fidelity, she eventually permitted him to walk her back to her lodgings. She knew the polite thing to do would be to invite him in, but as he stepped into her room he began to jabber as though worried that if he allowed the situation to lapse into silence this might be interpreted as a sign that he should conclude his visit and depart. He sat on the wooden chair and continued to babble as she rested on the corner of the divan bed, and then he told her that from the moment he had arrived at the drama school he had been forced to work hard to hide his contempt for the snobbery of the place. Did she not find the second- and third-years intolerable? He asked her three times before she finally nodded in agreement. Later that evening, after Harry had departed for his own lodgings, she lay back on her bed and kicked off both shoes and then sat up and curled her legs beneath her. Harry had tried to behave like a gentleman, but even as they had ascended the three flights of stairs to her top-floor room she could feel the poor boy's confusion. Having taken a seat, he wriggled slightly, as though he were ready to slip out of his jacket, but he appeared to change his mind. It was then that he began pressing her about her feelings regarding the school and the other students, and having agreed with him, she excused herself in order that she might go in search of some refreshment. When she came back up the stairs from the kitchen, she placed two cups of tea and a plate of biscuits on the table, and then she once again sat down opposite him. Harry leaned forward and gently cupped her left breast with his right hand as though weighing it. For what seemed like an eternity the two of them held the pose as though unsure what to do next. The contact felt stilted and unexpected to her, but finally she could no longer control the tickle in her throat and she coughed and Harry seemed to return to himself and he quickly withdrew his hand. Thereafter, a torrent of meaningless words began to spout from his lips. He promised her that he would always be kind, but why would he not be kind? She had done nothing unkind to him. Eventually he rose to his feet and shuffled nervously. "You can trust me, Gwen. You do know this, don't you?" After Harry's departure she thought that perhaps she ought to take the cups and saucers and the still-full plate of biscuits back to the kitchen, as her landlady had made it clear that she didn't appreciate slovenliness among her boarding girls. However, on this occasion the landlady would have to be patient, for she wished to sit quietly by herself, with her legs tucked beneath her, and wait until the room had emptied itself of Harry's ungainly presence and returned to its familiar sterility.

After this first visit to her room, Harry never again placed a hand anywhere near her breast. In fact, the boldest gesture he made was threading her arm through his as they began to stroll together after their weekly Saturday afternoon excursion to the cinematograph shows, and this gesture signalled the full extent of their intimacy. As they walked she would listen to him extolling the virtues or failings of whatever film they had just watched, and then he would leave her at the door to her lodgings and make no attempt to accompany her up the three floors to her room. In the evenings she would sit alone and push and pull her mouth into the shapes that she had been instructed in at school, and try to speak in a manner which she knew would please her frustrated teachers ("It's pronounced *frawth*, my dear"), but she always felt cripplingly self-conscious and inevitably discontinued the practice. Of course, lying in bed at night she soon came to realize that the person she was most afraid of disappointing was not herself but Harry, who appeared to have more invested in *her* eventual success than he did in his own.

One morning a visibly fidgety Miss Frances, the head of acting, ushered her into the empty staff room and politely asked her to take a seat. She listened to the treacle of the woman's voice as Miss Frances suggested that, after taking part in the school's short season in its own theatre, she might consider auditioning for a theatrical manager in the hope of securing an invitation to join the chorus of one of the many professional musical shows now touring the country. This would offer her the opportunity to display her dramatic skills, but without her having to complicate matters with speech. According to Miss Frances, two more years at Mr. Tree's school were unlikely to produce any tangible improvement as far as her diction was concerned. The following day she didn't feel well enough to attend school, and that afternoon Harry called to see her and she shared with him the news of Miss Frances's misgivings. He seemed shocked and ordered her to ignore Miss Frances's impertinence, and announced that on Saturday they would forgo their excursion to the cinematograph and instead visit the Natural History Museum. On Saturday, however, they progressed no further than the huge skeleton of a dinosaur in the lobby. They stood together to the side of the bony structure for what seemed like an age, and then slowly circled it, always, it seemed to her, pushing against the flow of other people. Harry explained that once upon a time these monsters ruled the earth and everybody cowered in the wake of their majesty. He paused, and then reminded her that dinosaurs no longer existed. "It's a queer business when you think about it, but not a single specimen survived. Can you imagine it?" But she couldn't, no matter how hard she tried. It was hard enough for her to imagine Harry's upbringing in Devon, and so she stood silently and stared at the unhappy dinosaur and simply waited until her friend had finished drifting in his mind and once again returned to himself.

On the final night of the student production, she sat with the hand glass and listened as the Turkish girl told her that the Count's latest "trollop" had now begun to make a mockery of her mother's life. Apparently the man had become bored with the wretch, but his spurned conquest had come knocking at the girl's mother's door, demanding to see "her man." She listened to the seemingly inexhaustible gush of words cascading from the lips of the peculiar girl, who was surrounded by baskets of flowers that had been sent by her devoted gentleman, and then she looked again at her own wan reflection and wondered if Harry had returned from visiting his mother in Devon. Before his departure, all Harry would say was that she was ill and he promised to be in touch with her once he returned to London.

After the excitement and confusion of the student production, life at Mr. Tree's school eventually returned to normal, although Miss Frances made it her business once again to suggest that she should consider a future outside the school. The woman even volunteered to write to her Aunt Clarice, but she very smartly persuaded Miss Frances this would not be necessary. At the end of the week she left school and presented herself at the ladies' undergarment counter at Selfridge's, where she bought an apricot-coloured satin nightdress, which the shop girl wrapped exquisitely and tied with a bow. She made her way back to her dismal room and slipped into the nightdress, but as soon as she stared in the looking glass she knew that she had made a dreadful mistake, for it was the wrong colour for her. In the morning, her landlady knocked gently at the door and brought her a cup of tea. She followed the woman's eyes as they drifted towards the discarded object pooled untidily on the floor, and as the landlady handed her the cup and saucer, the woman smiled. "Is everything alright, my love?"

An hour later, as the skies outside began to darken in anticipation of a storm, the woman again appeared at her door, this time cradling a large bouquet of gay flowers and asking if it would be convenient for her to show a gentleman caller up to her room. However, she could see Harry standing behind the woman, and so obviously the landlady had already decided that it *would* be convenient. As an unusually scruffy Harry sat down, she could see he was tired. He confirmed to her that he had been in Devon caring for his mother, who was now allegedly "ailing." He then announced that earlier in the week he had formally withdrawn from the school in order to be able to spend more time with his feeble mother. Harry looked surprised that she had not received his letter informing her that he was considering this option, but she suspected he had not written to her. And then he leaned forward and placed his lips against hers in such a manner that there was an efficient pressure to his dry kiss. "Would it be possible," he wondered, "for the two of us to go steady?" She nodded, but it was unclear to her what exactly the difference might be between this "going steady" and what they were already doing. With this matter settled, Harry relaxed a little and offered her a strangely opaque smile that he probably hoped was reassuring.

The rain spattered softly against the windowpane and the wind rattled the frame. She had thought about complaining to the landlady, for the noise often kept her awake at night, but she worried about stirring up trouble for herself. Harry appeared to be engrossed in the theatre column of the daily newspaper that he had brought with him, and then lightning suddenly illuminated the room and Harry raised his head.

"I forgot to carry an umbrella."

Quickly folding his newspaper twice along two creases, he placed it on the table.

"Look, as I thought, right here in this very newspaper there are plenty of shows you might audition for, but I'm still not convinced that you should leave Mr. Tree's school."

"But Miss Frances insists that I'm wasting my time. She thinks I should join a chorus and have done with it."

"And give up?" He observed her closely. "Listen, my girl, life's about making a fist of it. Take my fiancée, for instance. I tried to keep things going with her even after I met you. I still wanted to remain friendly, so I said to her, I've found another girl and try as I might, I can't be expected to split myself between the two of you, can I?"

"Did she understand?"

Harry laughed and took another sip of his tea.

"Not entirely, but I didn't give up. I attempted to be civil with her."

She looked at Harry and struggled hard to picture the poor girl, whom she immediately felt sorry for. It was then she noticed a small smudge of what appeared to be lipstick on his shirt collar just below Harry's left ear. Perhaps some girl had buried her face in his shoulder and then peered pleadingly at him. Or perhaps it was nothing more than a shadowy remnant of shaving cream, or hair gel. Whatever it was, she knew she would never feel comfortable asking Harry to explain himself. A few moments later Harry climbed to his feet, fastened the middle button of his jacket, and announced that, because the rain was now little more than a hesitant drizzle, he had better "push off." She would see him again soon enough, but meanwhile she was to banish all thoughts of terminating her association with Mr. Tree's school. She couldn't leave yet, not until she had made what Harry believed to be "an adequate effort."

The following month she took the birthday cake that she had bought for Harry out of its box. Her landlady had brought her a large knife and a plate so she was able to slice the cake and fan out the pieces in an almost floral pattern. Harry watched her do so and seemed genuinely touched, but in the early afternoon he claimed that he had to go to Devon to watch over his mother and he left abruptly. During the past few weeks she had slowly begun to understand the nature of her new arrangement with Harry. Apparently there would no longer be any walks together, or outings to the cinematograph, or trips to museums. Their routine appeared to involve his occasionally visiting her room for a bout of inelegant kissing and some desultory conversation, until the room became gloomy and Harry decided it was time for him to leave. As Harry had poked at his slice of birthday cake, he reminded her that his father had effectively disowned his mother, and although there were rumours that the man wished to remarry and start another family, Harry couldn't be sure where his father was, and didn't much care. As she listened to Harry, she picked up her own plate of sliced cake and then changed her mind and put it to one side. It was then that Harry began to press her about her history with men. He wanted to know why there had been none, for he understood that in hot climates passions ran high. She didn't fully understand what he meant by this, and assumed that eventually he would explain, but he simply pressed on. He boasted to her of his own experiences with a succession of young girls with full bosoms and shapely thighs, and he recounted his one liaison with an older woman who was the first to let him go all the way, and then he sheepishly asked her if she would like to go all the way with him. She lowered her eyes and knew instantly that this was a question she should not answer. "We can't do it here, of course, but I could arrange a hotel room." He seemed delighted by the prospect of planning an assignation, and as he spoke, his conviction grew, but she was already beginning to suspect that Harry was simply seeking a girl without experience, an innocent who would never forget him. Harry was clearly excited, but had he troubled himself to look closely at the young woman before him, he might have come to terms with the reality that this particular girl bore no resemblance to the shy English girl he actually wanted.

17

Anyone for Tennis?

That night she lay in bed in her top-floor room, and for the first time in months she found herself drifting back in her mind to her home. She remembered that Daphne Morrison was her first English friend, although it quickly became apparent that she had precious little in common with a girl who introduced the phrase "cracking form" into every other sentence, irrespective of the context. Her mother had encouraged her to befriend the Morrison twins—Daphne and Roger—pointing out that the soon-to-be ten-year-olds were her age, and for reasons her mother failed to specify, they would undoubtedly be "a good influence." Having arrived on the island, her parents had liberally scattered letters of introduction about the place and eventually declared that their intention was to establish a tennis and social club along the lines of the one they used to manage in Calcutta. Her mother told her that Mrs. Morrison was once judged to be the best lady tennis player in the west of England, but her mother had heard this from Mrs. Morrison herself and had no way of verifying if this really was the case. From the beginning her father disapproved of the new English family, especially when rumours began to circulate that since his arrival the astringent Mr. Morrison, with his wing collars and his hair greased down on either side of a severe centre parting, had developed a particular loathing for Negroes, whom he routinely referred to as "niggers." According to her father, a number of people had witnessed him punishing an elderly servant in the privacy of his backyard with an unnecessarily brutal laying on of a stick. As she mixed the evening cocktail and prepared to hand it to her father on the veranda, she overheard him telling her mother that the problem with English people was that they were always acting a damn part of some kind.

A few months after the Morrisons had embarked on their purposeful quest to establish themselves, Mrs. Morrison organized a significantly lavish birthday party for the twins. It was during this party that Mr. Morrison invited her into his study, claiming that he wished to show her the family crest. "Now, my dear, do you know what a crest is, or what it is meant to represent?" She shook her head and, clutching a glass of lemonade in both hands, followed Mr. Morrison into his book-lined retreat. She stared at the beautifully polished floorboards, and then she raised her eyes and took in the deftly carved chairs of a heavy dark wood she had never before seen. Later that afternoon, when she returned home, her mother looked up from her embroidery and asked about the party, but she knew that she must never tell her mother that Mr. Morrison had scratched her. She knew that she had done nothing wrong, but she remained dreadfully confused. She remembered Mr. Morrison pointing towards the image of a rearing horse on the gaudy plaque that hung above the mantel, and then he smiled and leaned in close and pressed himself against her, and she winced as she felt the exfoliating scrape of his unshaven cheek against her face. Through the open jalousies she could hear the joyous laughter of the other children chasing one another around the parched lawn and playing a game that Daphne loved, which involved flapping one's arms like a giant butterfly. They were, all of the children, very much enjoying the extravagant hospitality of the Morrison family.

18

A Weekly Bath

On Sundays she was accustomed to a routine of waking up late, long after the birds had sung every song in their repertoire, and then pulling on her dressing gown and padding her way down to the first floor, where the landlady drew a weekly bath for her at eleven sharp. The large spacious room had clearly once been a bedroom; the positioning of the bath in a far windowless corner suggested the clumsy haste with which the room had been converted. She was permitted to bring salts and oils, which she did, but the landlady reminded her that she was expected to lie there for no more than fifteen minutes, for there were other girls who also needed to use the bathroom. As she slipped into the water, she tried to imagine how Harry had passed his Saturday night. Every girl at the school seemed to have a keenly anticipated commitment of some description on this one night of the week, but Harry had never invited her to go anywhere with him on a Saturday evening. Before her skin began to soften and pucker, she hastily towelled herself dry and returned to her room, and soon after there was a gentle knock on the door and the maid entered carrying a pile of freshly laundered clothes, which she placed on the bed. It was her own task to introduce each article to the right hanger, or lay it flat in the correct drawer, and having done so she slid back under the covers and drifted across the broad expanse of Sunday afternoon and Sunday evening, all the while trying to hold at bay the depressing suspicion that she had been abandoned.

19

The Letting Go

When he finally came to visit, she could smell scent on him. He handed her a gift-wrapped box of chocolates and then sat down on the wooden chair and loosened his tie and proceeded to sink into a posture of unbuttoned ease. For a brief moment she felt as though she might cry, but she quickly composed herself and listened to his rambling story about a cousin called Lucy, whom he had known as a child. As their eyes met, she could see that behind his bluster Harry was exhausted. "She's like a sister to me, and she's found herself tied up with an absolute cad!" When Harry went over the story a second time, all the details were the same, except this time he had felt obliged to offer Lucy a shoulder to cry on.

"Do you remember when we sometimes used to go for a walk, Harry? And then talk about the films."

He seemed uncomfortable and laughed a little too loudly.

"A bit chilly for that today, isn't it?"

"How are things in Devon? With your mother. Perhaps one day you'd consider taking me there?"

"I'm not sure that you'd care much for the place. But perhaps I'm mistaken?"

She looked closely at him as he began to smell the air.

"I'm sorry about the foul odour, Harry. The landlady says something must have perished beneath the floorboards."

After Harry left, she put the gift-wrapped chocolates to one side. No doubt Harry would already be on his way to see his cousin Lucy. Once there he would explain to her that now wasn't the right time to end it, but soon he would be tackling the matter. Of course, poor Lucy mustn't concern herself, for he had everything under control, but he had to be careful not to hurt the foreign girl's feelings, for she was touchy. But she had already made up her mind. When Harry next deigned to visit she would tell him that she was sorry but she could no longer continue with their arrangement. The following week, Harry sent word that he would stop by on Saturday afternoon, and so she braced herself and rehearsed her words. It was early evening before she accepted that Harry was not going to visit, and she stepped meekly out of her clothes and into the apricot satin nightdress. Harry had passed out of her life and travelled back in the direction of his Devon, where he was no doubt trying to impress Cousin Lucy with his knowledge of a discriminating private hotel. She burrowed down under the blanket in an attempt to keep warm, but as the rain grew heavier, she heard the landlady knock gently on the door. After a moment the woman knocked again, but by the time the landlady decided to crack open the door she had closed her eyes and was pretending to be asleep. Only when she heard the door close did she open her eyes, and she could now see that her small room was completely shrouded in the bleakness of early evening.

20

Are We Drinking or Are We Gawping?

The three of them had left the rehearsal room together, but now they were simply idling by the door that led out onto the street and she was waiting for either Mabel or Ethel to say something. Eventually it was her new flatmate Mabel who, as she buttoned up her coat, suggested that they all go back to the flat for a drink. Ethel shrugged her shoulders, for clearly she had nothing else planned. "What about you, Gwennie?" asked Mabel. "Do you mind a little drink-up at our place, just for a lark?" She smiled weakly and explained that she was feeling a little giddy and she needed to sleep, but she told Mabel that she was content to lie down in her bedroom out of the way. Mabel looked exasperated.

"For heaven's sake, kid. When are you going to learn to swank a bit and have some fun?"

Ethel admonished her friend. "Give it a rest, Mabel. You know that Gwennie's not some happy-go-lucky flighty piece like yourself."

"Maybe I'll just sit with you both for one drink." She looked at her two friends. "If that would be alright?"

Mabel pushed open the door to the street and a frigid blast of air took them all by surprise.

"Alright, just the one drink it is, Gwennie. Then you can catch up on your blessed beauty sleep."

Mabel and Ethel were both from the north of England and they shared the same blunt vowels and slightly nasal enunciation. Attending drama school in London had brought them together, but they carried on as though they had known each other for years, frequently finishing each other's sentences and then collapsing into peals of laughter. Ethel was the younger of the two, and the more physically striking, with cheeks that dimpled. She had about her a commonsense aspect which suggested that she should have known better than to try for a career on the stage. Mabel, on the other hand, was impulsive, and what she lacked in talent she made up for in determination. Her voice was always distinguishable in the chorus, rising high above the welter of competing voices, and she was consistently keen to volunteer herself for any part no matter how unsuitable. In the presence of Mabel and Ethel, she felt like a younger sister who knew that the price of being in their company would, from time to time, involve her submitting to some form of teasing. However, more often than not, nothing was demanded of her and she was simply expected to listen to conversations she knew she would not be invited to participate in.

As Mabel led the way into their small second-floor flat, Ethel coughed and covered her nose and mouth with her hand.

"Your Ronald's been here, hasn't he?"

Mabel laughed as she turned on the lights. "Well, he does

help pay for the place, so I suppose he's free to come and go as he pleases."

"And take whatever he pleases," said Ethel.

She looked on as the two friends began to giggle.

"He smokes like a bleeding chimney," said Mabel as she picked up an overflowing ashtray. "I've told him it can affect me and Gwennie's voices and make us hoarse, but it's like he's got cloth ears."

Mabel emptied the ashtray into the bin, and then opened a cupboard and took out an unopened bottle of gin. She shooed the pair of them towards the sofa.

"Sit yourselves down, then. Gwennie will tell you, there's no maid service here."

She noticed that Ethel carefully dusted down the cushions on the sofa before lowering herself with a delicacy that couldn't quite disguise her unease at the state of the flat.

"There we are," said Mabel as she slopped the gin into three glasses. She passed them each a glass and then raised her own. "Cheers," she said as she slumped onto the sofa next to Ethel. She then turned to her flatmate. "Well, Gwennie love, are we drinking or are we gawping?"

Under Mabel's watchful gaze, she lifted the glass to her lips and took a small sip.

"It's a nice place, Mabel, but you and Gwennie really ought to get a maid."

"Ronald's not going to pay for that, too. He likes to think that he's keeping me upmarket, but he comes over here and never tidies up after himself. Bleeding men are all the same."

"Well, get shut of him, then. I don't see no ring on your finger."

"Then where am I gonna flaming well live? In a single

room like you, I suppose." Mabel paused, and poured herself a top-up. "I still don't see why you got rid of your Wilbur, you daft lump. He had some money, didn't he?"

"I'm a career girl. I've not got much in my grubby little room, but I'm glad that it don't come with a bloke telling me what to do. Nothing against your Ronald, but it's not the right time for me to be under some bugger's thumb."

"Well, you know it can be nice to have a bloke to buy you things, but old Ronald does get a bit carried away with the demands. And if you ask me, some of them's a bit kinky. I expect you hear all sorts of things you don't want to, don't you, Gwennie?"

She smiled, but said nothing. Then she watched as Mabel kicked off first one shoe and then the other, and began to massage her toes. Mabel gestured towards Ethel with her head.

"Gwennie, I swear sometimes I don't understand her. That Wilbur was a looker, and he had a bit of class. He was a notch above my Ronald, that's for sure."

She had met Ronald only once, and that was shortly after she had left Mr. Tree's school and joined the company and Mabel had noticed that the new girl seemed terribly lonely. ("Don't you have any chums?") Mabel wasted no time in suggesting that she move out of her lodgings and move in with her as a flatmate, but having done so, she still wasn't able to shake off her woebegone aspect, and so one Saturday night Mabel took pity on her and said she ought to come to dinner and meet her friend Ronald. Before the first course had even reached the table, however, she decided that Mabel had not, in fact, asked her along to the dinner out of pity, but had done so because she didn't want to be alone with this rotter of a man whose appetite was clearly whetted by a glimpse of any trim ankle. Apparently his family owned a shoe-making business in Leicester, and although Ronald was earmarked to one day take over the family firm, he harboured ambitions to write musicals for the stage. As he ordered yet another bottle of Champagne, Mabel placed her hand lightly on Ronald's arm in a gesture clearly meant to suggest moderation, but she saw this man violently brush Mabel's hand away.

"I'm spoiling you, aren't I?" He emptied his glass. "No, I've already spoiled you. You've gone off, Mabel. You're rancid."

Mabel laughed. "Really, Ronald, you're not nearly as amusing as you think you are."

He looked coldly at her, and then he tore his napkin from his neck, pushed back his chair, and strode silently away from the table.

"He's gone to the bar to smoke with the men," said Mabel by way of explanation. "I once met his family at their country house. They have deer on the grounds and little bunny rabbits who pop out from beneath the hedges at dawn and then again at dusk. I could see them from my bedroom window, but during the day the bunnies were nowhere to be seen. Imagine that. Along one side of Ronald's family's estate is the main London railway line, so you can hear the steam engines thundering by in the distance at all times of the day and night. It's so different from my world, I can tell you that."

She remembered looking closely at Mabel and seeing the tears that were now filling her friend's eyes, and hoping that this Ronald would spend the remainder of the evening smoking cigars with the men and leave her friend alone.

Mabel suddenly sprang from the sofa and disappeared

into the small kitchen. She returned with a large white bowl filled with grapes, which she offered to their guest, Ethel. Then she plonked herself back down and replenished her glass of gin.

"Sometimes I wonder if Ronald even remembers my name. He never asks me anything about myself. I once told him that I had a kid sister and he wanted to know if she was interested in the stage. When I told him no he just snorted and looked right through me."

Ethel reached over and took Mabel's hand.

"Mabel, you know my feelings about that pompous arse Ronald, so you'll not be getting any sympathy from me. You should be looking for a new feller."

She looked at a tipsy Mabel and a perplexed Ethel, and then she took another small sip of her drink and thought again of the letter from Aunt Clarice that she had received in the morning post. As she did, she realized that she needed to be by herself.

Mabel smiled, and then she got to her feet and fidgeted with the shoulder strap of her dress.

"Either of you girls up for a dance? I could put on some music."

Ethel pulled her friend back down onto the sofa.

"You're a lovely girl, Mabel, but you don't need that Ronald. Things are going to work out all fine and proper for you. You've got it on your face. My pa, he always used to say, 'Some girls got good luck stamped on their faces.'"

She watched as Ethel leaned in to give Mabel a hug, and then she stood up and stammered as she spoke. "I'm sorry, Mabel, but I've got to go out for a walk."

"A walk? I thought you were going to go and lie down and

get your beauty sleep. It's dark out now. Where do you think that you're going off to at this time of night?"

She didn't reply. She quickly made her way towards the door and plucked her coat from the rack. As she did so, she became aware that she was still holding her glass of gin, so she set it down on the table beneath the looking glass, where a small pile of unpaid bills were neatly stacked.

"Gwennie, did you hear anything I just said? I said it's dark and I've got a feeling it might start up raining."

"I'll be alright. Really, I'll not be long."

Out on the empty street she pulled her collar tight and began to walk rapidly away from the mansion block. She stopped at a broad junction and could hear footsteps approaching her from behind. As the man pulled level with her, he glanced across at her tear-stained face.

"Is everything alright, miss?"

She made a small dismissive gesture with her hand, and swallowed deeply as she did so. Then she blurted out the words.

"Thank you, but I'm fine."

So her father had unexpectedly died, and according to Aunt Clarice, her mother didn't appear to mind whether she returned home to the West Indies or remained in England. Her father was dead and her mother didn't care whether she returned home or not? A thin drizzle of cold rain began to fall from the sky, and she stared at the gas lamps that stretched in all directions, casting a series of pools of light onto the damp pavement at regular intervals. She knew that she would never be confident and brash like Mabel or Ethel, so why should she stay in England? She turned a corner where she noticed a gas lantern that was attached to a triangular wall bracket as opposed to a post, and then a man in a shop doorway hissed at her in an attempt to attract her attention, but she ignored him. With her head down and her eyes fixed firmly on the ground, she began now to walk rapidly, knowing that she would soon be thoroughly soaked, but she suspected that dawn might break before she felt calm enough to make her way back to the small untidy flat that she shared with her friend Mabel.

21

A Strange Bird

Her new boardinghouse was frigid, and because the maid had left for the day, there was nobody she might ask to lay a fire in her room. She wrapped a thin blanket around herself, knowing that if it got much colder she would most likely have to disturb the sour-faced landlady. After the news of her father's death, she had sensed that Mabel was having difficulty accommodating her depression, although her friend never said as much. However, rather than risk things between them descending into argument, she had decided to pack her bags and move into a cheap second-floor room that Ethel had found for her. She pulled the blanket up to her ears and blew out her candle, for the smell of jasmine was suddenly too overpowering. Ethel occasionally called her a strange bird. "You're a strange bird, Gwennie, but you'll soon pick everything up." Mabel would usually laugh, and then finish her friend's sentence. "Except men, that is." But she never did pick anything, or anyone, up, which seemed to frustrate Mabel.

"You've got to stop pretending you're a virgin, as that frightens them off. And you always look half-asleep, has anyone told you that?" Eventually she began to think of herself as not only a strange bird but a bird with a broken wing. In the middle of the long, cold night she realized that she was dreaming of Ethel, who, of course, was the only one of them who could really sing or dance. She saw Ethel in Leicester Square, where the unruly crowd were pushing and shoving one another in order that they might get a glimpse of the famous actress as she stepped out of a motorcar with her young swain. Ethel had everything now: a first night, money, glamour, and a puppy of a man on her arm who seemed both compliant and grateful. She was happy for Ethel, but she wondered if behind the smile that she was giving off, and behind the glitter of her fancy dress, this was still the same kind and considerate Ethel she had known. As the well-wishers began to surge forward, she found herself being jostled in the opposite direction until she fell out of the back of the crowd. She picked herself up off the pavement and understood that she was now standing alone. While most people continued to look at Ethel, there were some strangers who chose now to stare at her, but, unlike Ethel, she didn't smile back.

V

Love

22

Suede Gloves in One Hand

After the second show on Friday night, and as she made ready to drag herself back to her digs so she might nurse her cold, she momentarily stopped just inside the stage door, and that's when she met his eyes. He was standing uneasily on the pavement among the unseemly scramble of gentlemen who sported top hats and carnations in their buttonholes, all of whom were attempting to purposefully loiter, but this shy-looking man's quest to press his claims upon a soft-eyed, bonneted stage girl appeared to her to be halfhearted. She had just eased her way past the doorman (*"Good night, George"*) and out into the incessant drizzle of yet another Southsea evening, when the man stepped in front of her. He nervously ran his eyes over her from head to foot, and as he did so, she noticed the way he held his suede gloves in one hand and leaned against his cane. She was sure that he had no use for a walking stick beyond affectation, but she listened politely to the middle-aged man's stuttered proposition that she might join him for supper, and without understanding why, she agreed to accompany the handsome stranger. At the somewhat raucous supper party that he escorted her to, he was soon ignoring everybody except her. He ate very little, then fastidiously squared his knife and fork on the plate and pushed it to one side and asked where in England she hailed from, but before she could answer, he enquired as to whether she had enjoyed a long career on the London stage. She had, of course, encountered men like this before, although this gentleman appeared to her to be a little more unsure than most. Clearly wealthy, and with mature good looks and a tinge of grey about the temples, the man occasionally grinned like a Cheshire cat, but he did so as a substitute for sharing anything substantial with her. She listened to every other sentence, for she understood that this man's conversation didn't truly involve her, and his discourse was, in fact, little more than a short detour on a path towards once more discreetly raising a hand and ordering more Champagne.

A waiter dimmed the lights, and a cake that was illuminated by two dozen candles was carried aloft by the chef to the grand table at the centre of the room. Her dining companion joined in the general applause and encouraged her to put her hands together. Then, as he leaned back in his chair, the gentleman's face became clouded in shadow. It was as though darkness had suddenly descended, although a thin band of light from the chandeliers managed to illuminate his tired eyes. Over the clatter of the waiters gathering up their plates, he asked her, "Do you regard London as home?" She swallowed slowly before answering, but the man appeared to be lost in a dream world, and so she waited. Eventually he sat forward in his chair so she could once again see his face, and he brought both of his hands together as he announced that it was probably time for him to excuse himself and take his leave. "I'm afraid it has been a long and difficult week." He pushed back his chair and then gently took her hand. "Come, let us go." The sudden upsurge of noise from the centre table, as a young girl blew out the candles on the cake, provided a distraction which enabled the man to unobtrusively weave his way through the tables and hurry them both in the direction of the door. "I take it you have lodgings in Southsea?" Yes, she had lodgings. Weekly digs in a seedy backstreet with a drunk of a landlady who insisted on being called "Ma." It had stopped raining, and she stood together with her suitor on the pavement and watched as a motorcar splashed through the puddles and drew up before them. "I shall call on you in London, if I may." He paused and then gestured to the driver. "My man will convey you to your lodgings. I shall walk and clear my head." She turned to face her swell and waited for him to wish her good night, but an enigmatic smile fleetingly disturbed the gentleman's face and then he nodded slightly and began to walk away from her.

23

Romano's

A week after the conclusion of the company's Southsea engagement, she was back in London and dining at Romano's. She knew that to anyone seated at one of the other tables it would immediately be clear that she was a relative stranger to the man with whom she was taking supper. He had explained to her that Romano's was busy every night of the week, but at present it was particularly crowded, as the London stage was able to boast an unprecedented number of musical shows running at a dozen different theatres. This was a Saturday night, and without a reservation nobody—ostensibly not even a member of the royal family—could be sure of a table at Romano's, yet when her gentleman ushered her through the door and out of the mid-evening shower, Mr. Romano himself promptly appeared before them. Having diligently mopped the sweat from his brow with a folded handkerchief and snapped a quick bow to her as the lady of the party, the small, swarthy man with a large moustache personally escorted them to a corner table and snatched up the RESERVED sign before holding the chair for her, ensuring that she was the first to be seated. As she looked all about herself, she continued to feel apprehensive, for she couldn't imagine the crossroads where her life and that of her gentleman stockbroker might conversationally intersect. In fact, the stockbroker and the chorus girl sounded like an abbreviated summary of the plot of one of the many musical comedies with which London appeared to be so enamoured.

Having cleared their supper plates, the waiter refilled her patron's glass, which he lifted to his lips, and then her gentleman gazed directly at her, but she lowered her eyes and wouldn't meet his own. "Are you still hungry?" She shook her head, which was now beginning to feel dizzy as a result of the wine. Why, she wondered, was this man able to tolerate long periods of silence without displaying any anxiety? From the table behind them laughter began to spill, unhinged from meaning, and she wondered what lessons, if any, she could import from the wreckage of her friendship with Harry Bewes that might enable her to better comprehend her present circumstances. And then her stockbroker finally began to question her, one arrow after another. "Are your family truly beastly to the blacks?" "Do all of you stage girls have your eyes set on titled men?" "Come along, young lady, it won't do to keep an honourable chap waiting." He smiled. "Well? Lost our tongue, have we?"

They stood together on the Strand waiting for his driver to pull up the motorcar, and as they idled, he gallantly held an umbrella over her hat to prevent the arrangement of artificial flowers from wilting in the light downpour. Despite the hubbub of people arriving and leaving, she was struck by the relative peace of the London street after the ferment of Romano's. "To my club, then?" It sounded to her more of a statement than a question, but she couldn't be sure, so she smiled, as this seemed the safest thing to do in the situation. The car arrived and the driver quickly emerged from behind the wheel and opened the back door so that she might slide in and onto the cushioned seat. For a moment she sat alone as the man scampered around to the other door, which he then opened, allowing his employer to join her. "My dear child, are you comfortable?" He spoke without looking in her direction. "I don't imagine it will take us too long." With this said, the motorcar began to move off, and he turned towards the window. She began now to wonder if she should have politely declined this evening's invitation, and she found herself thinking longingly about her cheerless overfurnished second-floor room, with its peeling white paint and the cracked pane of glass in the single window. Yet she remained convinced that there was kindness in the eyes of this older man, and she trusted that in the end everything would be alright and at some point she would, indeed, return safely to her room.

Through the open door she could see that adjoining their private wood-panelled nook was a chamber which contained a bed. They ate cheese and figs, and Lancey unstopped a cut-glass decanter and introduced her to his club's special port, whose taste she found bitter and unpleasant. As though answering a question, he informed her that he had never married, although some years earlier a Miss Violet Hambro had led him a merry dance for a few seasons before jilting him. Apparently, when the lady finally rejected his proposal, Miss Hambro feigned surprise that he was even interested in girls. He laughed heartily at the absurdity of such an error, but she wondered why he was telling her this tale. In the wake of his disastrous proposal he admitted to having momentarily fallen into a sorrowful state, but his family had encouraged him to regain his mettle. According to his mother, the silly Hambro child was confused, having just lost her own mother, but if the poor foolish girl didn't want her son, despite the fact that he had managed to overlook her plainness, then her son was to remember that there were plenty more fish in the sea. Lanccy laughed and shared with her his surprise that his mother was familiar with such colloquialisms, and then he once again confirmed that he wasn't married, although she had demanded no such explanation from him. Her eyes began to drift in the direction of the slightly open door, and as they did so, her gentleman leaned in and attempted to kiss her, but she pulled back, despite the fact that a delicate sensation of pleasure quivered through her, for she liked this man. "I do believe you may have developed a gentle ardour for me, am I correct?" She smiled coyly, and then the thought struck her that perhaps Lancey was only now realizing he was attempting to engage his chorus girl in a game whose rules she was not yet familiar with.

24

An Oddly Vertical City

She watched as Lancey stepped out from between the sheets and picked up his dressing gown from the chair next to the bed. He draped it about himself before quickly disappearing through a door which she assumed led to a plush bathroom. She lay back and stared at the ceiling and wondered just how much of a disappointment she had been. Yesterday evening, when he asked about her previous experience with men, she had ignored his question, but he must now know that she had had no prior experience. She closed her eyes and reminded herself of how well the evening had begun. She had followed Lancey's instructions and his car had delivered her to his grand house in Mayfair's Charles Street at 7:00 p.m. precisely. A well-dressed manservant opened the door and ushered her into the drawing room, and a few minutes later Lancey entered and seemed delighted to once again have her company and expressed admiration for her appearance. The same manservant eventually escorted them to the dining room, and after supper they returned to the drawing room, where Lancey poured himself a brandy while she drank whisky. Mabel had told her what to expect. "He'll beat around the bush a bit all sly like, and then you'll have to reckon for yourself whether it's something that you're ready for." Long before arriving at his Charles Street house, however, she had already made the decision.

As Lancey relaxed with his brandy in the drawing room, he lit a cigar and began now to talk about his business affairs. "I had to call a young man into my office this morning. A lively, jocular fellow from the Midlands, and something of an experiment on my part." He paused to make sure that the cigar was lit, and once he detected a curl of smoke he resumed his anecdote. "He had made a terrible mess of some figures, and I should really have given him his marching orders, but I simply couldn't bring myself to do so." At this point Lancey leaned forward and topped up her glass of whisky. "You see, I was once in this young man's position, some years ago in America, in New York City, to be precise, a remarkable, oddly vertical city where chaps such as myself are often to be found as temporary, one might say exotic, additions to the business world. Late one morning my mentor, a genial American gentleman named Morgan, called me into his office, where I noticed that seated to his side was the company's accountant balancing some ledgers in his lap. Of course I knew in a jiffy that I must have made some unfortunate miscalculation, and try as I might to remember what this might be, my mind remained blank and so I was forced to wait until Mr. Morgan gave the accountant the floor. Thereafter, the little man began to complain about some minor accounting inaccuracy which, he claimed, had major significance for the company. Even as he spoke, it was clear to me that the man's real source of frustration was myself and not my blunder. Here I was, a privileged Englishman, Eton and Cambridge and all the predictable connections, but as far as the little American man was concerned, it was an outrage that I was behaving as though I possessed the necessary skills to assist these Americans in the running of their business. Mr. Morgan listened to the accountant and then turned to me and asked what I thought he should do. I was unsure as to how exactly I should respond; perhaps I should have volunteered to resign on the spot, but it hardly seemed fair to compound my clerical transgression with a further mistake and so I remained silent in the hope that my mentor might spare me the ordeal of making his decision for him. After what felt like an age, Morgan dismissed the malevolent accountant and announced that we two should take lunch together, enquiring if I had a favourite tavern or restaurant. Sure that whatever I suggested would be a disappointment, I allowed Morgan to choose the venue and accompanied him out onto the crowded street of Broadway, where I once again marveled at the tight crush of buildings pressing skywards."

Lancey knocked the ash off his cigar before settling himself back into his chair. He gestured towards the bottle of whisky, but she placed a hand over her glass and waited for him to continue, which he did after once more filling and then emptying his lungs. "As we completed our orders and handed the menus back to the waiter, Morgan didn't waste a moment, for he knew exactly what he wished to share with me. A man, he insisted, will make mistakes in life, for all of us are human—and therefore fallible. Only in the area of female companionship must a man be shrewd enough to always make the appropriate decision. It transpired that his own marriage was arranged and he discovered too late in the day that his wife suffered from a frivolity of mind. The fact was, although the woman was presentable, she was not entirely respectable. He said little more, but it was clear that his marriage had brought him great unhappiness and frustration, and he admired my caution in this department, although he was keen to stress that my personal life was none of his professional business. He was, he insisted, talking with me as a friend. Man to man, as it were. To his eyes, an accounting slipup was of no great importance; he employed chaps to repair such missteps. But the choice of one's partner required vigilance of a far greater magnitude and he urged me to continue to be heedful. Which is the same advice I gave to the young fellow today. Forget trivial mistakes in one's work. Look to one's life and try to avoid making rash errors of judgment in this department."

As Lancey poured himself another brandy, she knew that the man seated before her had shared this anecdote with her in order to help her better understand that wariness and tact would inform their friendship. He smiled and offered to find her more spacious and comfortable accommodation and insisted that he wished to pay her an allowance. She knew that Mabel would approve of this development, but it was then that Lancey posed his question about her previous experience with men, and believing that it was unlikely that a man such as this would have any desire to take on the responsibility of a novice, she said nothing and resolved to let the evening follow its course. Her feelings for him were such that she hoped to experience passion, but this would necessitate some zeal on his part and she suspected that his relations with women would customarily have an aspect of the businesslike about them. So it proved, and in the absence of fervour she chose to affect a passivity which she now feared he might well have interpreted as a lack of either interest or effort. In the bathroom she could hear water running and she assumed that Lancey was drawing himself a bath. Suddenly she was deluged with uncertainty. Should she vacate the bed and make ready to leave? Or should she wait until Lancey was dressed and then take a bath herself? The rules of engagement were a mystery to her. As the water continued to thunder, she decided to emerge from beneath the tangle of knotted sheets and put on her clothes. Having done so, she would wait in the chair by the bedroom window, thus neither truly staying nor going but offering Lancey the opportunity to instruct her.

25

Sunday Lunch

As she lingers on the train station platform, she follows Lancey's car as it continues to labour its way back up the hill, where it will soon crest and thereafter plunge out of sight. She can see that, as usual, Lancey is driving too slowly, but she hopes that before he returns to the depressing Victorian brick house that stands half-hidden behind a line of overgrown trees he will not have entirely emptied his mind of "Little Miss British Crown Colony." She had arrived at the rural train station only a few hours earlier, and while Lancey had initially greeted her with enthusiasm, as they began to motor the short distance between the train station and Cousin Julian's house, their conversation began to fade. She turned her attention to the dense thicket of hawthorn and bramble that lined the narrow country lanes, whose banks were dotted with bright flowers, the names of which she had yet to learn. She could sense an unease emanating from her gentleman, and once they arrived at Cousin Julian's house, lunch rapidly became an ordeal. The assembled pale young men and women, all of whom took pride in exuding an effortless sense of belonging, were clearly both fascinated and appalled by Lancey's choice of female consort. Sadly, having chosen to exhibit her in this fashion, Lancey proved himself to be singularly incapable of disguising his own embarrassment. Cousin Julian wore the confident demeanour of a bully, and spiteful jibes about "uncategorisable women" went unrebuffed by Lancey. From the moment she arrived, the arrogant young man's general disdain for her presence in his house was palpable. It was Lancey who eventually suggested that she might wish to catch an earlier train, and she promptly excused herself and retreated to the bathroom, for she didn't relish the thought of appearing visibly distressed in front of Cousin Julian and his kind.

She looks up at the road and stares hard at the point where Lancey's car is about to drop over the hill. She imagines that all must now be well in his world, for with his cashmere travelling rug protecting his shoulders, he is journeying back to the ugly brick house, where he will spend the weekend in the amusing company of his chums. She could already picture Cousin Julian with Champagne flute in hand, pushing back his flap of blond hair from his eyes and wondering aloud if dear Lancey's savage is not perhaps half-potty. She, on the other hand, will return to the rooms that Lancey pays for and sit alone on the divan bed and mark off the hours according to the pealing of the church bells. She will sit patiently by herself and simply wait for Lancey to once again propose a tryst, such is the nature of their arrangement. Having, at his urging, more or less given up the life of a chorus girl travelling from dingy town to dingy town with a small suitcase in one hand, enduring dimly lit stages and badly rehearsed orchestras, this waiting around is now her life.

Suddenly she is aware of an elegant bespectacled man on the platform who is staring at her with a practiced eye. He is slight of build but smartly dressed in a broad-shouldered navy blue suit, which makes him appear far more substantial than he actually is. She glances at the svelte fellow and is appalled to see him walking in her direction with a warm smile decorating his thin lips. When he reaches her, the man begins to laugh somewhat self-consciously.

"Well, my, what a coincidence." She watches the stranger scrutinizing her puzzled face until it finally dawns on him that he ought to introduce himself. "I'm Robert Carrington, Lucy's father." He pauses and ungloves a hand, extending it towards her in a gesture of sincerity. "We met in Lucy's dressing room."

"Why, of course." Even as she speaks, she wonders why this man assumes that she might remember either him or his daughter. Doesn't this Mr. Carrington understand that chorus girls are packed into dressing rooms like matches in a box and they seldom have the time or the inclination to exchange names?

The man hardly pauses for breath as he mentions two other West End shows that he has recently had the pleasure of attending, although neither of them featured his daughter. Eventually the ear-splitting whistle which signals the imminent arrival of a train rescues them both from the artifice of the encounter, but not before Mr. Carrington shares with her the news that she is indeed a very prepossessing young woman. "Might I ask, do you have a friend?" Sure that this man will be travelling in the first-class carriage, she smiles sweetly and prepares to take her leave.

"It was very nice to see you again, Mr. Carrington. Please do give Lucy my best wishes."

Robert Carrington unconsciously brings his heels together in a manner which betrays a military background.

"Would you, by any chance, be free for dinner one evening?"

Pretending that the roaring hiss of the steam train has obscured his words, she turns and quickly makes her way towards the second-class carriages.

26

His Father's Friends

She noticed Lancey playing nervously with the corner of his linen place mat. They were sitting together in Simpson's restaurant awaiting the arrival of his unpleasant cousin, Julian, who Lancey insisted was a good sort who regretted getting off on the wrong foot with her. She remained unconvinced, but felt she had little choice but to submit to this attempt to broker peace between them. In the meantime, she listened to Lancey as he tried to share with her what he referred to as "some fundamental family history." "You see," he continued, "Father died two years ago, which has left Mother quite distraught. He was in his mid-seventies, so it was a fairly good innings, but I don't wish to appear callous." He paused and steadied himself. "However, there's no getting around the fact that I fear I was a bit of a disappointment to him. After all, he was once the Governor of the Bank of England, and I think he expected me to achieve a more elevated position in society than that of a mere stockbroker." Again he lowered his eyes. "On the morning of the funeral, Mother asked me to meet with her at the end of the day, just before dinner, in Father's study. The actual service took place shortly before noon, and the guests returned to the house for a light lunch, which was swiftly concluded when my mother insisted that quite soon she would have to lie down and rest. Of course, everybody understood what she meant, and so they trooped out, leaving Mother and her children alone. It was then, for the first time, that I noticed there was an emptiness in the house that seemed to me truly disturbing. Shortly after the departure of the guests, Mother stood and excused herself, and we all watched respectfully as she opened the door and closed it behind her. Later that afternoon, as the light in the drawing room started to fade, it occurred to me that I should leave behind my brothers and sisters and take myself off to my father's study. Once there I discovered that Mother had changed into a black crepe dress. She was seated behind Father's desk, as though she were now in charge of his affairs, although we both knew this to be a preposterous charade. She came straight to the point. 'Your father has bequeathed me a small allowance, but the bulk of his estate has been left for you to administer. Your father intended that you should formulate some sort of distribution for your siblings.' I could read disappointment on her face, and I'm sure that if the light were better I would have seen bitterness, but I said nothing and simply averted my eyes and looked all around at the beautifully grained curves of the decorative wooden fixtures that adorned my father's study. 'I do hope,' she said, rising from her chair, 'that you will find it in your heart to be kind to your mother.' With this said, Mother smiled sweetly before sweeping past me and out of Father's study."

She continued to stare at Lancey, and having assumed that this was the climax of the story, she leaned forward ready to offer her condolences, but he held up his hand to let her know that there was more. "The following morning I trudged a half-mile down a damp and muddy country lane where the mulch of leaves considerably fattened the ground. It was my intention to call upon Wilfred Stevens, a retired doctor with whom my father played a weekly round of golf and who, sadly, had been too frail to be present at the funeral. My father used to pass each weekend tramping the fairways with old Stevens, before both men settled into the huge leather armchairs in the local clubhouse and proceeded to lose themselves in clouds of cigar smoke and tumblers of the finest peaty malt. On the increasingly rare occasions that I visited our Roehampton home, I tended to restrict my socializing to the confines of the family house, sure that Mother and Father's circle of friends disapproved of me and regarded my life in the city as little more than a gay circus of social frivolity. On the other hand, I regarded the world of my parents as frozen in a Victorian fantasy of an earlier England, where to show interest in the world beyond Dover was somehow indicative of a lack of loyalty to monarch and country. I knew Dr. Stevens to be in possession of a more worldly vision, however, and as he adjusted his position in his wheelchair and allowed the nurse to rearrange the blanket about his knees, he asked eagerly about traffic in Piccadilly Circus. 'I hear that it's impossible these days to cross the street without taking one's life in one's hands. And I believe things are worse in Paris, where the

French passion for anything fashionable has them craving to be the first to acquire the latest piece of useless gadgetry, be it a bicycle or an automobile. Really, they constitute a quite stupefyingly vain nation.'

"I watched as Dr. Stevens slowly, and deliberately, peeled an orange, using a dull knife, and then I told him about the difficulty of the situation with regard to my mother and my late father's will. However, I realized that the man was thoroughly preoccupied with the challenge of removing the peel as one long strip, and having done so, he began to split the fruit into its various segments and arrange them on a small white plate that he balanced in his lap. 'Your father meant for you to feel the inconvenient mess of responsibility.' He offered me a segment of orange pinched precariously between trembling finger and thumb, but I politely refused, at which point he popped the fruit into his own mouth. 'You see, your father was a man who made every decision with calculation. He left little to chance. It's partly what made him such an excellent golfer. Unlike the rest of us, who are content to practice as we play, as it were, your father spent two or three mornings each week by himself refining his grip and stance. Nobody bested old Hugh, and so he will have anticipated your discomfort.' I said nothing as Stevens pushed another segment of orange into his mouth. 'If he thought your mother capable, or even worthy, of assuming authority over his affairs, things would now be different.' He paused and studied me intently. 'For you both.'"

At this point she saw Lancey consult his watch and glance again towards the door of the restaurant. There was still no sign of Cousin Julian, and so he turned back in her direction. "You must understand that my mother is a difficult woman and things between us have never been easy. She would, I imagine, like to see me married and settled. I suppose all mothers feel this way about their children."

"About their sons, perhaps."

He placed one hand on hers and looked briefly into her eyes. Then he looked down at their intertwined fingers.

"Yes indeed, about their sons." Again he paused.

"Young lady, I have feelings for you." As though surprised by his own words, he coughed quietly and gathered his composure. "That said, if we are to continue to spend time with one another, it is only fair that you have some awareness of my family, even though you seem altogether reluctant to share any information regarding your own."

She looked at her gentleman, knowing full well that he had little real interest in her family, assuming them to be simply colonials of some description, but she felt it sweet of him to pretend.

"I'm sorry, Lancey, but I'm not hiding anything from you."

He offered her a tight, laconic smile, and then glancing once more at the door, he continued.

"Two months after my visit, old Wilfred Stevens passed away after a stroke had snatched the gift of speech from his lips. I went to see him the week before he died, but by then it was impossible to understand anything the poor chap was saying. After a few minutes of mumbled noises he simply turned his eyes towards his nurse, who swiveled his chair and rolled him from the room, leaving me all alone in front of a roaring fire. I now realize that in all likelihood I was his final audience. At dinner that evening, I tried to raise the sad topic with my mother, but she refused to be drawn on the matter. A week or so later, I came up from London for Dr. Stevens's funeral service, a dreary event attended by two representatives of the golf club, his helpers and domestic servants, and a distant cousin from Lincolnshire. After the proceedings I returned to the family home and asked my mother if she knew why Dr. Stevens had chosen to live such a solitary existence. I wondered, had there been distress in his life? Perhaps a betrothal gone wrong or a broken promise that had cleaved his heart? For the first and, as far as I can remember, the only time, I saw Mother's face curdle into open contempt. 'I think you'll find that your father's bachelor friend struggled to control his illicit passions throughout the course of his life. I suppose we should be grateful that at least that conflict has now reached a merciful denouement.'

"The morning after Dr. Stevens's funeral, I tramped my way through the morning mist to the home of Norman Lascelles, who was not only my godfather but one of my father's former business partners. For many years Mr. Lascelles's firm had taken care of my father's legal obligations and spared him the necessity of ever soiling his hands with such matters. Land transactions, estate planning, the complexities of corporation law, nothing was beyond the scope of Mr. Lascelles, and while my father was universally considered to be a steely-eyed, cold administrator, the squat, avuncular figure of Norman Lascelles appealed to those who preferred business matters to be conducted as though two school friends were sitting down for a light luncheon and the opportunity to catch up on old news.

"It was less than a mile's walk to Norman Lascelles's newly constructed villa, with its undeniably ostentatious long and winding driveway of crushed gravel and its high boundary wall of damp stone. To the side of the oversized front door was a wedge of hardwood flaunting a newly chiseled sign which duplicated the one at the gate; both signs announced one's arrival at Swallow Haven. His housemaid directed me to the morning room at the back of the villa, where I found my father's erstwhile solicitor wrapped tightly in his dressing gown and seated at a table on top of which were piled scrupulously organized pieces of paper that I assumed to be bills, which were receiving his full consideration. During the last phase of his life, my father had reassessed his opinion of Norman Lascelles. 'The man is a swindler' had been my father's new position. 'He'll have to get up early to hoodwink me, but what about the defenceless man in the street?' My father was an individual who found it difficult to accommodate imperfection, so he would perhaps have been disappointed that I made it my business to walk clear across the village and sit with Mr. Lascelles for the better part of an hour, during which time Lascelles had absolutely nothing to say about my recently deceased father beyond vague generalities relating to my father's sense of duty and his propriety of dress. 'You'd never catch Hugh receiving guests without a collar and tie and a smart jacket of some description.' When Lascelles laughed, he did so like a scout troop master trying to impress upon his boys the fact that he was one of them. However, as he continued to chuckle, I could almost feel the man's hand sliding into my pocket and beginning to rummage about for my wallet. How could my otherwise hardheaded and perceptive father have made such a mistake? Indeed, how could I have made the mistake of visiting this man?

"The carefully executed dissolution of my father's business dealings with Lascelles actually unsettled my mother far more than it did my father. Henrietta Lascelles, whom I always knew as Aunt Hen, had, until this parting of the ways, been the only friend with whom my mother might be described as being intimate. They met most mornings of the week for tea and cordial gossip, and never ventured forth to any social function without the other. Then, without anything being said, it was plainly understood that their friendship must come to an end and all ties were broken. As I sat with Mr. Norman Lascelles, I looked in vain for any sign of Aunt Hen; a photograph, or a familiar item of clothing draped casually over a chair. I'm not sure what exactly I was hoping for, but curiously enough, Aunt Hen appeared to be absent from Swallow Haven. I suppose I can now see that in some ways the termination of my father's friendship with Norman Lascelles, and the subsequent banishment of Aunt Hen from my mother's life, marked the end of my parents' marriage, and certainly the closure of my mother's relationship with any form of contentment.

"When Lascelles finally stopped laughing, I was startled to hear him launch into an ungenerous, and entirely inappropriate, assessment of my father's supposed avarice. 'The balance sheet, that's where your father's heart stopped beating, and your mother knew it all too well. Which, of course, is why she began to look elsewhere.' I listened to the man, expecting him to offer up some kind of clarification of his absurd and squalid insinuation, but he simply stared out the window, seemingly enchanted with the birds who were flitting about the naked tree limbs in search of any scrap they might peck at. 'A new gown, or a fresh coat of paint in the house, or perhaps a new set of furniture, we're all of us obliged to offer up these trifles to keep the ladies content, but not your father.' Naturally, I knew my father to be prudent when it came to balancing the books, but it was the implication concerning my mother's character that I wished Lascelles to revisit, for I found his tone offensive. 'In her youth your mother was a beauty and could have chosen any man she desired, but one should never forget that security and safety are in their own way quite attractive. But really, what a terrible nightmare for the poor woman.'

"As I walked away from Swallow Haven and slowly crossed the gloomy village, I now understood why my father could not find a way to work with Lascelles. No matter how skilled a lawyer he might be, or how adept he was in the kind of social settings that my father found vexing, Lascelles was not an honourable man, and try as I might, I failed to understand why my father, who was a generally perceptive individual, had tolerated this partnership for so long."

Lancey suddenly stopped speaking and lowered his eyes. "I'm sorry, but since childhood there has always existed some estrangement between myself and my father, and I suppose I am still trying to understand this rift. But clearly I should never have sought out Lascelles." He paused, and once again looked up at her. "What's more, I'm afraid that my mother's recently developed bouts of anger and impatience are issues that I am also still trying to come to terms with." He shook his head and once again cast his mind back. "Later that same night I sat in the kitchen with my mother. The servants had long ago been dismissed for the evening, and it seemed unnecessary to ask the resident housekeeper to run upstairs to lay a fire in the drawing room while there was still adequate heat in the kitchen. I confessed to my mother that I had called upon Norman Lascelles. Mother looked exasperated, and would not meet my eyes. 'Despite the awful row between the two men, your Aunt Hen never said a word against her husband.' She paused and her voice dropped to a bemused whisper. 'I'll go to my grave not understanding her. Once upon a time I believed such behaviour, such loyalty, to be virtuous.' Then Mother fell silent, and her attention appeared to be seized by the undisturbed surface of her brandy. I knew full well that the only other words she would utter would be 'Good night,' and that the words would only fall from her lips when she determined that *she* was good and ready."

Again Lancey turned and stared plaintively at the restaurant door. It was becoming clear that Cousin Julian had changed his mind, and so in an effort to spare Lancey the inconvenience of admitting that he had been deserted, she picked up a menu from the tabletop.

"Perhaps we should order?"

"Yes, of course. You're absolutely right."

She looked at Lancey, who began to scan the menu, and although she could see that her gentleman's eyes were fixed on the card, it was clear that poor Lancey's mind was elsewhere.

27

Discretion

Eventually she learned to fall asleep beside Lancey, but never in his arms. She would lie next to him on her back and remain as stiff as a corpse, for she sensed that Lancey preferred the formality of uncoupled distance, and the gap seemed an apt conclusion to their judicious lovemaking. After a short while, she would inevitably discover herself dreaming some variation on the same familiar shards of memory. Home. Always home, and a succession of troubling images, all of which involved her walking hand in hand with her increasingly distracted father through thick tropical forest, or beside a tumbling river, or towards a place they never seemed to reach. At some point in the night she would turn over onto her side, but when she felt the morning light striking her face, she knew that she should now dress quickly and leave Charles Street before Lancey's manservant arrived at the house.

As she stepped down onto the pavement, she would routinely chance upon the dawn patrol of silent men in rubber boots who efficiently hosed down the streets while scorning all passing strangers. She generally liked to stroll without any destination in mind before the city became impossibly busy with the bedlam of a new day, but this morning, when she attempted to cross the broad expanse of Piccadilly in order to better witness Green Park emerging as the mist cleared, she was nearly run over by a motorcar whose driver seemed disinclined to slow down even though she was sure that the fellow had seen her. She instantly stepped back, and a burly labourer touched her arm. "Oi, you'd best watch what you're doing." She stared into the distance after the automobile. The man spoke again, this time with more sensitivity in his voice. "Well, love, you crossing to the other side or not?" She looked at the inquisitive lout and unsealed her lips to thank him, but there was something about his aspect that made her uneasy, so she gave the man her back and moved off towards her bus stop.

Lancey had recently established her in a larger set of rooms in Chalk Farm, but she found both the flat and the neighbourhood drab and uninspiring. Having safely returned to her new abode, she sat in the dismal living room and stared out through the window at the incongruous cherry blossom tree and wondered if she would ever see it flower. There were weekly singing lessons, which Lancey paid for, and the occasional audition that out of habit she felt obliged to attend, but in the main she played the role of a girl who waited patiently until she was summoned and who, sometime later, left silently before her beau opened his eyes and was forced to confront the tactlessness of her presence. Of course, only her heart prevented her from spurning this role altogether, but what she truly desired was more visibility. Sitting alone in this unfamiliar part of London, she felt embarrassed, and it troubled her that some distance appeared to have developed between herself and Mabel. Her friend seldom wrote to her, and on the one occasion that Mabel had bothered to stir herself to get on the bus to Chalk Farm, they sat together uncomfortably, the pair of them seemingly determined to steer the conversation away from any topic related to Lancey, whom Mabel appeared to have taken against. This wasn't the same tittle-tattle Mabel of old, and she couldn't help feeling that by agreeing to this arrangement with Lancey she had some-how let her friend down. However, unless Mabel took the trouble to help her understand what, if anything, she had done to cause offence, then she would have to remain mired in a state of confusion, for there was nobody else to whom she might turn for an explanation, as Ethel was away on a twenty-week tour of Australia, with four weeks in India. Unlike herself, Ethel was busy; unlike herself, Ethel had not stooped to love and thereafter found herself sitting idly about waiting for a man to whisper kind words in her ears as he unfolded his wallet.

28

Less of a Man

Earlier in the evening, after the departure of his manservant, and during the quiet time when they usually sat together in the drawing room, he asked about her father. However, the abruptness of her answer ("He's dead") caused him to look across at her and then, not wishing to cause any upset, avert his eyes and decide not to ask anything further. Sadly, he knew full well that his own father would have regarded the girl as a "mongrel" who could never be part of their world and who therefore did not deserve his son's time or attention. After a fitting period of silence, he coughed quietly in an attempt to break the tension, and then he relit his cigar. "When my own father returned from South Africa he informed my mother that he would collect me from school, even though my mother insisted that it had been arranged that, as usual, one of the servants would be travelling to Eton to escort both myself and my trunk home. However, my father would have none of it, and one snowy December morning after breakfast

I discovered him lurking furtively in the hallway outside my rooms with a black felt hat in one hand, while with the other hand he was adjusting his Gladstone collar, which was fastened by a simple gold stud. When he finished we shook hands rather stiffly, and then he said we must hurry, for he had promised Mother that we would return home in time for a family dinner.

"As the carriage proceeded to move off towards the train station, the snow began to fall with increasing vigour and thicken around the wheels, which naturally enough caused us to slow down. Father speculated that the train might well be late, but even so, at this pace we were sure to miss the connection. Suddenly the carriage drew to a halt, and the driver dismounted and opened the door so that the swirling snow blew in on us. He pointed a short distance up the road and announced that a tree was down and blocking our path. According to the driver, if we doubled back and took the side road we might still catch the train, but the man seemed to think it best to stay put, for he deemed it quite likely that the potholed side road would also be impassable. The driver let my father know that in such conditions it was customary for the local farmer to hitch up a pair of horses to a cart and venture out in search of those in distress. The man was confident that help would soon arrive and the tree would be cleared from the road, but 'soon' was never going to be good enough for my father. He shouted impatiently to the driver that we should try the side road and so, after a momentary pause in which the man obviously determined that it was pointless to say anything further to my father, we unhurriedly turned and made our way through the snow in search of the alternative route.

"Some few minutes later we skidded off the icy side road, narrowly avoiding a frozen pond. As we eventually came to rest in a ravine of a ditch, I heard the axle break. Father didn't say anything, but I knew that he was no longer absorbed by thoughts of the train, or how we might keep warm, or who might discover us; his entire thoughts were with Mother and her inevitable displeasure when she realized that we had not arrived home for dinner." Lancey paused and refilled his glass. "Truly, I am not sure why I am telling you this. For the best part of his life my father was an admirably cautious man, but at times he was possessed of an impulsiveness that I have spent my life running from. Does this make me less of a man? A coward, perhaps?" He waited, as though half-expecting her to answer, but she said nothing. "As you know, Father died a little over two years ago, so I think I feel something of your loss. In fact, not a day goes by when I don't think of him, but I wish I were in possession of more palatable memories to help counterbalance the distressing ones." He laughed uneasily. "You know, I caught a dreadful cold that night, and spent most of the Christmas hols in bed coughing and spluttering. If I remember correctly, the doctor had to be called out when my fever soared, but Father never expressed any regret. It was nearly dark by the time we were rescued, and we spent that particular night at the Station Hotel, an extremely ugly brick monstrosity where a platoon of similarly marooned patrons ate and drank cheerlessly before sloping off to the games room to indulge themselves with tedious hands of bridge or frames of billiards before retiring to their rooms. I remember looking out of the uncurtained window at the snowflakes, which had once again begun to swirl and eddy according to the whimsy of the wind. My still fully clothed father lay back on his bed, and just before I drifted off to sleep I watched him take a silver pin and set about cleaning out his pipe before turning to me and proposing what I hoped he wouldn't propose. He suggested a different story that we might tell Mother. One that didn't involve an alternative route. 'Lancelot,' he said, for he never called me by my nursery name. 'Even as we speak, your poor mother will be standing by the door in her button boots and with her winter hat clamped to her head, ready to hasten out into the night and greet us on our return.' The essence of the tale was to be truthful: snow, a broken axle, the driver trudging for miles on our behalf, an interminable wait, bitter cold, eventual rescue, and then a shared room in an unsuitable hotel. But we agreed that no alternative route had been taken; there had been no mistake. None whatsoever." Lancey laughed quietly as he relit his cigar, but he avoided eye contact. "No alternative route. What do you make of that?"

29

Men with Pencil-Thin Moustaches

The light and airy dining room is empty except for the solemn-looking man by the window who keeps glancing in her direction and smiling. She is sure that he must be a resident of the hotel, for he has about him a peculiar unencumbered aura. The waiter hovers in silence by the door, longing for one of them to finish so that he might clear away their plates; however, she takes her time with her bowl of soup. She feels vulnerable dining alone, but Lancey had warned her that his business affairs might delay him, and he had instructed her that after a half-hour she should begin without him. The waiter moves towards the man who, having finished his lunch, now rises from his seat and begins to approach her table. He wears a pencil-thin moustache that she imagines to be the custom of an earlier period, and he is dressed somewhat formally, even for an establishment such as this one. "May I join you?" He nods his head slightly as he speaks, and she gestures with an upturned palm indicating that she would have no objection to his taking the seat opposite her. As he introduces himself, she can see the waiter looking in her direction as he begins now to clear the man's table. Unfortunately, it is not possible for her to discern if she is being warned of impending danger or if the waiter is merely curious to see how this encounter might develop. As the now-seated man continues to speak, she watches his mouth move and understands that Mr. Fresh is eagerly telling her all about himself.

The man asks her again if she has ever been to Canada, and again she tells him, "No, I have never been to Canada." He continues to talk, informing her that he is waiting for the first ship to take him home to Canada, for he has a sick father he would very much like to see before it is too late. The man pauses and wonders aloud if he is being anti-British wishing to flee the country for purely personal reasons. "Mind you, despite all the talk, a full-scale conflict seems highly unlikely, don't you think?" Without waiting for her to respond, he convinces himself that he is doing the right thing, and then he confesses that Britain makes him feel a little trapped. But really, what does this man know about feeling "trapped"? She speculates as to what might have delayed Lancey, and in her mind she begins to rehearse a sharp, entirely undeliverable sentence with which to greet him. Meanwhile, her uninvited raconteur continues to talk about himself. It is only now that she notices that the man has a bread crumb lodged in his moustache, which has the effect of making him appear foolish, but she understands that it would not be politic of her to alert him to this fact.

30

A Disappointment

After nearly two weeks of silence, he sent her a telegram inviting her to meet with him at Simpson's for afternoon tea. When she arrived at the door to the dining room, the manager gestured towards the table in the far corner, and it was then that she saw Lancey seated with an implacable-looking older lady. Of course, she knew immediately who this must be, and so she composed herself and allowed a liveried young man to marshal her across the full expanse of the restaurant floor. Lancey rose from his seat and introduced her to his mother, whose lizard eyes had not left her from the moment she had entered the room. She stared at the large stones on the woman's slender fingers, and in this instant felt as though there was something terribly illicit about her own waiflike presence in the world. Who, the woman wanted to know, were her people, and from where exactly did she originate? Lancey's mother managed to fire off these and other equally intrusive questions before the woman eventually succumbed to what was evidently boredom and decided to order tea. Feeling humiliated, she looked hard at the menu and wondered why Lancey had established this audition knowing, as he surely must have, that she would fail. Why deprive her of the opportunity to prepare herself?

She had no memory of eating any crumpets or smoked salmon sandwiches, or sampling the wide selection of scones and cakes. She remembers being aware that Lancey's mother was attempting to disguise her flaccid neck by appropriating a high collar, and then the woman resumed the conversation and occasionally asked if she knew this person, or that person, but she was clearly a disappointment, for she knew nobody. As the older woman's skepticism deepened, the questions once again began to dry up and Lancey made no effort to rescue her from the situation. After a second cup of tea, his mother quietly folded her hands together, which was Lancey's prompt to spring into action and assist the clearly dissatisfied woman to her feet. The older woman bade her son's acquaintance a pleasant farewell, and she watched as Lancey escorted the grande dame from the dining room. She sat for a moment with a solitary glass of ice water for company, but she had no desire to either disturb the skin of the water or stimulate a gentle tinkling of the ice. It was unclear whether Lancey intended to return, but when it became apparent that the eyes of the other diners were now trained upon her solitary presence, she took a deep breath, gathered up her few belongings, and prepared to quietly depart the grandly ornate room.

31

A Serpent in the Bed

A week or so into the new year, Lancey finally contacted her and sent word that his driver would call for her, as he had made a reservation at a new restaurant in Piccadilly named Marco's. Once she arrived at the restaurant, she discovered Lancey on the pavement nervously smoking a cigarette, which he quickly stubbed out without either complimenting her on her appearance or wishing her a Happy New Year. "Shall we enter?" They were summarily greeted by a hireling in a top hat who held open the heavy, oversized mahogany door for them to pass through. Once inside, Marco himself welcomed them, attired in a plum-coloured suit with an astutely contrasting lilac silk handkerchief flamboyantly stuffed into his breast pocket. Lithe and olive-skinned, Marco had white hair and thin wire glasses which made him appear older than he was; however, the proprietor successfully exuded both flair and gravitas in equal measure. The host made a performance out of addressing Lancey by name, and then taking her own hand and lightly kissing it. "Please," he said as he led them past a fountain and into the candlelit interior of the restaurant, where he offered them a table with a clear view of the full splendour of the establishment. Once they were comfortably seated, Marco bowed slightly, then stepped back from the table. "My dear friends, I am at your service."

Lancey placed his hand over his glass to prevent the anxious waiter from pouring him any water. "The wine list, please." They both watched as the young man scampered away, and then Lancey continued to survey the room. "I hear that once upon a time this Marco held a position at the Ritz in Paris. I'm not clear what led him to join us here in London, but everybody is talking about the man's supposedly exquisite sense of fashion." She looked around at the decor and could see that original paintings seemed to cover every inch of the walls, although it was difficult for her to appreciate what most of them were meant to represent. She felt a sense of relief when she spied the occasional fruit bowl, or a sunlit riverbank, among the strange shapes and odd angles which seemed to dominate the majority of the canvases. "Allegedly in his youth the man knew Wilde. In the last year or so of Wilde's life." It was clear that were she a good conversationalist she would, at this juncture, have had a comment or observation to make, but once again she felt as though she were failing Lancey.

"A bottle of Champagne." He handed the wine list back to the waiter, who continued to hover with pen and notepad in hand. "Well, what are you waiting for? We shall order our food when you return with the bottle." She winced with embarrassment as the suitably admonished waiter beat a retreat. "Quite extraordinary. You would have thought that having made such an outlay on this business the man might find himself decent staff. And what am I to make of this menu?"

"It's in French, Lancey."

"Of course it's in French. I know that, but *why* is it in French?"

Marco smiled as he passed by with another couple, whom he seated in an alcove that was half-hidden from view. She noticed that before leaving the alcove their host summoned over a more senior waiter than their own, and then Marco stood sentry while the senior waiter made note of the couple's order. Eventually both Marco and the waiter moved away from the secluded table, but this time Marco travelled a more circuitous route and avoided their own table as he hurried back to his station near the door.

Having approved the Champagne, Lancey ordered for them both and then handed the menu back to the young man, who hovered timidly in an ill-fitting suit. She looked at the overstarched collar of the waiter's white shirt and could see that one tip had escaped from beneath the lapel of his jacket and was turned upwards like a small pyramid. She felt sorry for this disquieted man whom Marco had foisted upon them. "Anything else, sir?" Lancey waved a dismissive hand and then raised his glass and waited for her to do the same. "To the new year," he declared as they touched glasses.

A plate of bread arrived at their table, and although she felt that the slices had been cut too thickly, Lancey didn't seem to care as he broke a piece in half and crushed it into a petal of butter.

"Remind me, do people speak French on your island?"

She once again confirmed that English was the native tongue, and then she continued and explained how on a clear day it was quite possible to see Martinique from her mother's family estate, but Lancey had already lost interest.

"There's something unpleasant about this foreign intrusion, don't you think?"

She sipped at her Champagne but said nothing, while secretly wishing that Lancey would take the trouble to clarify whether he still maintained tender feelings for her. Please, Lancey, if you loved me just a little, I might not feel so lost. But Lancey said nothing and continued to talk. Had she done something to offend him, or was he now simply displeased with her presence on the perimeter of his life?

"But I imagine that's how the American chaps regard me, as part of some foreign invasion. I'm afraid New York can be a damned unrefined place to do business."

"How long do you think you might be away?"

He laughed as he replaced his glass on the table. "Really, my dear, you're such a funny little thing. It's just as well that I'm going to America so we can have a little respite from each other, don't you think?" She occupied herself by breaking off a piece of bread, which she then set on her side plate. Lancey pressed her. "Well?"

This was how the girls said it usually happened. Some incidental talk about being busy at the moment and not wanting to feel rushed or under any pressure, and then a gradual separation. Apparently, sometimes they offered money, but if there was any protestation or hysterics, then they might threaten a girl with the police. If that happened, then you could be sure you'd never see them again. She watched as Lancey's smile widened and his mouth began now to dance in the frantic mode, although she could hear no words. She remembered being surprised by that first attempt at a kiss at his club and hoping that everything would be alright; hoping that she would eventually be safe and looked after. That was over a year ago. How stupid. How bloody stupid.

The young waiter placed a second bottle of Champagne on the table and then readjusted the white cloth that was draped over his arm. Having untwisted the wire, he pulled at the cork, which, to the poor man's evident dismay, broke off in the bottle. The waiter began to fish in his pocket for a corkscrew, but Lancey held up his hand.

"Oh good Lord. What on earth's the matter with you? Well?"

The flustered waiter muttered something in French, which elicited from her a sympathetic smile, and then Marco arrived at the table and swiftly picked up the discarded piece of cork.

"Monsieur Hughes-Smith, I am so sorry for the inconvenience." With this said, Marco dismissed the young man from his presence with an extravagant twirl of his wrist.

"Please, the new bottle will be on the house, of course."

"But your staff don't speak English."

Marco laughed nervously. "They speak the international language of cuisine, but naturally some are more fluent than others."

Marco moved away from the table, and a deeply irritated Lancey threw down his napkin. "Do you suppose that chap imagines that he is amusing?"

Under different circumstances she would have reached across the table and taken his hand, but the air between them was thick with frustration and it was clear to her that the evening had already been lost. If only he could find it in his heart to drop a hand to her knee beneath the table, as he had often done in the past, then things between them might yet be rescued. That's all I ask, Lancey. After all, please tell me what unkindness have I ever done to you?

It was the senior waiter who attended to them for the remainder of their meal. While he was clearly more experienced than the young waiter, their new server seemed determined to talk incessantly in his highly accented English and Lancey could barely contain his annoyance with the garrulous fellow. Eventually coffee was served. "Sugar?" The senior waiter gestured towards the silver chalice that was brimful with cubes, but Lancey shook his head. "I want proper sugar, not these stupid bricks." The waiter nodded sympathetically. "Yes, of course, sir," and he removed the offending item.

"Do you think," she asked, "that we might write to each other while you are in America?"

Lancey turned his head from the retreating waiter and looked incredulously at her, as though astonished that she didn't understand how these matters were supposed to work.

"Write to each other? About what exactly?"

It had been a risk to say anything, and she straightaway felt flushed with humiliation, for it was her naive desire to be safe with him that had led her to forsake her common sense. She stared at Lancey, suspecting that her gentleman had known all along that she was simply not transferable into his world. Did he not feel any responsibility for her buoyant heart? Had the attitude of his mother successfully corroded whatever affection remained unspent? Please, Lancey, talk to me. She had given herself away, and it appeared as though the remainder of her life's journey would now have to be completed without the consolation of his reassuring presence. A year ago it was Lancey who had helped her to understand how things might begin, but she had received no instruction from him in how to navigate the short, jolting course towards separation. Perhaps, unseen by her, a serpent had been slumbering in their bed from that very first evening at his Mayfair townhouse. She looked up as the experienced waiter warily made his way back in their direction with a conventional sugar bowl cradled in his hands. He placed the silver chalice on the table halfway between them both, and then he stepped back.

"Thank you, sir." He offered Lancey a deep bow.

Lancey ignored the man and applied himself to the sugaring of his coffee. Only when he had concluded his task did he once again acknowledge her.

"I'm sorry," began Lancey. "We should never have come to this place. This Marco clearly wouldn't know what to do with a brace of pheasant or a quail. Furthermore, a man who boasts of an association with Wilde is quite simply not qualified to manage a London establishment."

She listened, but her eyes were trained upon Marco, who at that moment was standing by the oversized door and fingering his way through a huge vase of ruby red roses and looking for just the perfect stem that he would present her with as she left the restaurant.

32

Ramsgate

Having boarded the train for Ramsgate, she took up a seat in a compartment that was already occupied by an elderly couple who were sitting quietly together. Through the window she saw a handsome young man holding the hand of a young boy, and they were both waving at the old man and his wife. The couple turned slightly and waved back, and as the train began to labour its way out of the station and set out on the two-hour journey to the coast, the couple continued to wave until long after the son and grandson had passed from view. Thereafter, they readjusted their positions and said nothing. The man removed a pair of spectacles from a stiff case he carried in his inside pocket, and he unfolded a newspaper, which he proceeded to read. A half hour later, as the train pulled away from yet another small rural station, the woman reached into her handbag and produced a packet of sweets, which she painstakingly opened and held in front of her husband. He took one without either looking at her or saying "Thank you," and then returned his attention to his newspaper. His wife, mean-while, set about emptying the packet of its contents. She looked at the old couple and wondered if this is what Lancey had in mind for his own future, a comfortable descent into old age with a presentable lady whose role was both to serve and to be grateful, and who would continue to behave in such a manner until the bitter end. Lancey's latest curt telegram had clarified things with regard to their own situation: She was not to contact him. He had already suggested that she take a short break on the coast, at his expense, to "recover herself" after the procedure that he had paid for, and he had sternly coun-seled her to be more selective with regard to "male friends," unless she wished to submit to another such undertaking. His allowance aside, he reiterated that she must now learn to live without him, for it was not possible for his name to be associ-ated with a person who now appeared to be making herself available to the type of men who habitually preyed upon young women suffering from low self-esteem.

The light seemed to change as they approached the south coast. The sky became brighter and seagulls spun into view on tilted wings, but the noisy rattle of the train meant that the screeching birds could not be heard. Then they plunged into a long tunnel, and when they emerged, the train slowed to a walking pace as it began to sidle its way into the station. "The selfish bleeder's right, you do need a bit of a rest" was Mabel's verdict. "Now that you've got rid of the kiddie, take his money and have a bit of a spree. Put some colour in your cheeks. Whenever we played the seaside towns you used to like the Punch and Judy, didn't you? Try a donkey ride, or buy yourself a stick of rock, live a bit. But I'm worried about you, love. You've got to lay off the booze and stand up for yourself and stop letting blokes take what they want. Are you listening?"

She was listening, but she decided that Mabel must be talking about somebody else, because she loathed the English coast and the grey, lifeless sea, and the stupid ice-cream sellers and noisy clowns on the pier, and the wind whipping along the beach, and the mist creeping up the streets towards the narrow cobbled alleyways in which every second house appeared to be a glum bed-and-breakfast of some description. "I don't think you're well, Gwennie, and I know you're hurt, given how he just dropped you, but you're getting a bit of a reputation, you do know this, don't you?" She watched as the man carefully folded his newspaper and then stood and reached out a hand to help his wife to her unsteady feet. The grateful woman smiled and then passed him the now-empty packet of sweets, which he crumpled and pushed into his jacket pocket. The couple straggled out of the compartment and into the corridor, and she followed and took up a place behind them. All three of them waited for the carriage door to be opened from the outside. It was then that she noticed the man had taken his wife's hand in his own and was holding on to her in a manner that left her unsure as to which one of them was most in need of comfort and support.

33

Christmas

She spent the days leading up to Christmas by herself in the Chalk Farm rooms that Lancey paid for, as she was fed up with the league of morose men who at the end of the night might push a sovereign into your bag. On Christmas Eve she finished a second bottle of red wine and then sat quietly by herself combing her hair. She missed her head being fogged in the manly scent of his shaving cream; she missed the sweet aroma of his superior cigars; she missed walking with him. She knelt down by the side of the bed and tried to dredge up a prayer that she might place on her tongue, but her memory would not release one. She felt his loss as a wound, but nothing really mattered a straw. Out of the corner of her eye, she saw her stockings hanging out to dry on the back of a chair in front of the gas fire, but she hadn't the energy to find a coin to drop into the slot meter, which would have enabled her to turn on some heat. Perhaps it was her imagination, but she suddenly felt as though she was being menaced by mosquitoes, and then the sound of excited voices in the passageway startled her, but why bother to get to her feet? Happy Christmas, Gwennie. But there was no shouted friendly greeting, for she didn't know these people and they didn't know her. In the cupboard there were water crackers and some milk chocolate and a little whisky, and she felt ashamed of how she had allowed Lancey to undo her in this way, for there was nothing dignified about wanting a person who didn't want you. It was shameful. That was it, shame. She tried to recall the lyrics to a mournful song that spoke of shame, but her mind began to spin. It was Mabel who was looking down at her when, on Christmas morning, her eyes hatched and she began to swim back to the world. The doctor wore no expression and he spoke first in a crisp, well-pressed voice. "Sit up properly, miss." She could see Mabel in a modish new hat starting to cry, and then she saw her landlady quickly pull a handkerchief from her apron pocket and hand it to her friend. Mabel unfolded the handkerchief and balled it up in her face. "Oh, Gwennie, how could you do this? Why didn't you let me know you were feeling wretched?" The doctor asked her friend to stand back and give him some room, and the landlady took Mabel's arm. But Mabel kept repeating herself. "You should have let me know. Listen, love, I'd have come round straightaway if you weren't feeling yourself. There's no need for you to have gone and done this."

34

South of the River

Late one morning, she lay sprawled on the bed in her room staring impassively out of the window. It was almost noon when she hauled herself upright, and through the oval that she created with her hands she could now see only grey sky, and she tried hard to empty her mind of the events of the previous evening, including the man's name. Once again her memories came rushing back, and her fingers began to quiver and the oval frame collapsed, and she decided to roll over onto her side and curl up into a ball. With Mabel's assistance she had left Chalk Farm and found a new place to live in Bloomsbury, and once she was settled, she informed Lancey that she had relocated and gave him the address to which her monthly allowance cheque should be sent. She then did as Lancey had demanded and returned his letters and messages, but after countless months of hearing nothing further from him, it was Mabel who insisted that she should stop feeling sorry for herself and finally put "that rotten bastard" out of her mind. "You need to get yourself back into the swing of things and start to see some decent new gentlemen."

They had sat in the back of a motorized taxi as it bullied its way past a few horse-drawn hansom cabs and then continued to speed its way through the lamplit streets of the city. They were leaving behind the elegant squares and sumptuous terraces of the well-heeled, and it soon became clear to her that they were now moving purposefully in the direction of the river. She had already marked Mabel's friend down as a dull man whose company at dinner had been unrewarding, to say the least, and whose clumsy attempt to reach across the table and stroke her cheek had established a trying tone to the evening. Having traversed the moonlit black water, squalour hurried into view and closed in on them as the pavements were suddenly crammed with dirty-faced ruffians. On certain streets it seemed to her that whole families had banded together and were wandering aimlessly, as though refugees from some great catastrophe, but she found it difficult to watch them, for she knew that by doing so she was simply reducing them to the role of filth-encrusted street performers. Down a side street she could just about make out a ghostly pack of dogs who appeared to be freely scavenging, and still this man had not turned from the window to face her and let her know what, if anything, was coursing through his closed mind. The man continued to sit perfectly erect, with both hands clamped tightly on top of his cane. She presumed that for her escort this was most likely a journey into a familiar underworld where the prospect of showing this sylphlike girl a desolate part of the city no doubt caused him some tremor of amusement. She looked at the man and imagined that were she a more compliant character they would most likely be relaxing in his

Chelsea drawing room with glasses of Madeira to hand and a bedroom in their future, but instead they were plunging ever deeper into this abyss, and the man continued to say nothing at all and simply stared vacantly out of the window.

Some moments later, she noticed that her companion had slipped down a little in the seat and his head was now swaying in time to the lurching of the vehicle. The views of the world beyond their taxi were becoming increasingly disturbing, and for a moment she toyed with the idea of touching Mabel's friend on the arm and waking him from his slumber. She didn't wish to kindle any emotion within the man, however, and so she clung to the door handle as they rose and crossed a small wooden bridge, which deposited them even deeper in the heart of London's filth. A whistle rent the silence and a gangly man burst into view, his arms and legs moving in seemingly random formation, and then the man ducked hurriedly into an alleyway and passed out of sight. She heard voices raised in anger, and again a whistle burst through the night air, but nobody else appeared. Her gentleman friend opened his eyes and turned now to look at her, and by squinting slightly, she was able to detect a self-conscious smile on his face. "It was very unkind of me to disregard you in this way." His face was disguised in shadow, so it was difficult for her to see his full expression, but now that he had spoken she felt somewhat safer. To be fair, he didn't appear to be judging her, or silently laughing at her, as some of Mabel's other men friends had done, but she knew that it was foolish of her to have agreed to dine with this man in the first place, for she wasn't in the right frame of mind to spend time with anyone.

How long would it be before he would let her go back to her room in Bloomsbury? She didn't want to appear ungrateful, but the tedious meal and now this strange journey were already more than enough adventure for her. How much further, she wondered, before these roads spat them both out into the countryside below London? Her companion leaned over and ever so gently removed the pin from her hat, and then lifted the bonnet from her head and set it down on the seat in between them. "There," he said, "surely that feels better?" If he had taken hold of her dress and stripped it violently from her body she could not have felt more naked than she did in the wake of his gesture, but then the vehicle stopped and she could see that they were now on a broader street that was blessed with some illumination from gas lamps that were bracketed onto a large brick building. She guessed that they were outside a public house, for music was spilling from the building and out into the street with a clamorous confidence with which she was familiar, although it felt like an age since she had last stirred herself to attend an audition, let alone set foot on a stage. The driver turned off the engine and she was relieved that it appeared as though they might well be about to enter company, for her gentleman would now be subject to the scrutiny of other eyes.

As he stepped from the motorized taxi, Mabel's friend extended a helping hand, and her attention was once again temporarily captured by the worn condition of the engraving on the gold band that decorated his wedding finger. As the driver shut the door behind her, she looked around and saw an unshaven man sitting on a low wall staring steadily at them both. His hand levered a brown bottle to his face and he drank deeply before once more lowering the bottle. It was then that she noticed the man's chin jutting out with a defiant confidence that directly contradicted the evidence of his situation, and then, with a movement that seemed comically contrived, the man cautiously lifted his hand to the brim of his cap and touched it in a gesture of both greeting and humility. Behind him the noise of music unexpectedly rose again as gusty pub voices began to sing along to the piano, but her escort ignored the pandemonium and simply took her arm and nodded in the direction of the Star and Garter. "I believe we might secure a nightcap here, unless you would prefer somewhere a little quieter."

The brass-trimmed interior of the pub was overly bright and crammed with people singing and playing cards, all of whom were caught up in a joyful atmosphere that bore no relation to the misery of the world that lay beyond the venue. The man held on tightly to her arm and steered her towards a door at the far end of the public bar. Once they passed through the door, a brawny brute with a ruddy complexion anticipated their needs. "A perch for two, sir?" He quickly led them to a table by the window and produced a cloth from his apron which he flicked onto the tabletop as he encouraged them to sit. "Beer for you both, and will there be anything to eat?" She shook her head and then watched as the fellow passed through a set of swing doors which led into what she inferred was the kitchen. Their entrance had disturbed a dog sleeping beneath the neighbouring table, and the mangy hound looked up at them. In this part of the pub people neither played games, nor did they listen to music, but its strains were clearly audible. The unwashed clientele huddled over their drinks and, unlike the dog, showed no interest whatsoever in the newcomers. But why bring her to such a place? Did he really imagine that she might enjoy an evening in this frightful pub? The swing doors were flung wide open and a boy, no more than ten years of age by her reckoning, set down two glasses of foaming beer before nimbly scooting away. Her gentleman lifted his glass to his lips and encouraged her to do the same, and for the first time it occurred to her that this man might well be lonely, but it was no business of hers. As she replaced her glass on the tabletop, she noticed the elderly couple at the next table clamber unhurriedly to their feet and lean into each other as they began to dance to the muffled music from the public bar. They moved together, their arms circling each other's waist, their feet scuffing through the sawdust, their two clouds of beery breath becoming one as they forgot themselves. She guessed that their embrace marked the end of a day of labour on some market stall, a day that had most likely commenced before dawn in the darkness of a noisy London back street. Now they were able to press up against each other and, bathed as they were in sweat, feel the cool calm of a familiar body. She knew what it was that she was watching, but she dare not call its name. She stared as the couple turned slowly before her eyes, for she had not expected such passion to show itself tonight; and not here, in this place, south of the river.

On the return journey north neither of them said a word. The motorized taxi had waited for them, and although she had felt content watching the dancers turning silently as one, after a second glass of beer her gentleman was ready to leave. It had begun to rain, and as they approached Westminster Bridge, her eyes followed a homeless old woman who trudged, with a bundle across her back, up the incline, but as the fatigued apparition stepped into a cone of light, she could see now that the sour face was actually that of a child, and her heart sank. She listened to the mournful bellowing of a foghorn as an unhurried vessel eased its way downriver towards Greenwich, and she asked herself, Is all happiness extinct in this city? Once again it occurred to her that she should simply renounce this place and go back to her island and leave behind the haunted faces of London, for, after all, her efforts to establish a life for herself trapped towards the rear of a stage had proved futile. Really, why stay? And then she felt the touch of the man's hand on her own. He leaned in and kissed her, with his beery breath, before asking if she wished to take a turn in Regent's Park, but she understood full well what he was asking of her. A curtain would be pulled to and she would be expected to submit to this man as they joined the parade of carriages and motorcars crossing the park in the darkness. She looked closely at him, but there was something pathetically halfhearted about his suggestion. After a short while he spared her the embarrassment of having to respond. "Tired?" She nodded. The couple would still be dancing together in the pub, she was sure of this, but she was equally sure that as the night progressed their feelings for each other would only deepen.

35

The Deadline

They are now sitting together in his study, and she is fully clothed. An hour earlier she was lying back on his bed in the lace underwear that he liked her to wear, but as he started to unbutton his shirt, she began to scream, and he immediately asked her to please get dressed and follow him out of the bedroom. On entering his study she had demanded a glass of water, and then she began to count out the pills as though they were confectionery. He eventually persuaded her to return the pills to the bottle, replace the top, and hand the infernal thing over to him. "Thank you," he said as he placed the bottle on the highest shelf of the bookcase. He stares at her, unable to understand why her normally accommodating behaviour has, of late, become hostile and sometimes hysterical. Sadly, he now accepts the fact that he has little control over the woman he has moved out of her Bloomsbury room and into his Temple flat. She glares at him and then suddenly she smiles, but he is unsure of what exactly it is that is amusing her. She begins to giggle and then addresses him. "It's hopeless, isn't it?" He waits for her to continue, but she momentarily has trouble remembering his name. "Max?" At this point her laughter becomes uncontrollable. "Pour me some whisky, Max."

He looks at her closely and concludes that she really is a fine-looking young woman, although clearly not to everybody's taste. He assumes it is the exotic part of her nature that contributes to her allure, but in some rural parts of England she might well be mistaken for the slow girl in the village. Her eyes, for instance, are perhaps a little too close together, and he often observes her sitting perfectly still in a trancelike state of wonderment, with her lips slightly parted. Once again the telephone rings out, but he ignores it, for he knows that his impatient employer is expecting the revised article before midnight. Unless the woman can be persuaded to calm down, he shall once again miss his deadline, and this time there will certainly be talk of his newspaper moving him on.

Three months ago they began their arrangement. He surprised himself by making moderately improper overtures at their first dinner together, and shortly thereafter he asked her to end her unregulated friendships with other men and consider moving into his flat. He boldly announced that there would no longer be any need for her to pose nude for so-called artists, or waste her nights drinking at the disreputable Crabtree Club. He told her that he too was prepared to forgo casual friendships with females, and in this way they might build a future together. But she has deceived him, and tonight, after she put on the lace underwear, he could no longer help himself. However, instead of complying with her entreaties and taking possession of her with quiet force, he simply stood over her and unleashed his accusations, which were met with frenzied hysteria and her subsequent childish attempt to swallow pills.

He hands her a glass of whisky, and she takes the drink, but her eyes don't leave his face. He speaks quietly. "You have let me down." He is repeating himself, for he knows that she heard this same line in the bedroom. "I felt safe and content with you, but what am I to do now?" She refuses to answer, and so he crosses to the window and looks out into the night, where he sees a lad turning the corner with a package under his arm. The gaslight is fully illuminating his young face, and he notices the carefree bounce in the fellow's step. He immediately understands that his employer has sent this boy to collect the article, and most likely drop off some research for the weekend column, and so he steps back from the window and waits for the knock on the door.

"Well," she says, "aren't you going to see who that is?" He watches as she gulps down her whisky. Again there is another knock on the door, which she takes as a signal to hold out her glass. "I would like another drink, please." As he pours more whisky, she begins to laugh at him. "You needn't worry, I'll soon be gone, and then you can get on with your work."

"Don't talk like that."

"Give me back my pills." She gestures with the full glass and spills some whisky onto the rug. "My pills!" she demands.

"Please keep your voice down."

She raises the whisky up high as though greeting him across a crowded room. "Cheers," she says, before lowering the vessel, and then with her finger she traces a circumspect circle around the lip of the glass.

When he first met her at the Crabtree Club, she had a drink in her hand, and while the other girls appeared eager to talk or dance, her whole body seemed to be bent over the bar and focused on her whisky. Shyness, he assumed, which was partly what attracted him to her, but two weeks after he began seeing her, Percival Whittaker, the Home Affairs editor, called him into his office and asked him to please close the door behind him. During the preceding week he had twice delivered copy late, but it would be difficult for him to confess to Whittaker that he was having some trouble with a mercurial girl who appeared keen to be mauled, with or without tenderness, and who seemed reluctant to allow him to disentangle himself from the muddle of the bedsheets. The editor smiled at him with his nicotine-stained teeth, and stubbed out his cigarette in the ashtray that sat on top of a pile of old newspapers on his desk. As Whittaker started to speak, it was clear that the man was trying to make their meeting appear to be more conversation than admonishment, but his intention was clear. As his editor spoke, the man's face temporarily hidden behind wisps of dying smoke, it occurred to him that he was actually frightened of this new girl, and his reluctance to attend to his work had less to do with her charms and more with his having imported a dangerous lion into his life. "Well, Max, what are we going to do about your late copy?" His editor looked at him over his half-moon spectacles, but he wasn't sure how to respond to Whittaker. Surely he wasn't the first bachelor reporter whose infatuation with nightlife and saucy girls had caused a dip in the efficiency of his work. However, after a few minutes of apparently affable conversation, it became clear that his editor was simply letting him know that the problem was his to solve, and warning him that he should do so quickly.

Tonight he was determined, without any prepared statement, to draw things to a close and launch the girl onto a new path, but he wished to do so without her feeling as though the palm of his hand was resting against her back. The detour into the bedroom had been her stratagem, and he had nobody but himself to blame for his weak submission to her aberrant behaviour. But now, as he refilled his glass and replaced the decanter on the tray, he began to search for the right words. Mercifully, Whittaker's boy had stopped his knocking, but as he composed himself, he could hear muffled sounds of laughter in the street as late-night revellers passed by. He decided to wait until the noises faded, but the girl's patience had clearly expired.

"You know," she began, "there was somebody before you, but I told you this, didn't I?"

"Yes, you did."

"You act as though you're the first, but I've been let go before."

"But you are still seeing other men. How do you think I feel?"

"I don't know how you feel. All of you men have such strange names: Max, Lloyd, Algernon. Maybe that's what I like about you, Max? Your strange name. There must be something that I like about you." He watches as she swirls the whisky in her glass as though searching for ice. "But the first man was very different from you. I believed, at least to begin with, that his intentions were quite honourable, but it appears that I wasn't able to make any real contribution to his life." She pauses. "The truth is, I never really discovered what his intentions were."

He sinks into the armchair opposite her, but the fey girl won't meet his eyes. She stares instead at the space between her splayed feet.

"Do you remember when you took me to the races at Ascot and I met your newspaper friends and you included me in the conversation, even though I knew so very little. You gave me money to buy a new dress, didn't you? And we laughed and you made sure that everybody knew we were together, and I thought that it was always going to be like that day at Ascot, but I'm so naive, aren't I?" She looks up and pierces him with her eyes. "But in this sense you're just like the other men with their silly names. In the end I'm not what you want, am I?"

"That was a marvellous day at Ascot, and there's no reason why it can't be like that again. But I've told you, you really must clarify your situation with regard to your men friends."

He smiles at her, and a smirk slowly begins to appear on her face. Then he notices that she is pouring what remains of her whisky onto the rug, letting it cascade gently from the glass, more dribble than waterfall, and then she begins to study the dark, wet spot as it blossoms between her feet. He shakes his head and stands and crosses to the window, knowing that he should immediately order her to leave his flat, but understanding that it would be unwise to do so. And then he sees Whittaker's messenger boy, who is standing at the foot of the steps that lead up to the front door and leaning against the iron railings. The boy holds the package in one hand, and his other hand is pushed deep into his trouser pocket against the chill of the night. Clearly the lad is under instruction that he should go nowhere until he delivers the material in person.

36

A New Family

When she saw the bus come to a halt in the traffic around Piccadilly Circus, she stopped running, for she knew that it would be alright and she was now certain to catch it. But then the motorcars suddenly began to move and the bus began to accelerate towards the stop, and so she raised a hand to hold her bonnet in place and began to barge her way through the crowd. Just as the bus was pulling away from the stop, she jumped up onto the step and squeezed in and took up a seat next to a shop girl whose head was buried in a cheap paper book whose sensationalism was evident from the number of exclamation points on the pages that were visible. But who was she to judge? The girl seemed contented, and so she turned to the window and could see that the rain had once again begun to fall and was making the streets glassy and causing the lights of the shops to glisten like fairy lights in the murkiness of this early Saturday evening. Where was everybody going? Home, she imagined, after a day of work or an afternoon spent tramping the streets of the West End shopping for items that were now crammed into burdensome bags that spilled out into the aisles of innumerable buses. Her feet were wet, as she had stepped in a puddle racing for the bus, but she hoped that they didn't begin to attract any attention, for the smell of damp leather could sometimes be unpleasant. She closed her eyes and listened to the drone of the vehicle as it lurched and then stopped and then lurched again with erratic regularity, and then she once again became aware of the girl next to her eagerly turning the pages of her book and nudging her each time she did so. Eventually she guessed that they must be getting close to her stop, and so she opened her eyes and rose to her feet and grabbed the overhead rail and began to stumble her way towards the back of the bus.

The bus deposited her a short walk from her rooming house on Torrington Square, but not having an umbrella, she bent her head and leaned forward into the spiteful London wind so that she could see only her feet and a few yards of pavement ahead of her. She cradled the small ribboned box under her arm, tucking it away as best she could to protect it from the now lashing downpour, and she could feel the bitter cold beginning to sting her face. Whenever she heard a pair of footsteps, she looked up to make sure that she was avoiding a collision, but inevitably the person had already seen her and was moving out of her path. Once she reached the house, she scampered upstairs as quickly as possible so that she might shun having to engage with any of the residents who, during this time of war, appeared to be a strange assemblage of Continental transients and strays hiding out in London—but from what or whom she could never be sure. And truthfully, was she that dissimilar to them? During the week she worked at a canteen near Euston Station serving soldiers and other lost souls, and in the evenings she would unhappily slouch back to her room and wait. But for what? For the war to end, of course, but would it ever end? And the longer it went on, the more she felt trapped in England.

She closed the door to her room and put the box of cake down on the sideboard. She was too tired to lay a fire, and so she would have to move briskly. She slipped out of her damp shoes and then hung her sodden coat on the back of the door. Then she stepped clear of her best skirt and unbuttoned her blouse before sitting and peeling off her stockings. Her old dressing gown lay corpse-like across the bed where she had left it this morning, so she picked it up and belted it around herself and then emptied the contents of the ceramic jug into the tin basin and cupped the icy water to her face. She was safe now, back in her room, and unless one of the eccentrics knocked at her door and tried to persuade her to come downstairs for dinner, she was comfortably beyond human intercourse for the remainder of the evening.

She stared out of the window as the rain intensified, and she thought of all that had happened on this strangest of Saturdays. She had deliberately woken late, as though keen to bypass the day that lay ahead of her, and then she dressed slowly and attempted to time her exit from Torrington Square so that she might dodge any prying eyes, for the bonnet she was wearing was bound to leave her susceptible to unwanted questions. She found the church easily enough and took up a seat in the rearmost pew on the side that looked as though it belonged to Mabel's family and guests. Then she fidgeted as she waited. She could see the back of two dozen heads and guessed that some of them were stage girls, but she had long ago left that world behind and so she knew that it was unlikely that any of the girls would be familiar to her. After migrating to Australia, Ethel had written her a peach of a letter telling her all about her new husband, who owned a travelling circus, and so there was only Mabel left to remind her of what she once was. And then the music dropped full-on, deep disturbing organ chords which announced something ominous was about to transpire. All about her, people rustled to their feet, and so she did, too. The matronly woman next to her was wearing an extravagant hat set off with a peacock feather, and she watched her neighbour lean forward and pick up a hymn book and raise her voice together with the rest of the congregation. But why were they singing a hymn? Surely the bride was supposed to walk up the aisle to just music, but because she'd never before been invited to a wedding, she couldn't be sure. Then Mabel passed her by dressed in a white satin gown with a lace veil, and she could see that her friend was leaning on the arm of an older man who she assumed was Mabel's father. Mabel looked uncertain, but her father seemed proud, and the people continued to sing their hymn, and then Mabel reached the altar, where a man named Billy was waiting for her, a man to whom her friend had never introduced her, for, according to the note that Mabel had scribbled on the back of the invitation, everything had happened really fast.

The fellow was attempting to eat a piece of cake with a fork. "Have you ever ridden in a motorcar? Another year or two and I'll have one for myself."

She stared at the ruddy-faced clown who had followed her down the nave and then out into the cold and around the back of the church to the hall in which the wedding reception was to be held. How clever this chap must think he is, talking to Mabel's peculiar friend and attempting to work out if he is in with a chance. She ignored him and peeked over at Mabel, who was trying to mingle with her guests and appear happy in the large draughty hall. But Mabel didn't seem happy, and she wondered if perhaps an unwelcome baby was on the way. She observed her friend closely as she continued to whisk her way around the hall with a smile stitched to her face, and then she came to rest by Billy's side and touched her husband's arm as though keen to indicate that this man meant everything to her.

"Hey, you're not listening to me, are you?"

She blinked at the fellow, unsure of what exactly he expected her to say.

"I asked you if I could call on you, but if it's not convenient, then just say so. It's not nice to keep a chap hanging on like this."

She looked closely at the man, and then across at a beaming Mabel, then back at her admirer.

"Listen, wee lassie, you should go home. I hope you don't mind my saying so, but you don't seem well. But don't forget to pick up your little box of cake. Nice touch, don't you think. Typical of our Billy to think of every last detail."

It had stopped raining now, but she continued to sit in her old dressing gown and stare out of the window and down into Torrington Square. Mabel had tried to persuade her to stay

("There's plenty of interesting blokes here besides Billy's big brother"), but she told her friend that she had a headache. ("Well, I expect to see you after the honeymoon. Billy's taking me all the way to Scotland. It's where his folks are from.") It was some time now since Mabel had wistfully announced that she was putting aside her hopes of enticing a wealthy "sugar." ("Let's be honest, I'm turning blousy, and when the petals start to fall off the rose, the bees don't come around anymore.") Today her friend Mabel had snagged a modest type of fellow, and she was pleased for Mabel, while having no aspiration of her own to be similarly encumbered. Mabel now had a husband, and she in turn had a little box of cake, and earlier in the day she had given Mabel a hug and then dashed off to try and find a bus back to town, where she knew she would have to change at Piccadilly Circus.

She pulled the dressing gown even closer and realized that she should withdraw from her seat by the window and climb into bed and try to keep warm before she caught a cold. She knows that Mabel isn't coming back from Scotland. Why would she? Mabel has willingly costumed herself in a white dress and veil in exchange for the guarantee of an escape route. As she turned over in the icy envelope of the bedsheets, she tried to feel pleased for Mabel, but she worried that Mabel's brother-in-law might well be representative of Mabel's new family, and if this proved to be the case, then she feared for her friend's future happiness.

VI

Continental Drift

37

The Great War

After weeks of scouring the notices in newspapers, she eventually secured a job near Euston Station and started serving food and drink to men returning from the horrors on the Continent. These were truly broken men who lined up before her, and any temptation to wallow in self-pity over her post-chorus-girl years of drinking and ill-chosen men seemed inappropriate. For many of these gallant soldiers shuffling towards her counter, death on the field of battle might have been a benevolent gift. Having dragged themselves back home she guessed that a great number of the men had now discovered themselves adrift among family and friends who no longer recognized them, nor did they know what to do with these ghostly apparitions. The men smiled pluckily when the bashful lady handed them a bread roll and a cup of tea, but she wasn't fooled by either their civility or the bulky confidence of their brown greatcoats, for she knew that beneath their buttoned shrouds of rough wool these men were skin and bone and the occasional charitable "meal" wasn't going to help. Just what actions had they witnessed that caused these young souls to wear such looks of abject bewilderment? Having eaten, some of them could barely manage to drag themselves to their feet and leave, while others finished their tea and bread and then grabbed another roll and scooted for the door as though ashamed to be seen taking handouts of any kind. Some few, of course, had never fought in the war and were simply down on their luck and drifting around fogbound London when they happened upon the canteen by good fortune, but uniformed or not, neither she nor the other women made any distinction once a weary man stepped through the door in search of food and drink and a temporary respite from the late-autumn chill.

Her rooming house was crowded with refugees from every corner of Europe. On the evening that Monsieur Lenglet visited, she instantaneously noticed his stiff white collar and tie, and his handsome dark eyes, and the unkempt hair that swept down across his forehead betrayed the fact that it was unlikely he had ever seen the front. He sat near the head of the dining table and spoke softly in French, but every time she looked up, the confident stranger was staring in her direction, and long before he eventually turned to her she knew that he would find an excuse to address her. Would she perhaps be able to join him for lunch tomorrow at a Soho restaurant with which he was familiar? English people seemed to dislike her voice and so she had long accustomed herself to speaking in a whisper, but this meant that her words were often lost in the welter of noise generated by competing conversations. He asked her again, displaying quiet elegance in a language that was not his own, and this time she nodded as she answered "Yes," but she was careful to make sure that their eyes did not meet.

The following evening they sat together at the Café Royal and stared out of the window at the elegant sweep of a busy Regent Street. As they did so, the waiter removed the cold ornamental plates that boasted the restaurant's name and replaced them with marginally larger warm plates that lacked decoration of any kind. Their silences were long but never ungraceful, and she liked the fact that this foreigner felt under no obligation to entertain her with sweetly dealt words. In fact, he behaved towards her as though women were to be admired as opposed to desired, and a man had never before appeared to simply delight in her company. Lunch had been easy. He had waited patiently for her in a shop doorway, and only when she came into view did he step forward and offer his arm and gently guide her into the dimly lit Soho restaurant, where he finally asked her, "Are you English?" She paused and lowered her eyes. "Well, I suppose I've tried to be, but no." After lunch she strolled along Piccadilly on the well-favoured man's arm, and he bought her cigarettes, scent, and powder, and then said he thought her wise to have renounced the stage, for it was beneath her. He then enquired if she might be available for dinner.

The waiter placed the dessert tray on the table in front of them, and only after the attentive man withdrew did she begin to tell Monsieur Lenglet about Aunt Clarice. Over pre-dinner cocktails he had asked about her family, and unsure how to respond, she had changed the subject in the hope that the business of ordering food and wine might deflect his attention away from this topic. However, now that they had reached the culmination of their meal, she felt comfortable enough to speak a little of her Aunt Clarice, whom she summed up as "disapproving." Having shared this information, she quickly moved on and told him that after arriving in England she had been relentlessly teased by the girls at her school. As she spoke she could see a cloud of hurt descending across her new friend's face, as though it was he who had been the victim of the schoolgirl bullying. He reached across the table and took both of her hands in his own, and then he paused as though unable to comprehend that such cruelty might exist in the world. "I am so sorry, but now I understand why you appear to be so frightened. These girls, they really hurt you, didn't they?" She had never thought of her eighteen months as a schoolgirl in Cambridge as possessing any real significance, partly because so much unhappiness had been visited upon her during her subsequent years in London. "Yes," she said, her voice faltering slightly. "I think it was difficult, but once I left the Perse School and came to London and started at Mr. Tree's Academy of Dramatic Art, I soon forgot all about the girls."

Monsieur Lenglet let go of her hands and sat back in his chair and looked at her as though he had never before met such a creature. Although she was unsure of what he was thinking, it was suddenly clear to her that this mysterious but nevertheless charming man seated across from her represented the possibility of an escape to some kind of a future. On each evening of the same week he escorted her to dinner, where by degrees she learned a little more about his past. He told her that he was fluent in at least four languages and that he had been sent by the French government into Germany. But to what purpose? she wondered. The Germans were the enemy. She listened and he talked, and even when the impossibly expensive dinners ceased and were replaced by long evenings at her rooming house with a bottle or two of red wine, she continued to listen diligently. One night they charged out into the first sprinkling of snow and stood together in the cobbled courtyard behind the house like guests who had turned up late for a party. When he asked if she might consider crossing the Channel and joining him on the Continent once this damn strife finally came to an end, she felt able to whisper, "Yes." However, later that night it occurred to her, join who exactly? All she really knew was that this man's past seemed to lead to the muddy crossroads of Belgium, Germany, the Netherlands, and France, and he spoke cautiously to her out of the hodgepodge of his many languages. Obviously he had a history, but nobody at the Torrington Square house seemed able, or willing, to assist her in understanding what it might be, although she had gleaned that he bought and sold things that she suspected were not always his to sell. But did it really matter? Her life in England had now been reduced to a job in a canteen near Euston Station spooning out rations to the unfortunate and the afflicted. She turned over in bed and looked out through the uncurtained window at the black starless sky, and once again she asked herself, did it really matter that she knew practically nothing about this strange Monsieur Lenglet, who had offered her no blandishments and, unlike the others, did not appear to be in a hurry to try and make his tongue gambol in her mouth.

38

A Modern Marriage

The train ceases its rattling march and slows down as they near the Gare du Nord. As it does so, she presses her face up against the window. Where is the world of wide, inviting boulevards populated by fashionable Parisians? Where are the garrulous French bohemians who choose to sit at splendid sidewalk cafés drinking coffee and liqueurs, as opposed to hiding themselves away in pubs? Nearly a year after the armistice, the façades of some buildings remain boarded up; brickwork appears to be pockmarked and she can see many broken windows. As the train eases its way into the station accompanied by an ominous metal grating, she stares at the flurry of itinerant soldiers and scurrying vendors and keen-eyed porters. After five months in Holland she understands that, for better or worse, this is now her world. Her slumbering husband continues to breathe with a hoarse regularity that she worries might thicken into a snore, and so she leans forward and gently pushes him awake. Monsieur Lenglet rubs a hand across his face and seems distracted, as though momentarily trying to remember her. Is it possible, she wonders, that she might well be participating in a modern marriage: attachment and detachment at one and the same time?

She steps down onto the platform, clutching her brown valise, and scans the disembarking passengers to her left and right. A barrel-shaped man in a purple gown, with slippers to match, gestures with his little finger towards a pile of luggage that he expects a bemused porter to convey for him. The flamboyant man smokes a cigarette with a filter, and she can see that the thin sheen of perspiration on his brow will eventually cause his makeup to run. She gazes at her tired husband, who seems to be affecting boredom with this chaotic foreign terminus. No doubt her Aunt Clarice would have pursed her lips and without any words made it clear that this alien was exactly the type of untrustworthy dawdler she anticipated her twenty-nine-year-old niece would end up with. Lenglet throws down his cigarette and smiles at her and tries to simulate an ease with the scene, although she suspects that her husband's immediate impulse is to get back on the train and escape this furor.

"You need to rest." He gently touches her pregnant stomach, then he steps back and takes her in from head to toe. "And we will have to get you some Parisian clothes."

But the city would have to accept her as she is, for experience has already taught her that making any kind of effort never seems to result in anything but disappointment.

"Won't you look at me?" He lifts her chin with his index finger. "You're supposed to be happy now." She gives him her eyes and then bursts into laughter, a habit which creates pockets of awkwardness which she knows Lenglet finds difficult to abide. And then she attempts to hide behind her nonexistent mane of hair. Her husband has already accused her of looking at him as though she has gone back to her childhood, but why not go back to a time when she was relatively content?

Lenglet takes the valise from her and slips his free arm around her waist. As he does so, she is once again assailed by the same sense of fatigued resignation that five months earlier almost smothered her as she made the short sea journey across the turbulent Channel to Holland to rendezvous with her suitor. And now they are married, and she is pregnant, and they have left Holland, and finally they have arrived in the city he had promised her from the beginning—Paris. They walk quietly along the platform and she allows Lenglet to steer her bulk between the dense press of people. She finds it strange to see men who don't appear to feel it necessary to wear a hat and who seem perfectly at ease sporting themselves bareheaded, and then her child moves and she wonders if anyone has noticed her momentary alarm. It will eventually have to be clothed and fed and given a name and offered guidance and advice as to how to pass safely through the world beginning here, in Paris. She drops a discreet hand to her stomach. So, she thinks, this is my life. This is my new beginning. Our new beginning. This is the city Lenglet vowed he would offer up to me. This is Paris.

39

The Negress

One evening, while slowly making her way to the hotel dining room, she saw the back of a gaunt Negress who was quietly disappearing into a room at the end of the long passageway. She stood transfixed and stared in the direction of the closed door and wondered if her imagination might well be playing some diabolical trick on her. Despite the cumbersome evidence of her pregnancy, of late she had taken to walking lightly, as though keen to leave no footprints, and so she continued on her dainty way. The clumsiness of enforced conviviality depressed her, but having glimpsed the Negress, she was somewhat cheered to be in possession of a secret and determined not to alert her fellow residents to the woman's présence among them. However, as she took up her seat, the bellicose Monsieur Gaston, whose bald head was decorated with pink blemishes, pushed his soup plate disparagingly away from himself, wiped his mouth on his still-folded handkerchief, and then asked the two women at the table if they were aware that a nigger was dwelling among them. Dame Olivia promptly turned on him, her face colouring as she spoke. "I will not tolerate that kind of talk at the dinner table. Kindly confine your prejudices to less public places." With his familiar contempt, Gaston ignored the elderly English lady, whose drooping face hung loose off its moorings, and he addressed the hotel proprietor and demanded to know why the city didn't provide such people with their own places to lodge. Why must they reside, even temporarily, among decent people? *"C'est une honte!"* The hotel proprietor barely looked up as he cleared the man's soup plate, but without raising his voice, he made it clear that the Negress was an entertainer of some distinction and she could stay for as long as she wished. He added that it was she who had chosen to eat alone in her room, but his guest was in no way compelled to do so. A florid-faced Monsieur Gaston snorted in evident disgust but said nothing further.

The following day the Negress left her window open and played gramophone records from early morning to late in the afternoon. By sitting near her own window she was able to listen to the infectious beat of the Negress's music, and in this manner while away the solitary hours in her cramped hotel room, occasionally feeling the cotton curtain being blown inwards by the draught and brushing up against her bare arm. In the evening the hotel proprietor announced that his absent tenant would imminently be performing a dance recital at a nearby theatre. It now made sense to her. She imagined the Negress in her room practicing steps to the music and contorting her body into all manner of different shapes, a suspicion that was given some credence by the fact that the woman had a tendency to play the same song repeatedly, so either she was busy rehearsing or the poor soul had lost her mind. Her husband would have an opinion, but these days Lenglet seldom bothered to show his face at the hotel before midnight, and on most mornings of the week he was gone again shortly after dawn, and it was therefore unlikely that he would ever see or hear the beguiling woman who now dwelt among them.

On Sunday, Monsieur Gaston presented himself at breakfast in his finest clothes and announced that he was going to church. Nobody had asked him about his intentions for the day, but Gaston was obviously keen that everybody should be apprised of this new development. "The church near the Gare du Nord seems respectable" was how Gaston introduced the subject. Dame Olivia peered over the top of her spectacles and stared directly at him. "And are you familiar with their service?" After Gaston had left the dining table, Dame Olivia reached over and placed a comforting hand on her arm. "He is a Jew, you do know this, don't you?" Monsieur Gaston's heritage held no interest for her, and this knowledge was unlikely to colour her already jaundiced impression of the man. Dame Olivia continued. "Are you waiting for me to leave so that you are free to take your husband his breakfast?" She felt herself blushing, but she chose to say nothing in response. "My dear girl, you remind me of an *ayah* we had in Ooty during the interminably long hot summers. A snippet of a thing she was, and the fragile girl said precious little." It was undeniable: On Sunday mornings her husband expected her to bring him breakfast, and so she had been deliberately lingering in the hope that

Dame Olivia would leave. Once she was alone, the hotel proprietor would invariably hand Madame a small tray, for he had evidently seen something in her plight that encouraged him to feel pity.

That Sunday morning she left her husband's breakfast tray of café au lait and fresh rolls and butter on the chest of drawers while he continued to sleep, and then she did as Dame Olivia had suggested. She knocked gently on the Englishwoman's door, and as Dame Olivia ushered her in, she discovered that the old lady's room was much larger than her own, and being at the front of the hotel, it was also brighter. Through the open window she could clearly hear the loud, competing bells of distant churches, and there was also a clamour of raised voices in the street below, but this discord was preferable to the clatter of the courtyard at the back of the hotel, where her own room was situated. "Well, sit, sit." Dame Olivia briefly surrendered to a fit of coughing before clearing some newspapers from a chair and practically pushing her down. "Now," she said, eyeing her closely, "you must tell me the truth about yourself. You are not happy, are you? With either yourself or that husband of yours." She opened her mouth to speak, but Dame Olivia's hand shot up like a signal. "No, I won't hear a word of protest. You *will* talk to me, young lady, even if it means keeping you here all morning."

Two days later, the hotel proprietor told them over breakfast that the Negress had departed and they would not, after all, be able to make a group excursion to see the woman onstage. Purportedly her project had collapsed due to some financial misdealing, and although the proprietor didn't appear inclined to offer up any facts, she suspected that the man knew more than he was willing to share with them. Both she and Dame Olivia thanked him for the news, but as he made ready to leave the dining room, the proprietor spoke again. "Madame Venus is her name." He paused. "Her name for the stage."

Lenglet moved a protective arm around the back of her chair, which had the anticipated effect of silencing Dame Olivia, who simply smiled in the direction of the married couple and said nothing further. As soon as it was apparent she might give birth at any moment, her husband had fallen into the new habit of returning to the hotel in time for dinner. Once they were back in their room, an agitated Lenglet paced the floor and nervously sucked on a cigarette. He turned to face her and gestured with the cigarette. "We can't stay here, do you understand? I told you not to talk with these people. Why does the old woman need to know that we spent five months in Holland? You're a damned fool." She looked calmly in her husband's direction, but felt as though she had suddenly fallen through a gap in the floorboards. Having rediscovered her balance, she searched for the right words, but they eluded her. Why would Lenglet shout at her like this? It was true that dinner had been trying, but surely Lenglet understood that diplomacy was hardly Dame Olivia's strongest suit. The elderly lady had oddly uncoordinated hands that she moved with great animation whenever she wished to emphasize a point. "And so," she said, "I believe the child was conceived in Holland during a short five-month stay, is this not the case?" Dame Olivia had addressed the question to them both, and as the persistent Englishwoman continued with her attempts to ensnare them in conversation, she felt Lenglet move his arm around the back of her chair. And now, having returned to their room, her husband stood over her and continued to fume. She heaved herself to her feet and reached for her coat, and then she remembered her friend Mabel's words. "Trap you, that's all some men ever want to do to a girl. Just get you where they want you." She ignored Lenglet's protests, and as she left their room, she gently closed the door behind her.

The following week William Owen Lenglet was born, and when they brought him back to the hotel, they placed the tiny child in a small basket and stared at him, neither of them having any clue as to how they might integrate the child into their lives. Sometime later they noticed that not only was their baby refusing food, the diminutive tot's colour was changing, and so, having accepted advice from the hotel proprietor, they took their son to be cared for at the hospital for poor children. Reluctantly, they left him there and returned to their dour hotel room, where they were now both keen to avoid prying questions from Dame Olivia. Soon after, the hotel proprietor received an urgent telephone call, and having replaced the receiver on its cradle, he slowly climbed the stairs and informed the anxious couple that William, their three-week-old son, had died of pneumonia. *"Je suis vraiment navré."* Once they reached the hospital, the kind nurses ushered the confused couple into a small windowless room and asked them to please take a seat. Having done so, they informed the bereaved parents that they had taken the precaution of baptizing the infant before his death in the hope that this might ease the child's passage into the next world. She felt her cheeks beginning to flush red, and as her husband reached over to take her hand, she pulled it away in a gesture of calculated rancour.

40

A Child

She lies on a bed in a darkened room in a small town near Brussels. She looks up into the bright blue eyes of the woman who hovers above her and realizes that these are the same judgmental eyes that stared disdainfully at her when she danced onstage in the chorus. This time, instead of suppressing the longing to curse, she looks into the woman's eyes and gasps an oath, for the pain is once again opening her up and she knows that she is making a commotion. The woman ignores her profanity and, with the aid of an assistant, raises her hindquarters and slips a coarse towel beneath her; a layer of rubber is leafed between towel and sheet, and her hips are now encouraged to fall back onto the bed. *"Détendez-vous et continuez à respirer profondément."*

It is two years since the first child died. She remembers hurrying to the Parisian hospital and looking down at the three-week-old doll. He had been scrubbed clean and was laid out in a cardboard box that had been emptied of its original contents; the nurses had stuffed crumpled wads of old newspaper into what little space remained. Shortly after their loss, she and Lenglet left for Vienna, and then Budapest, and now Belgium, but weary of this aimless wandering, she is now determined to make her way back to Paris with or without her husband. The blue-eyed woman places a cold hand on her clammy forehead and once again orders her to push. *"Nous y sommes presque."* As she makes one final effort she closes her eyes and remembers the keen young chorus girl who quickly grew to dislike both herself and those who gawped at her. Mabel understood the truth of the situation: "Trust me, Gwennie, I'm your friend, and I'm telling you, love, you're not cut out for this life." The woman removes her cold hand, and she can feel a small run of blood on the inside of her leg, and then an inert warm bundle is placed in her arms. She continues to be embarrassed, for she knows that her ill-fitting gown is far too short. But why is there no crying? She opens her eyes and stares at her still-bloodied child's tiny fists and she wants to apologize, for as yet she has no name to offer this girl. I'm sorry, she says as she stares into her daughter's face. I wish I could tell you that I spoke with you before you arrived, but I didn't know what to say. The silent assistant hands the nurse a jug of steaming water, and then the moon-faced girl crosses to the window and draws back the curtains, revealing a rooftop view of black chimney stacks, above which hovers a grey, cloud-choked sky. Will her daughter forgive her? Already she feels guilty, for she knows she is making mistakes. O Holy Mother of Jesus, a child can never run away from an unhappy childhood. She knows this. Eventually the poor girl will become trapped by her childhood memories. She must at least make some effort to offer the poor innocent a name. "*Soutenez la tête. Voilà, comme ça."* After a few minutes the blue-eyed woman loses patience and reaches down and gently takes the newborn from her arms, and she is unburdened. *"Il faut dormir maintenant."* She feels defeated by a feverish desire for a large glass of rum or brandy, and then she surreptitiously brushes away a tear and wonders what Lenglet might make of this peculiar late-morning Belgian scene.

41

Parc Monceau

Sitting alone on a gracefully curved bench in the Parc Monceau, and watching her breath cloud in front of her face, her mind returned to that initial dinner at the Café Royal. With his enticing accent he abruptly asked her if she had ever considered leaving England, which made her heart leap with unexpected excitement. She watches children feeding the ducks and rolling around on the grass under the vigilant eyes of their primly dressed nannies and wonders why this man who rescued her from England now seems to have lost patience with her. Has he looked closely and finally come to the determination that there is nothing there? Her child is staying temporarily with a family in Versailles, and so when she is not posing as a mannequin for one of the fashion houses in the Place Vendôme, she prefers to sit in this park and watch other people's children giddily chasing one another along the dusty paths and testing the patience of their frustrated guardians, as opposed to moping in dimly lit bars which mock her loneliness.

She leaves the Parc Monceau and meanders along the shadowed side of the café-cluttered boulevards outside of which the French seem determined to loiter in order to advertise the virtue of leisure over business. She suspects that it is some unfortunate repercussion of Lenglet's illegal business dealings that has caused him to disappear from her life and that of their child, and she knows she will never truly forgive him for this abandonment. As the sun begins to dip in the sky, and shine first through the top of the trees and then descend even further, so that it is now visible from under the awnings of the establishments, it is the women who seize her attention with their stylish haircuts and false eyelashes, and the open fretwork of their stockings, and hems that expose ankles that taper down into shoes that are laced with ribbons. As she stares she wonders if she should dye her hair blond or simply change her name to something more seductive, for these delicate sylphs still possess what she appears to have lost, which is an intimation of the boudoir.

Eventually she reaches the sluggish Seine, where she tries and fails to visualize the sea, but her eyes are always caught and held by the surprising spectacle of men fishing with rods and lines. She walks further and begins to peruse the contents of the oddly shaped bookstalls that, at the end of the day, fold back into strange green boxes. As ever, she finds herself ignoring the trays of books and focusing her gaze on the maps and then the photographs, a great number of which feature images of sad-looking women clad only in undergarments. Suddenly she looks up, for she sees a young boy who is holding a stick on the end of which a blue balloon is being buffeted by the wind. The boy stands forlornly with his mother, and the pair of them appear to be stranded and unable to cross the road, for there is no break in the motorized traffic. Although the dancing balloon is clearly making the helpless pair visible to all, nobody shows any inclination to stop, and after a while the distraught boy begins to cry in the same blubbering way she cries at night in the privacy of her cheap hotel on the Rue Vavin, and as she imagines her daughter might cry in the safety of her pleasant room in a strange family's home in Versailles. When she can no longer bear to look at mother and child, she turns again to the bookstalls, but she has now lost any appetite to continue her inconsequential browsing.

42

A Knight in Shining Armour

She wakes up in the middle of a noisy Parisian night and discovers him sitting on the solitary chair nervously smoking a cigarette. She can see that Lenglet is agitated, but she rubs her eyes and tries to remember what he is doing in her hotel on the Rue Vavin. She craves a drink, but knows that her solitary bottle of whisky is now empty and any mention of alcohol will only stimulate her husband's judgmental nature. Then through the thin walls which separate the rooms in this run-down establishment they both hear a woman scream, and then the report of a slap—an open hand against skin—and Lenglet quickly stabs out his cigarette on a plate that lies at his feet. A few moments later they hear the woman scream again, but this time her cry is pitiful, almost a resigned whimper.

"Do you have to tolerate this every night?"

She sits up in bed and then looks over towards the corner of the room where the tap has begun to drip.

"It's not every night." She pauses. "Most nights, but not every night."

"But can you not find somewhere else to stay?"

She listens with dismay to the aggressive manner in which her husband is questioning her, and her mood plunges. After all, it is she who, in the absence of his having made any other arrangements, generously invited him to share her high-ceilinged, carpetless room.

"I can only afford this arrondissement."

"Well, why not a better hotel in this arrondissement?"

As though on cue, the muffled sobs of a baby crying begin to rapidly escalate until the child maintains a constant wail, and then they hear the loud clatter of a chair being knocked over by somebody hurrying to leave the room, and then a door slams. Lenglet stands and runs one hand back through his unwashed hair. His face has a hollow, anaemic aspect to it, and as ever, she imagines that her husband is managing to remain only one step ahead of whatever authorities are pursuing him.

"For Christ's sake."

For Christ's sake what, she thinks. You are here for one day, two at the most, and we have things to talk about, and then you can leave and go back to your Holland. You don't have to live here, so what gives you the right to complain? She scrutinizes her husband as he crosses now to the window and stares down into the street, where he notices a cat weaving a hesitant path in and out of some rusted railings.

"I don't believe it. The man is standing in plain sight relieving himself against the façade of the hotel as though it's a public toilet. How are decent people supposed to live side by side with this trash?"

He retreats from the window and lights another cigarette, and then he turns off the dripping tap before he once again sits, this time on the foot of her bed.

"Have you ever seen the woman and child in the next room? And why the hell does the brute beat her?"

She says nothing, but she suspects that the boy does not belong to the man. The man is hefty and blond, while the child is dark and emaciated, but because she has never exchanged anything other than the occasional raised eyebrow of recognition with the woman as they pass each other on the narrow unilluminated staircase, everything is speculation.

"Are you going to continue to make me sleep on the chair?"

She looks at Lenglet and nods, but she has no interest in pursuing a conversation. She understands that she is being tested.

"You won't share a bed with me? I disgust you now, is that it?"

She remains calm and does not take her eyes from him. Does he not understand that she would stiffen at his touch?

"We talked about this yesterday when you arrived."

"I am still your husband." He pauses in order that she might have time to absorb the import of the word "husband," but she remains unperturbed and decides to take the initiative.

"Have you made any decision regarding Maryvonne? I no longer wish to leave her with the family in Versailles."

"It was you who abandoned her. What kind of a mother are you?"

"And what kind of a father are you?" She stares hard at him. "I temporarily gave my daughter to a kind family who are better able to care for her than I am." Again she pauses. "Look, I have no money, but we both know Maryvonne needs a home."

"I refuse to allow you to bring our daughter into this place." He gestures all around at the grimy room. "I will not permit my daughter to grow up in filth."

"But I told you, I have no money."

"Then it's decided. I shall take her with me until you take control of your deplorable little life." He looks angrily at her. "Well, are you listening?"

"What if she doesn't want to go with you?"

"It doesn't matter, she's coming with me."

He gets up from the bed and sits down heavily on the chair.

"I see." She pauses and decides to try and defuse the awkward silence. "Thank you."

But "Thank you" for what? For finally acting like a father? For pretending to be a knight in shining armour on a charging white steed? Brave Lenglet has thundered across the border from Holland and arrived to rescue the situation. Sadly, the charming, secretive man who captured her imagination in London has allowed life to harry him so that he is now little more than a dreadfully unsteady parody of the enchanting foreigner who night after night escorted her to the Café Royal. But this is her own failure, for life in London should have already taught her to accept that some men are handsome in a way that will inevitably bring only disappointment. In the morning the pair of them will travel together to Versailles and reclaim their daughter, and then in the afternoon she will accompany her husband and daughter to the Gare du Nord and wave them farewell as they board the train for Holland. Farewell, not goodbye. She is fully aware that Lenglet has come to Paris to rescue their child, so why, she wonders, does he pretend that he also wants her? It is the habitual stupidity of men that she has never really understood. The pretence. The utter compulsion to pretend.

Next door she can now hear the couple talking with less anger in their voices. She is familiar with the concluding act of this drama. The bed begins to squeal as the man climbs into his sweetheart's arms and legs, and a rhythmic creaking commences. She can feel frustration rising within her. Why, nearly every night of the week, this same depressing farce? And what is the child witnessing? Tomorrow, with a heavy heart, she will allow Maryvonne to leave for Holland with her father, for at the present time, it is he who appears to be managing life in this world. She snakes out a hand and turns off the bedside lamp, plunging the room into a semi-darkness that can never fully close to blackness because of the luminous moonlight.

"Do you have nothing further to say to me?"

"Please, go to sleep. Tomorrow will be difficult. For everybody."

"And that is all you have to say?"

She pulls the sheet tight around herself and turns on her side and faces the wall. In the next room the woman finally gasps and then begins to sob, which is the man's reminder to comfort her. She listens as Lenglet settles himself on the irksome chair, but she knows that neither of them will sleep, for the ordeal of their marriage has collapsed to the point where neither of them feels it necessary to struggle towards the courtesy of compromise. There will be no temporary resolution. In a few hours, dawn will find them sharing a room in painful silence, with each one of them convinced that they are doing the right thing for their daughter.

VII

Mr. and Mrs. Smith

43

Seeking Refuge

She has been waiting on the unsheltered south coast train platform for nearly an hour. During this time the rain has begun to fall with increasing steadiness, but without an umbrella or even a serviceable coat to prevent her from getting a soaking, she has reluctantly accepted that she now has little choice but to seek refuge in the small, grim-looking waiting room. As she pushes open the door, she discovers that there is nothing in the place except a bench, a table, and a pile of old magazines. The tiny place reeks of stale cigarette smoke, but at least it is quiet and she is alone. It occurs to her that she might have to go back to the ticket office and ask the station master what exactly is happening with the trains to London, but the answer will almost certainly be "I don't know, love," which she recalls is the more polite form of "How am I supposed to know?"

It has stopped raining now, but there is still no sign of the train. An hour ago the weasel of a man threw open the door and excitedly informed her that there had been a signal failure somewhere up the line, but he assured her that the train would arrive in twenty minutes or so. He lit a cigarette and hovered eagerly, as though waiting for her to thank him for this information, or perhaps he expected her to ask a question, but she had nothing to say to the common man. She watched as he touched his cap, and then closed the door behind him, trapping still more cigarette smoke in the tiny room. She has enough money to pay for a few nights at a modest London hotel, but she has decided that after she meets with her sisters and attends her mother's funeral, she will return to her solitary life in Paris.

Once again the station master opens the door, this time slowly, which serves only to amplify the creaking of the unoiled hinges. He is carrying a cup of tea, and as he eases the door shut behind him, he offers her an apologetic grimace. "I'm sorry, your train's been cancelled, but another one should be along within the hour." He sets down the cup of tea on the table. "I've brought this for you, but we're out of sugar." She thanks him by simply nodding, and then she rediscovers her manners. "That's very kind of you." He nods and touches his cap, and he mutters, "You're welcome, miss," which makes her want to laugh. Does she really look like a "miss" to this man, or is he simply trying to make her feel better about herself? If so, there's no reason for him to bother. He casually slaps a pack of cigarettes against the heel of his hand and takes one out. He offers her one, which she refuses, and then he points. "The tea, I hope it's alright." She shares with him the creased smile of a woman who is becoming increasingly familiar with Pond's cold cream. "Thank you, I'm sure it's wonderful."

44

Sister Love

She sits by herself at the dining table and pours yet another measure of red wine into her glass and smiles at nobody in particular. "Well, this is quite nice," she says. She drinks deeply and then, her hand having never left the bottle, she refills the glass.

"Don't you think you should be going back to your hotel now, my dear?" Her sister Brenda tries to take the bottle from her, but not wishing to become involved in a tug-of-war, Brenda adroitly changes her mind. Minna's stage whisper echoes around the room.

"She shouldn't have come in the first place. Neither to the cemetery nor back here to the house. She's a disgrace."

She ignores both Minna and Brenda, for she knows that they are grief-stricken and probably not entirely sure of what they are saying or doing. She continues to smile and tries to be forgiving, for the pair of them have been the unlucky ones who, once it became apparent that their mother could no longer cope with either her financial difficulties or with Negro resentment at home in the West Indies, were forced to uproot their lives and journey to England to live with their unhappy parent in this mundane house in Acton. Soon after their arrival in London, their mother's health began to fail, and shortly thereafter the tawdry realities of English life began to dumbfound the matriarch and her mind began to flicker away from lucidity. And now that their mother has departed, her two sisters don't seem to understand that it was impossible for her to leave Paris and come and help, for she had a husband and she has a child. I'm sorry, she thinks, but the pair of you have neither a husband nor children, so of course Mother was your responsibility. What is it that you don't understand?

Again Brenda reaches for the bottle of red wine, but she refuses to let go of it.

"Gwen, are you sure you're alright, my dear?"

She is not alright, and she swallows deeply as her stomach begins a slow, churning circle, but she manages to keep everything under control until her stomach completes its manoeuvre.

"Ask her why she felt it necessary to carry on that way at the funeral service, screaming at everybody and acting as though she had taken leave of her senses. Well," said Minna, "ask her, for she's nothing but a vain, spoiled brat."

Brenda tries to usher her angry sister away, but Minna shoots the visitor a vindictive look and will not be moved.

"I despise her, do you understand? I don't want her in this house."

She listens and suppresses a giggle. "I'm sorry," she says, "but I was late and a teeny bit flustered and I lost my balance.

Anyhow, aren't I allowed to be a little emotional? She was *my* mother, too." She pours another glass of red wine and offers them both a smudged lipstick smile. "For heaven's sake, can't either of you ladies find it in your heart to forgive me? I meant nothing by it."

"She makes me sick."

Brenda looks genuinely shocked. "Really, Minna, there's no need to persist with this kind of talk."

When she wrote to tell her mother that she was staying on in England and planning to attend the Academy of Dramatic Art, her mother didn't trouble herself to grace her with a reply. Perhaps she didn't receive the letter? She has always liked to believe this. In fact, she likes to believe anything that will cause her less pain, but today nothing seems to be helping.

She pours the last drop of wine into her glass and only now does she relinquish her grip on the bottle.

"You do have a hotel room to go to, don't you?" Brenda picks up the empty bottle from the table.

"Yes, but I'm not ready yet. Do you have any more wine? I'm glad you didn't ask Aunt Clarice. She never really liked me."

"Gwennie, Aunt Clarice is dead."

"No, Brenda, you're being silly. Mother is dead."

"Gwennie, they're both dead."

She smiles at Brenda and tries to remember why they are all huddled together in this horrible house in Acton. She places a hand on Brenda's arm.

"Will you ever go back?"

"Go back where, Gwennie?"

"You know what I mean."

"You mean home? The West Indies?"

"Yes, that's what I mean. I'm going back to Paris now. Will you come and visit me in Paris? Where's Owen?"

"In Australia, Gwennie. And brother Edward is a doctor in India. It would appear we've lost both of our brothers to the colonies. We really are quite a clumsy family, aren't we?"

45

Mr. Smith

It was he who wrote first, saying he had come across her writing in a fairly obscure literary journal and wondered if she had anything else "on the go." The brief handwritten note from the English literary agent instantly rescued her ailing spirits, and all day long she carried it with her from one coffin-quiet bar to the next, and then, late in the evening, back to the despondent hotel room on the Rue Vavin. That was almost two months ago. Now—having travelled to London to be present at her mother's funeral—she decided that before leaving again she would make it her business to seek out the seemingly curious Mr. Leslie Tilden Smith. She had made up her mind to affect a casual, disinterested air with this Mr. Smith, in the hope it would be clear that *he* was not the reason she had come to London. But the truth was, after nearly a decade on the Continent, the zest of Paris had become decidedly passé. She needed money and she needed help, and she already understood that she would not be averse to the devotion of a suitable patron should such a person present himself.

The tall, angular Mr. Smith was more loose-limbed than she had imagined, and on first glance he appeared to be smartly dressed; however, she was adept at spying kinship in a frayed cuff or a missing button, and so she knew that all was not what it seemed to be with this rather shy man. He cleared some manuscripts from a conspicuously unstable chair by simply tossing them to the floor alongside others, and then Mr. Smith invited her to take a seat in his cramped office space which he announced he shared with an elderly part-time reader. Her suggestion of an early-morning appointment had obviously caught the literary agent off guard, for he had not adequately prepared for her visit, but she smiled as the courtly man continued to tidy up, and as she crossed her legs at the ankles, she allowed a slim foot to slide partway out of her shoe. To her eyes, it was immediately apparent that this man was a kind person, and as he began to speak, she realized that he genuinely admired her writing. Therefore, when Mr. Smith eventually found the courage to stammer an invitation to join him later that same day for dinner she saw no reason to refuse, although judging by the downcast, nervous manner in which the poor soul had framed his overture it was evident that he expected her to be otherwise engaged and had already anticipated rejection. She understood that Mr. Smith would most likely not have the resources to reserve a table at the hotels and restaurants that she recalled from her time in London before the Great War, but perhaps such places no longer existed? After all, London had changed. This morning, while making her way to her appointment with Mr. Smith, she had undertaken some rudimentary exploration. The grimy city had now lost what bloom it had once possessed, but then again, so had she. The streets appeared to be narrower and the people miserable, but it was the vast quantity of street traffic that made this new London hazardous, with its riot of noise and the endless surge of spluttering automobiles that chaotically congregated at unmonitored junctions.

The restaurant was cheerless and she felt certain that the food would be bland. She stared at a bickering couple at a neighbouring table and waited as Mr. Smith ran his eyes up and down the menu, unable to decide what to order. This, she knew, was not a good omen, but she remained calm and decided to continue to show him her best powdered face. The green-jacketed waiter was lingering in anticipation of an order, but her host didn't seem to notice. Then Mr. Smith looked up and smiled and turned to the waiter and said, "I'll have whatever the lady is having," and her heart momentarily sank, for it was now clear what kind of a man she was dealing with. Nevertheless, by the conclusion of the meal she had made a decision to extend her stay in London, and during the course of the week Mr. Smith brought her back to the same dispiriting restaurant without asking if she would prefer to dine at some other establishment. On their second visit, she watched his eyes gleam as he announced that he felt certain that he might well be able to secure for her a publisher's contract, but this news aside, he had, by this stage, effectively given up talking about matters related to the world of books. He was now attempting to interrogate her about her life, and she smiled sweetly and managed to distil the narrative down to the skimpiest of plot lines: colonial girl comes to England to seek her fortune and eventually escapes the misery of the postwar years by leaving for the Continent, where she quite unexpectedly takes up writing in a series of melancholy hotel rooms. He demanded more storyline, so she provided details of parents, a journey on board a ship, a wicked aunt, and even an unhappy interlude at an English boarding school, but she decided against giving out any more information, for she had no wish to be judged. Then Mr. Smith changed his tack. The conversation was now about Mr. Smith's life: his former wife and his daughter, the girl's impending marriage, his service during the Great War, his unsatisfactory time at university, and his aging parents. Fearing a return to the indignity of trying to find work posing for the fashion houses in the Place Vendôme, and her increasingly indigent life walking the lesser streets of Montparnasse before the inevitable late-night return to her austere hotel room, she listened with calculated attention, until it became perfectly obvious to her that Mr. Smith's stories served only one purpose, which, on a particularly blustery and inclement London morning, he finally blurted out.

As arranged, she came to his office shortly before noon in order that she might sign an agreement with his agency. A bespectacled girl brought the document and two saucerless cups of tea to the small desk, on top of which were piled stacks of newly published books. It was clear that the girl was some kind of personal assistant, for she behaved with great deference towards both Mr. Smith and his client, but her agitated manner suggested that the girl had been briefed with regard to the significance of this particular visitor. After she had signed the proffered document, the flustered girl reappeared and took up the agreement and quickly withdrew. "I am aware," began Mr. Smith, his voice imbued with a by-now-familiar rectitude, "that married life on the Continent has been a less than happy affair for you." He took a sip of his tea and then looked up and offered her the opportunity to either agree or disagree with him, but she reached for her own cup and waited for him to continue. "This being the case, from everything you have told me I think I should extend to you an invitation to remain here in London in order that you might pursue your work." He paused. "We do understand each other, don't we?" She peered beyond him and out through his small office window. The poor man was now attempting to sow the seeds of what *she* already understood might one day become a harvest of disorder. On the wall of a distant building she could just about discern a huge painted sign advertising BOVRIL. A young boy sat in his mother's lap holding a steaming mug in both hands, and their faces gave out beaming, self-satisfied smiles. "I fully understand that you probably require more time to think about this matter. I imagine that my proposition must have come as something of a shock to you."

46

A Confession

A week or so after Mr. Smith had nervously proposed co-habitation to her, he asked her to once again dine with him at his favourite characterless restaurant. From the moment he greeted her at the entrance to the establishment, she could see that something was troubling the frowning man. She worried that either he or one of his publishing contacts had changed their mind about her abilities, but as soon as they were seated at their table, he reaffirmed his enthusiasm for her writing, and he talked of the popularity of the coming-of-age novel and his high hopes for her future. She listened carefully to this Mr. Smith's words, but as he continued to speak, she detected a new impatience informing her benefactor's conversation, and a quizzical look of perplexity never left his face. Their last meeting had taken place in Mr. Smith's office at his literary agency. It was a cramped shared space, although his elderly colleague had failed to make an appearance on the two occasions that she had visited. In the week between Mr. Smith's stammered proposal and this summons to dinner, she had managed to find a quiet room in Finsbury Park and as a result escape the expense of an extended stay at her modest London hotel. However, despite this necessary industry, she knew full well that she had been remiss in not offering the poor man even a morsel of communication, wishing as she did to maintain the upper hand in their friendship.

Once the plates had been removed and the dessert menus handed to them both, Mr. Smith placed his card facedown in front of him and then asked her outright if she had ever been on the stage. "Believe me, it is not my intention to upbraid you, so you may as well tell me the facts." The muscles in her throat tightened as though somebody was squeezing them in a viselike grip, and she gave him a look intended to indicate that she didn't quite understand what he meant, but this merely fed the literary agent's resolve to pursue his line of questioning with regard to this unsavoury topic. According to Mr. Smith, a distant but credible relative of his recalled some vague reference to his new author having perhaps been a Gaiety Girl before leaving England for France. She felt tears forming behind her eyes, for although she hadn't lied to this Mr. Smith, she had also not told him the whole truth. Why should she? A cigarette butt that had been left behind by a diner on a neighbouring table had been inadequately stubbed out and the smoke was wafting into her face, but she tried to ignore it, and she gathered herself and assured her interrogator that it was many years now since she last had any connection with the stage. The apprehensive waiter reappeared at their table, but with poorly disguised irritation Mr. Smith informed the man that they would require a few minutes more before deciding upon dessert. The waiter moved away, and she could feel Mr. Smith staring intensely at her. "I wasn't hiding anything," she said. "I'm not ashamed of having been a stage girl, but it's just that people always draw bad conclusions." He reached across the table and took her hand, and she now sensed that his annoyance was more rooted in confusion than displeasure. "I want to help, but how am I to promote you if you insist on hiding these rumoured irregularities from me?" She felt herself relax a little, for it was now clear that the troubled man didn't understand. How was she supposed to write if she didn't hide things? Life hides things from her, people hide things from her, and in her quest for clarity she in turn hides things from herself; it's what she does. If this man truly yearns to spend time with her, then he will have to learn to stop telling her what to do. Sadly, even at this early stage of their arrangement, she could already see the full extent of the problem with this Mr. Leslie Smith. When the waiter returned, her friend ignored the dessert card and ordered a brandy. Mr. Smith asked if she wanted one, too, but he did so in a casual manner which suggested that he was sure that she would refuse. However, she nodded, and the literary agent was forced to recall the waiter to the table and ask for a second glass. She saw the not entirely approving look that the waiter shot her, but it was one with which she was familiar. She turned to face her pedantic dining partner, sure that he must now be beginning to experience the full weight of uncertainty, but she could find no consoling words to share with him. Mr. Leslie Tilden Smith, if I were you I would just concentrate on pushing my work to your publisher friends, for anything beyond this is just going to become too complicated for you. You *do* know this, don't you?

47

Waiting for the Rain

He stared out of the small office window and could see the rain continuing to lash down. However, he would have to wait for it to cease gunning against the metal awning above the door to the street, for despite this morning's forecast, he had forgotten to bring his umbrella. He glanced at the compact, framed photograph of his wife that he had placed on his desk in such a manner that her bewitching eyes appeared to be constantly watching over him. While he worked alone in his congested office space, he was spared the upset of their commonly contentious interaction, yet a photograph meant that he was still able to enjoy the warmth of her silent presence. It was some years now since he had been let go by his publishing firm, after which he decided to establish his own agency, but things were not going well. Financial difficulties had recently left him with little choice but to exchange their Holland Park mews accommodation for a pair of somewhat uninspiring rooms in Bloomsbury, and this unfortunate development had only exacerbated the tension between them. Sadly, things had continued to deteriorate on the financial front, and he had now resigned himself to the fact that at the end of the month he would be forced to vacate his office and work from home, for he could no longer afford the expense of leasing the property. Of course, he had yet to share this news with his wife, for the moment never seemed expedient.

This morning, having shouted through to the bedroom and bidden her farewell, he realized that his favourite fountain pen was not in his inside jacket pocket, where he usually clipped it. It then occurred to him that he had most likely left the pen on the small table to the side of his bed, and so he quietly set down his briefcase and moved towards the slightly ajar bedroom door. As he glanced in, he saw his wife standing naked at the side of her bed, with her back to him, and she appeared to have assumed an artistic pose which he imagined might prefigure some kind of dance performance. He stared transfixed and could feel himself awakening, and he started to feel somewhat ashamed, and then he returned to himself and quickly reclaimed his briefcase before stealthily tiptoeing from their rooms.

Once he reached his office, he dropped the briefcase to the floor, sat at his desk, and allowed his head to fall forward into his hands. Time had not eroded his desire, but her continual criticism and fault-finding had eaten away at his confidence and he had gradually lost his way. It had been like this with his first wife. His fumbling for words. The elation of her accepting his proposal. Thereafter, the slow corrosion towards a permanent state of disappointment on both sides, and her interest in the flickering world of Eros finally burning itself out. The separate beds. The lack of conversation. The separate rooms. Then eventually his first wife's betrayal when she went off with her Basil chap and began to build a new life for herself in India.

He could hear the rain intensifying as it drove hard against the window, and far off in the distance the sky cleared its throat and prepared to bellow. He lifted his head and glanced at the photograph on his desk. At least they still shared the same bedroom, and as far as he had been able to determine, there had been no duplicity. But still, he could not remember the last time he saw her naked body, and he had no idea how to govern the feelings his wife still stirred in him. He wondered, Does she slip out from the tight pouch of the sheets and pose naked like this every morning? Why could she not have waited until she was sure that he had left for his office before denuding herself in this shamefully irregular manner? Why had he forgotten his damn fountain pen in the bedroom?

He now heard thunder, and he looked around at the useless manuscripts that littered his desktop. These were, in the main, submissions from bored ladies and retired gentlemen with no evidence of talent. These days, such people constituted his so-called authors. However, at the end of the month he will jettison everything in the office except for the solitary photograph in which his wife stares coquettishly at him. If only he could replace this image of her fickle eyes with one of her naked body, for this would at least enable him to imagine the pleasure of once again having knowledge of her. When the rain stops he will walk back through the puddled streets, and once he reaches their new rooms, he will attempt to initiate an agreeable conversation with his wife about the events of the day. Perhaps he ought to confess to her what he truly desires, but he understands that in her mind he is fixed as a grey man docked in the middle station of life who is beyond passion, and for some time now, he has not said or done anything that might persuade her otherwise.

48

New Rooms

Now that he no longer has an office to go to each morning, her husband has begun to display a hitherto hidden talent for dissembling. He rises before her and breakfasts on toast and jam with black tea, and then he prepares a tray for her, which he brings through into the bedroom. Thereafter, he retreats to the main room and pretends to be reading an important manuscript of some description that calls for his appraisal. He stations himself in the armchair, thus ensuring that the small dining room table is available for her to work at once she leaves the bedroom and ventures out to join him. She sits at the table and steals glances at him, but she knows that there are no important new manuscripts; her husband simply leafs through old dog-eared submissions. Then at some point he will light a pipe and turn his attention to the previous evening's newspaper before once again making a halfhearted effort to reach for a previously scanned manuscript. It is painful for her to witness, and by lunchtime she generally submits to her uncontrollable urge to flee the claustrophobia of their rooms and bolt in the direction of the pub on the corner, thus leaving her poor husband to his own private pantomime.

A month after relinquishing the lease on his office and initiating this new practice of working from home, her husband asked if a certain Wilfred Rogerson, a comrade from his service in the Flying Corps during the war, might visit with them for a light supper. He informed her that the reclusive Rogerson resided in his native Cornwall and had not been up to London for over a decade, but her husband had got it into his head that it might be pleasant for them all to meet and share a social evening. Despite her considerable reservations, she said nothing and simply unearthed a vaguely presentable mauve dress, but when she saw the bedraggled man who appeared at their door she realized that she need not have bothered, for their guest had clearly already indulged himself with some alcoholic refreshment prior to his arrival. Rogerson was shorter than her husband and balding, and what thin wisps of hair remained fell forward and were being continually swept back by the application of an irritating hand that was pressed into service as a comb. Their visitor clutched a bottle of sweet sherry, and she unhesitatingly detected an arrogant yet insecure man who most probably recoiled at the idea of conflict of any kind, verbal or physical, but who would undoubtedly revel in the imagined respect bestowed upon him by ticket collectors, lift operators, and uniformed attendants of all descriptions. As the evening wore on, her husband's hopeless attempts to build temporary bridges of communication among the three isolated individuals collapsed as a nervous Wilfred Rogerson drank glass after glass of wine. The man continued to thrust cheese and crackers into his mouth, and whenever his upper plate became unstuck, he would push it back with his tongue. He began to lecture her about her own husband. "You must be aware that Leslie has suffered the indignity of desertion, so I feel compelled to ask, are you being kind to him? I do hope so, for he's a thoroughly decent sort." She watched her husband drop a hand onto his chum's shoulder in an attempt to staunch the flow of the man's well-lubricated tongue, but from the moment they submitted to the experiment of having a guest step into their Bloomsbury rooms, they both knew that yet more damage had been done to their already unsettled marriage.

After the man's departure, she lay back on the sofa and took yet another sip of red wine. Through the uncurtained window she could make out the quarter crescent of a moon that tonight would keep her company. What remained of their supper lay scattered across the tabletop, and her husband was now scurrying about trying to clear up the mess, while she made a point of ignoring him. Wilfred Rogerson, it transpired, was a farmer of some description who considered himself too clever for his job, yet he appeared to be too lazy to develop a coherent interest in anything else. She had quickly deduced that her husband's friend was hostile towards women, for no doubt some supposedly selfish creature had once refused to behave towards him with the inarticulate devotion of his mother and had therefore poisoned his attitude towards her gender. She was unsure if her husband noticed this streak of antipathy in his friend, but if he did, he said nothing. At some point in the evening the thin-haired farmer started in on the bottle of sweet sherry that he had brought with him, but by this stage she had tolerated enough and she noisily demanded that the fool leave their rooms and never return. Her husband's protestations had been feeble, and after the stumbled leave-taking of his so-called friend, she had offered him the choice of the bedroom or the sofa and refused to listen to his apology for having foisted this man upon her.

The following morning she lay prostrate on the dimpled-leather sofa and through bleary eyes observed her husband seating himself at the small table with his black tea and toast. He then announced that he would be going out for a few hours. As she propped herself upright, she felt a sudden jolt of pain shoot from one temple to the next, but she gathered her wits about her, for there were some words that she wished to share with her husband. "Leslie, you don't have a job, so where do you suppose it is that you are going?" But she said nothing, for it was woefully transparent that her husband's inability to secure work that might provide for them both was causing him a great deal of anguish and she had no interest in pressing the issue. She watched him rise silently from the table, knowing full well that he intended to seek out a public space where he might read his newspaper in peace. In the event of inclement weather, he would no doubt find shelter in a library or museum where he might masquerade as a diligent scholar of some description.

"May I," he wondered, "pour you some tea before I leave?"

"That would be nice, Leslie. Thank you."

As he reached for a cup and saucer, she glanced at his briefcase and marvelled at his newly acquired talent for dissembling. This evening, after he returns from his wandering, she will return to their shared bedroom and tomorrow offer him the opportunity of resuming his morning routine of bringing her breakfast in bed. There will be no more Wilfred Rogersons in their life. There will be no more visitors to their new rooms. And perhaps, she thinks, one day she and her tall, considerate husband might yet discover a way to live peacefully with each other. Perhaps.

VIII

Two Journeys

49

An English Husband

She settles down in a window seat, knowing only the name of the train station to which she is travelling, but having little understanding of what lies between London and the presumably grim suburban outpost that her brother has chosen to make his home. But who is she to judge, for her own life has been reduced from a carriage house in a Holland Park mews to two cramped rooms in Bloomsbury. Her sisters, she imagines, will continue to live out their isolated spinster lives in Acton without any desire to communicate with her, and heaven only knows what has become of their oldest brother, Edward. Which leaves only Owen, who, having returned from Australia with his tail between his legs, has not bothered to answer her last two letters, although she was simply writing to let him know that she would do her best to honour his wishes once she reached the West Indies. As she stares out the window, she moves her head first one way and then the other, and tries to catch a glimpse of herself in the glass, even though she knows that she will not necessarily like whatever it is that she happens to see. The train plunges past the lower-class destitution at the periphery of the city, and suddenly there are green fields, but she has not been paying attention and so she now wonders if she has boarded the wrong train. Eventually the train enters a tidy little station, where on the opposite platform she can see female passengers who are presumably waiting to journey into London to do their shopping, and she feels reassured. The train starts up again, and then she hears the guard's voice bellowing the name of the next station, which she believes is her destination.

In her darkest moments, she thinks, Poor Owen is quite possibly being held against his will by this Dorothy, and if this is the case, the very least I can do is make an effort to travel out and see him. In the past, he had written and confided in her with regard to his wife ("Things are never easy with Dorothy"), and although she initially wondered if his litany of complaints constituted another of Owen's attempts to evade responsibility for his actions, she has begun to build up in her mind a picture of a woman who arranges flowers and keeps a neat house and thereafter devotes the remainder of her time to passing judgment on her brother's life, both past and present. In fact, her brother suggested as much in his last letter. He concluded: "If only we had a weekend, or even an evening, in which we two might sit and talk, then my heart might find some of this burden lifted from it." And then there were no more letters. What on earth has this woman done to her Owen?

The train begins to slow, and once again she hears the

guard bark the name of her station, and she receives it as less of an announcement and more of a warning. The last time she saw her brother was before she left for England nearly thirty years ago now. Will she even recognize him? Her mind begins to race. She envisions a short walk to his door, and then a rattling of the letterbox, and she gradually begins to come to terms with the reality that she will most likely soon be standing face-to-face with Owen's wife. It hadn't occurred to her that she might actually like this Dorothy, but if this transpires, how on earth will she balance her protective instinct for Owen with her surprise at having discovered a kindred spirit in Dorothy? She leaves the compartment and begins to inch her way towards the train door, but the corridor is blocked by people seemingly keen to idle there in anticipation of the train's arrival. She will have to be patient with these loafers, and then she realizes that she has been remiss in not bringing a present of some kind for their child, her nephew, but it is too late now, and as the train shudders to a halt, the guard insists on yet again announcing the name of the station.

It is a servant girl who opens the door to the semi-detached house, and her initial thought is that the girl has lips that look like they can take a kiss, and she's sure that this one's not going to settle for a life of beating the knots out of pillows. However, the real mystery is why such a modest house possesses any servants at all. She tells the girl her name and lets her know whom she has come to visit, and the young girl stands to one side and ushers her into the narrow hallway and then into the first room on the right, which is an overly furnished, somewhat funereal front room, which obviously exists for show as opposed to habitation. She takes a seat on the sofa, and the girl announces that she will go in search of Mrs. Williams, but she has already guessed that the lady of the house is most likely upstairs by her brother's bedside. From the moment she crossed the threshold she could smell sickness in the place, and so she simply watches as the doe-eyed girl leaves the room without offering her any refreshment or even asking if she might take her coat. As she waits, she notices that late-morning light is slanting through the net-curtained windows, but the light fails to illuminate the dull, lifeless room and instead seems to cause the shadows to deepen further, thus establishing a joyless tone which she imagines radiates throughout the whole house.

She hears a whispered conversation in the hallway and then the door opens. A stout grey-haired lady, whose mane is curled and clipped to the top of her head, and whose heavy woollen clothes suggest no real shape to the lumpy body they cover, enters and scrutinizes the wayward sister who has made this unannounced visit.

"Gwendolen—if I may—how very kind of you to travel all this way to see us." The woman extends a limp hand. "Dorothy, Owen's wife."

It is only when she releases the woman's hand that she realizes that the servant girl is standing to attention by the door and awaiting instruction.

"Would you care for some tea?"

She nods and watches as Owen's wife makes the smallest of dismissive gestures with her hand, which suggests that the woman is familiar with the business of organizing domestic help.

"I apologize for not giving you notice, but I have been worried about Owen. My last two letters have gone unanswered and I thought it best to seize the initiative."

"Of course, I understand." The woman takes a seat in the armchair opposite her. "My husband is resting at the moment, but since our return from Australia, things have not been easy for him. However, he always speaks of you with fondness. You're up in London, aren't you?"

"At the moment, yes. My husband works there."

"Forgive me, but I thought your husband resided on the Continent. Perhaps I've been misinformed?" She laughs, which involves displaying all of her teeth while emitting very little noise.

"I have another husband. An English husband."

"Oh, I see." She pauses. "Please forgive me for any embarrassment I may have caused."

"And the doctor? Does he have an opinion about my brother's condition?"

"Doctors have many opinions, not all of them free of error."

"But may I ask, what exactly is the problem?"

"My dear Gwendolen, there is no need for alarm. Now do tell me a little about yourself. We mustn't be strangers."

Again the woman laughs before asking another question, and then yet another. It quickly becomes apparent that, as far as this Dorothy is concerned, time spent on conversational superficialities is an acceptable way to pass the morning, for the woman appears to be in no hurry to introduce her into her brother's company.

•

As the train pulls away from the station, she searches in her bag for a handkerchief and she finally finds a small lace one. She reclasps her bag. It had been established that the young servant would walk with her back to the train station, although there was no need for her to do so, for she had found her way to Owen's semi-detached house without any hitch. However, she agreed to this escort in the hope that the young girl might reveal something about her brother's situation. Sadly, they walked together in silence and her attempts to open up a confessional exchange with the girl ("How long have you worked for my brother?" "From where exactly in Ireland do your family originate?") were either ignored or met with the briefest of responses. An hour earlier the servant had led her up the stairs to the room in which her brother lay on his back with his eyes shut, tumbling in and out of a feverish sleep. She recognized Owen's ailment as one which had not originated in Australia but had plagued her brother since his youth, causing him to suffer from delusions and bouts of agitated mania, which she knew Owen would endure until he ultimately sweated it out of his system. Under the watchful eye of the Irish girl, she sat on the side of the bed and took Owen's clammy hand in hers. She understood. Her now middle-aged and significantly flabby brother would soon return to the world and respond to her letters, but first he had to make his hot, perspiring journey through the tropics. The young girl continued to stand sentry by the door, but eventually they both heard Owen's wife making her slow, controlled way up the creaking staircase, and so she released her brother's hand and rose to her feet. She had absolutely no intention of granting this woman the victory of suggesting that it might now be best if she allowed her brother to rest. By the time Dorothy appeared in the doorway, she had already picked up her handbag. She was ready now to walk back to the train station and return to London and her English husband.

50

A Continental Lunch

She stopped at the corner of the street and on impulse bought a bunch of winter tulips from an old lady who appeared to be blind. She opened her purse and took care to press each coin individually into the outstretched palm, and then she thanked the woman. The somewhat surly old lady weighed the coins by impatiently moving her hand up and down, and then the woman muttered something inaudible under her breath. Leslie took her arm before she could say anything to the flower seller, and then, without making any attempt to smell the flowers, he commented on the agreeable fragrance of the tulips. This was his first time in Holland, and as they walked together on this unusually bright late December morning, she listened as he praised the elegant lines of the lofty houses on either side of the canal. Suddenly a wind rushed up the street and she swiftly dropped a hand to prevent her skirt from ballooning skywards, but her husband pretended not to notice.

"Look at the patterns," he said, gesturing towards the metallic water. "You can see why they are a nation of painters. I imagine it's the combination of light and shadow and, of course, the reflections."

She glanced in the direction of the canal. "Well, the Dutch take the trouble to look and see things, but that's because unlike some people, they've got cities worth looking at."

Leslie said nothing and continued to take in his surroundings. He had made up his mind. This was her day and there would be no arguments.

"And does your father choose your clothes?"

Her daughter ignored her question, and the girl's eyes followed the flies that were now buzzing around the limp-looking salad on the plate. The three of them were taking lunch on a small balcony overlooking a canal, and the weak sun filtered onto them through the almost naked branches of a towering screen of trees. Leslie reached for his water but appeared to be frustrated by the excessive amount of ice he would have to navigate. Crooking a finger beneath the lip of the glass, he flipped some ice out and placed it back into the jug. The bright-eyed waiter hurried to the table to ask if everything was alright, but the adolescent girl with the heavy heap of brown hair ignored the fuss and continued to follow the flies. Eventually she turned and faced her mother.

"Will Papa pick me up here, or has it been arranged that you will walk with me back to the house?"

"Well, it's a pleasant enough day, so we thought we might perhaps deliver you back to your father's residence."

She glanced over her daughter's shoulder and into the

dim interior of the restaurant, where the regular diners were preoccupied with their *prix fixe* lunches before presumably ambling their way back to the drudgery of office work. She then returned her attention to the narrow balcony, where it was getting cold, and she worried that it might rain. Her husband cleared his throat and prepared to try once again to engage the bored girl. Meanwhile, she could see that down below a steady stream of cyclists continued to trundle by in both directions, and out on the canal the occasional low hum of a motor signalled the surprisingly graceful passage of a barge.

The girl discarded the salad and set aside the fork with a clatter. She looked at her daughter's lustrous silver necklace and wondered who had given it to her, but she knew there was little point in posing a question that was likely to be met with scorn. When she had written to Lenglet and informed him that, before embarking upon a voyage to the West Indies, she and her husband were considering a short visit, he replied and told her that he thought it a good idea. However, when they arrived at their hotel and telephoned his house, her former husband sounded less certain and suggested that they begin with a lunch, but he made it clear that he would not be in attendance, for he felt it important that Maryvonne spend some time with her mother. The bored girl stared into the middle distance and began to loop her curls around a forefinger and then indulge in the filthy habit of chewing her hair, but her mother had already come to the depressing realization that without the aid of the child's father, it was going to be impossible for her to establish any real connection with her moody daughter.

Maryvonne was now walking together with Leslie some

few yards ahead of her. She had excused herself and stopped to buy chocolate as a gift for her daughter, but having left the shop, she now felt a demoralizing compulsion to simply lag behind, as opposed to rejoin, the two of them. She assumed that the girl liked chocolate, but she felt queasy with embarrassment at the clumsy predictability of her stupid gift. Once again, her eyes settled upon her daughter's green socks and her heart sank, for the evidence of her neglect was unequivocal. She would never, under any circumstances, let a child of hers wear anything green, let alone such ridiculous anklets. As they neared a busy junction, a light speckling of rain began to make the cobbles slick. Quickly wiping away a tear, she slowed to a halt and found temporary shelter in a shop doorway. As the rain intensified, she looked at her husband and daughter and fought the urge to turn and walk briskly away, thus allowing Leslie and her child time to get to know each other.

IX

All at Sea

51

On the Train to the Ship

Leslie had purchased first-class train tickets for the passage to Southampton, where they would rendezvous with the S.S. *Cuba* and begin their sea voyage to the West Indies. Unfortunately, the anticipated pleasure of a comfortable journey failed to materialize, for they found themselves sharing their accommodation with a well-dressed man who seemed determined to secretly peer at her. He had boarded at Weybridge, and although she suspected that the other compartments were most likely empty, he had insisted on coming to sit with her and her husband. The vain man adjusted his collar and pretended to be minding his own business, but he really wasn't much of an actor. She continued to gaze out of the window at the colourless landscape that was Leslie's beloved England, but the man wouldn't leave her alone. He kept sneaking a look at her, although the fool didn't appear to realize that by simply glancing at his reflection in the glass she could see exactly what he was doing. After a while, he spoke to her husband, but he talked down to Leslie as though addressing a person of inferior rank. Unhappily for this interloper, she immediately recognized the man's laboriously cultivated tones as those of a pretend-toff. She imagined that the dissembler was most likely the son of a menial tradesman or else the occupant of some equally mediocre step on the English social ladder. Having softened up her husband with a profusion of inane observations about the weather, the man enquired about their destination, as if this were any of his business, and then he commented on how annoying it was that the trains appeared to be frequently delayed. Apparently the situation was different on the Continent, especially so in Germany, where Herr Hitler had been busily encouraging everybody to pull up their socks. She looked directly at the man and offered him a smile calculated to let him know that during her time in his country she had met people of all backgrounds and therefore she would not be participating in his game. She turned away and focused her attention on Leslie's England.

A grey, foggy shroud made it impossible for her to see the full expanse of the bucolic landscape, but occasionally the bleak curtain would unexpectedly part, enabling her to glimpse a cluster of cows huddled together in one corner of a field, or the distant outline of a small farmhouse flanked on either side by pyramids of hay. Without any warning, however, this pastoral world would again disappear behind the grey veil and she would be left to exercise her imagination. Somewhere in the distance perhaps there were villages, and small streams, and gracefully swaying trees, and on another day such scenes might well be visible and bathed in glorious sunshine, but not today. As the train continued to fumble its slow way through the chilly late-morning murk, she searched for the words. I'm sorry, Leslie, but I don't think I'm quite ready to go home. Her husband couldn't hear her, and so she carefully unsealed her lips. I think I need a little more time, that's all. The man continued to attempt to engage her husband. Visiting Maryvonne in Holland has somewhat upset my equilibrium. I can see that my daughter needs a mother, even if it appears as though this mother is incapable of offering anything to her child. So what am I to do? Is it not selfish of me to be chasing off like this across the ocean? To be going home. Does this make me a poor mother? Surely this makes me a poor mother. Please, Leslie, it is very kind of you, but perhaps we might obtain some form of reimbursement from the shipping line? By the time the train reached Basingstoke, the man had given up trying to talk to her now taciturn husband. Soon after, and without excusing himself, the irritating intruder simply got to his feet and left their presence. Feeling relieved, she closed her eyes, and she must have nodded off, for the next thing she remembered was the guard poking his head through the door of their compartment and shouting, "Southampton next! Southampton!" The fellow then slid the door shut and moved down the train. Did the guard imagine they were deaf?

Having alighted, they passed through the main entrance to the train station and out onto the street, and suddenly it all came flooding back to her. Her life after Mr. Tree's school. Her life in the chorus. Endless travelling in cramped third-class carriages. Frightful belching trains crawling the back way into miserable industrial towns. Arriving at yet another soot-blackened train station. Finding suitable theatrical lodgings with Mabel. They played many seaside towns where she was always disturbed by the smell of stale English sea air, but sadly these were the only places she found even vaguely tolerable. She stole a quick glance at a tired-looking Leslie, who held a large suitcase in each hand, and then she drew a little of the sea breeze into her lungs. It all seemed so long ago now, traipsing from one dismal town to another and enduring the smug condescension of landladies who considered them all to be little more than tarts. She learned how to put up with substandard soap that wouldn't lather and how to make the best of stiff thin towels; she quickly became familiar with how to disregard the leering male lodgers who would shave and clean their teeth in the kitchen sink; and then each evening she would perform the same old songs, with Mabel.

When she and her husband reached their hotel, the superior attitude of the desk clerk irritated her. The young man barely made eye contact, and having registered them, he asked an elderly bellman to show his guests to what she knew would be an unprepossessing room at the back of the establishment. A few minutes later she watched as the bellman placed the key into her husband's proffered hand, and then the leather-faced ancient hovered for a moment or two before finally grasping that there would be no tip and he turned down his mouth before leaving their room. On this blustery February afternoon, she tried hard to forget both the cavalier desk clerk and the shuffling bellman and generate some enthusiasm for the voyage that lay ahead, but English people continued to bemuse and disappoint her. So much wasted energy. So much posturing. She sat on the solitary wooden chair and surveyed the familiar threadbare carpet and shoddy curtains and understood that she was tired in both mind and body and she desperately needed to sleep. It was then that she felt Leslie slip a comforting arm around her shoulders.

52

Wine, Please

After she had made it clear that under no circumstances would she be dressing for dinner, Leslie decided to take control of the problem. Well, why would she return to the dining room after the ship's steward had looked down his nose at her? The previous evening her mind had been distracted with memories of her father, when the tyrant of a steward smiled and asked again if he might clear the table for the second sitting. The man had the obnoxious habit of pointing with his chin as he spoke, and his air of patronage put her back on those stupid trains trundling around England from one unkind venue to the next. The steward's smile died quickly, and with malice, and she wondered just who the hell did this conceited wretch think he was. Eventually Leslie understood that he should discontinue his attempts to persuade her to join him for dinner, and he announced that he would presently return. Fifteen minutes later there was a gentle knock on the cabin door, and when she opened it, she discovered her husband standing before her with a tray full of food. He stepped past her and set everything down on her bed. "On top of everything you aren't well, but you have to eat, for it's the only thing that will improve your health." For a moment she saw her husband's eyes drift towards the chair in the corner of their small cabin as though he was ready to desert her and sit, but she knew that he wouldn't. Leslie would continue to help. He removed a bottle of red wine from the tray and she watched as he began to apply the corkscrew. "You may be feeling a little diminished at present, but we'll soon have you restored to your former glory."

The wine bottle is empty, as are two others. She turns over onto her side and realizes that in less than an hour it will be light. She could reach out across the gap between the two beds and just about touch Leslie if she so wished, but she simply watches the poor smitten man thrashing about as he attempts to find some sleep in his cramped cot. Why, she wonders, does he persist, for he must know that she is undeserving of such devotion. Her father, she suspects, might well have approved of Leslie's loyalty, but he might also have wondered why she had not done a little better for herself. He's a decent type, Gwennie. Keeps you in check, does he? Above Leslie's quiet wheezing and occasional tight cough, she can hear the clanking noises up on deck which announce the impending arrival of day. She understands that it doesn't matter where you are, on land or sea, you always hear the noises before you see the light—and then soon after, the new day will arrive to torment you.

53

An Unpolished Performance

She sat in the chair in the corner of the cabin and once again unfolded Owen's meticulously corrected typed letter. In the wake of her recent visit to his suburban home, she searched for any clues which might help her to better understand her brother's present predicament. Owen's letter betrayed no insight with regard to his feelings on the subject of marital unhappiness, however, but instead confined itself to the vexing matter of his West Indian progeny. As far as she was concerned, her brother's confused rush of words constituted a desperate, unpolished performance, and with each rereading his letter continued to disappoint. A father's duty, like that of a mother, was to be with his offspring, and unlike her brother, at least she was trying. There had been no relinquishing of her daughter, despite the difficulties of geography and her child's temperament, but Owen's behaviour was in part inexcusable. Her husband was asleep, but she continued to have trouble accustoming herself to the movement of the ship as it rocked over increasingly sizable swells. She folded Owen's letter and placed it back in its envelope. He was asking her to intervene in his affairs as though he bore no responsibility for his actions. Clearly, it was her guilt-stricken brother who ought to be on a ship sailing home to the West Indies.

54

All at Sea

She is guessing that it must now be about seven o'clock in the morning, for the harsh light is bleeding around the edges of the miniature curtain where her husband had failed to properly draw it across the porthole. Last night she noticed his oversight but was too tired to bother adjusting it, and then she must have dozed off. She has on all her clothes, including her shoes, and she is lying on top of the covers, which makes her feel a little queasy, for she already suspects that these French stewards do not value cleanliness. As she sits upright, she can see yet another tray of untouched food on the chair in the corner, for she is still refusing to visit the dining room, and this being the case, every evening her husband continues to act as her personal waiter.

She swings her legs out over the side of the slender bed and rests her feet down onto the small rectangle of rug. Then she tries to stand, but is suddenly overcome by dizziness, so she remains seated. She feels fragile and would give a shilling for a glass of water, but she knows that there is no longer any-thing to drink in this cabin. She looks across at her sleeping husband, who must surely be wondering why he has inflicted this suffering upon himself. Mabel always insisted that the key to happiness was to simply stay quiet and make them fall for you. Eventually she learned how to do this, but it was afterwards that always proved difficult, when she invariably decided that she no longer wished to remain quiet. That's when they would start to inch away from her, but not Leslie. She would observe them beginning to distress themselves with indecision, for they were never entirely sure as to how they might delicately set the untamed creature to one side, but not Leslie.

55

Walking the Decks

The French barman doesn't say a word as he places another whisky in front of her. He's not said anything since she asked him if, given the size of the measures, they were rationing drinks on this ship. He cast her a look which indicated that she had crossed a line, but it's not as if he were friendly before this apparent faux pas of hers. Anyhow, if she were he, she would keep quiet, as his tourist-class bar is empty and she is clearly his best customer. It is a reasonably pleasant afternoon out on deck, so he could offer this as an excuse, but the truth is, given this man's regrettable personality, she imagines that every day is most likely a little slow in this particular bar.

This morning she and Leslie shared a late breakfast together. She had finally decided to resume taking meals, and so her relieved husband escorted her into the dining room, where two places had been set at a table by the window. They took up their seats, and it was the same disagreeable French barman, in the guise of a waiter, who brought in her scrambled eggs and two slices of bread and butter on a side plate and set them down in front of her. At least the eggs were warm, she could say that for them, but beyond this, there was little merit to the breakfast. She looked out of the window and could see that it was a blustery morning, but it wasn't raining, so she decided that once she had finished her eggs she would leave her husband, who had already declared his intention to go back to their cabin and read, and go out on the decks for a walk.

By eleven she had abandoned her walking and taken up a seat on a canvas-backed chair. She was minding her own business and watching the sun dissolve what remained of the morning haze when the pair of them strolled by. They pulled on their cigarettes and nodded a curt greeting in her direction, and in their wake they trailed a fume of what she surmised to be an expensive scent. The young men weren't talking to each other, which was the first odd thing that she noticed about them, for she'd long ago come to the conclusion that men didn't know how to walk with each other without talking. It was also clear that they were both misty-eyed, which immediately made her wonder if they had spent the night in the ship's casino. She watched them amble off, and she followed them until they vanished into the bend near the bow of the ship. No sooner had they disappeared from view, however, than they must have decided to return, for they were quickly walking back in her direction. For a moment she thought about getting up and fleeing before they reached her chair, but not wishing to behave in a way that might be deemed unfriendly, she sat rigid and waited.

Before either of them could say a word, she invited them

to sit with her, and both men were unable to disguise their delight. They each shook her hand, and then sat down in adjacent chairs and announced that they were from Buckinghamshire and taking a holiday together, as they had lost one of their friends. She had no interest in their history, but Leonard, the taller of the two men, seemed keen to share their personal details, and so she let him talk himself out. "And that's about it. Some diseases can be cured and some cannot." Colin, the younger and more diminutive of the two, who possessed an unfortunate pockmarked face, simply nodded. "Yes, that's right," he said, but he seemed a trifle overcome with shyness and embarrassed to be mouthing even these few words. Leonard stared out to sea, and then he turned to look at her as though suddenly remembering that he was in company. "But of course we mustn't depress you." He glanced at his wristwatch. "We'd be awfully thrilled if you'd submit to join us for a late-morning tipple."

She and Leonard sat together in awkward silence at a table in the far corner of the bar, while Colin ordered the drinks. She understood that her looks were not what they had been, and she had gained a little weight, and these days found herself much more reliant upon her eyes, but it still surprised her that Leonard appeared to be thoroughly indifferent to her presence. After all, nobody could accuse her of not being splendidly attired, Leslie having finally responded to her hints about the necessity for a new wardrobe by allowing her to indulge herself on Oxford Street. She smiled sweetly while her new friend took an abbreviated drag on his cigarette and then blew a puff of uninhaled smoke upwards before stubbing the cigarette out, as though finding the whole experiment unsatisfactory. When Leonard saw his friend gingerly making his way over to their table with his hands cupped like a ten-fingered blanket around three glasses, he came to life and pushed back a chair for Colin to sit down. "Whisky for the lady," said Leonard as he reached over and took her drink from his friend and placed it in front of her. She looked at this Leonard and realized that one day he would make some lucky girl a good, loyal husband, for he had a gallant eagerness about him which suggested that his present station in life was not a place where he was prepared to remain stranded. Unlike her husband, Leonard possessed ambition, and perhaps some talent, and she felt sure that his good manners and keenness to give out the right impression would ensure his progress. His friend, on the other hand, was a follower who she imagined would be susceptible to being easily led by both men and women, and for whom the apology, both the short humble version and the long and exasperating variant, would undoubtedly be a part of his future. Neither of them wore rings that might suggest an affiliation, but Leonard had about himself an aspect of great vigilance, which led her to believe that the next young woman who crossed his path was likely to be seized upon and offered the possibility of a lifetime of companionship.

After the third drink, it was Leonard who suggested that he and Colin had better be making their way back to their cabin. They both hoped that her husband would soon feel better and they were grateful to her for spending some time with them. There was a sudden ungainliness about their decision to leave, and she thought that it might be connected to her asking the barman if they were rationing the whisky on this ship. The barman had been attentive enough to come to their table, tray in hand, but he had clearly been offended by her comment. The two men stood, and so she too got to her feet. Leonard said they would like to walk her back to her cabin, but she told them there was no need, for she was going to move from their table and sit at the bar and have one more drink, as she had a number of things to ponder. As she took up her seat on a bar stool, she watched them pass through the door. It was then that the sullen barman simply placed another whisky in front of her before turning his back and continuing to wipe clean some glasses.

56

Other Women

This morning there are two other women sitting out on deck. She said a polite "Good morning" to them both as she took up her seat, but received only the briefest of smiles in response. The birdlike younger one with plucked eyebrows, who is dressed in a navy blue twinset, is easy to sum up. No doubt she is returning to the islands to continue to help her husband manage an estate after perhaps visiting relatives, or even a child who has been shipped off to a minor public school in the English countryside. The matronly woman is older, closer to her own age and perhaps not yet fifty, although the muscles on this woman's face have slackened dramatically. She reads an out-of-date newspaper like a man, with the sheet spread out and occupying her full wingspan, but there is plenty of room on deck, so why not? Occasionally she leans forward and licks a finger to make turning the pages a little easier, and her guess is that the woman is a schoolteacher of some description, for her shoes seem more functional than fashionable and lying on the seat next to her is a briefcase. She has noticed that women today no longer seem to feel the need to justify, or even explain, why they exist independently of men. Progress, she assumes, and a part of her envies such modern women, but are they any happier? Do they truly know what to do with this freedom? She wonders, Is the stern-looking woman sitting opposite her, with a man's briefcase on the neighbouring chair, really what the suffragettes were dreaming of when they chained themselves to railings and threw themselves beneath the feet of galloping horses?

57

The Bluest Sea

The schoolteacher has neatly folded the newspaper and slipped it into a briefcase. She didn't even offer to share it and give her the opportunity to catch up on the news. Now both the sensibly shod schoolteacher and her twin-suited friend are blissfully dozing, their heads occasionally snapping to attention before they once again readjust their positions and fall back asleep. She recognizes that her quandary with Leslie might best be described as unhappy, but not desperate, and she realizes that there is a difference. In the distance she hears a clap of thunder, which wakes the schoolteacher but leaves the younger woman still dreaming. The older woman looks around as though momentarily unsure of where she is, and then the rain cloud bursts and the torrent begins. The woman leans back in her chair and proceeds to try once again to rest. They are all three seated beneath the bridge, so unless a strong wind begins to blow, they will remain dry.

But what to do now? Really, the woman might have offered to share her newspaper. At least she has married a decent man who has made an effort to help her, although at times he has tried a little too hard. However, she is adamant that she doesn't want to do anything that might cause Leslie hurt. After all, it is clear that whatever professional capital the poor man once possessed, he has recklessly spent it promoting her own stumbling career, and his present unemployed condition must surely be causing him both grief and embarrassment in equal part.

She looks again at the sleeping schoolteacher, and then from her pocket she draws a violet headscarf and fastens it tightly about her head, although the odd shred of hair insists on breaking cover and flying free in the forceful breeze. My husband and I no longer enjoy any intimacy. So this is my situation. I don't anticipate your sympathy, nor do I wish to receive your judgment. I'm sorry, but I say this just to clear the air. Given the fact that they will presently be approaching the tropics, she wonders if at some point soon the schoolteacher is perhaps contemplating a change in travel costume, from heavy tweed to light cottons. My husband hasn't done me any actual wrong that I can identify. If anything, Mr. Leslie Tilden Smith has been too devoted, and not infrequently he has left me feeling claustrophobic and angry and I've lashed out. People say that time heals, but it doesn't. You just train yourself to forget the ugly incidents, but it only takes one thing to bring it all back again. In fact, the only thing you really learn is how to forget temporarily. My husband miscast me. Sadly, these days my Leslie's thoughts about me are difficult to discern, for they are well hidden behind a mask of diligent formality. Unfortunately, I fear that I may have robbed him of the capacity for happiness. But she says none of this, and turns from the slumbering woman and stares now at a suddenly deep blue sea that rises and falls under a stormy sky.

X

A Now Empty World

58

Home

From the deck of the S.S. *Cuba* she gazed at the densely textured slopes of the St. Lucia hills. They were thickly matted with foliage which exhausted every possible shade of green and capped by an azure, cloudless sky, and she breathed out with relief, for she was home. They would remain here for a few days before taking a smaller vessel that would convey them north to Dominica and her reconnection to a world that she hoped would lift the burden of anonymity from her tired shoulders. She looked at the lush island landscape and journeyed back in her mind to her childhood. She remembered her mother busying herself in the living room rearranging her father's books and newspapers, or meticulously draping the polished table in a lace cloth, which always seemed to remain stubbornly decorated with a lattice of stiff folds; she also remembered her mother seated squarely in her bedroom before the looking glass and staring fixedly, as though unable to see her own reflection. As the years passed by, she began to notice that her mother was becoming progressively more careless about polishing her nails, and increasingly disinclined to trouble herself with the task of rouging her lips. She remembered her father, whose distrust of the English she now understood, but over the years she had trained herself to exercise caution once her father made an appearance, for *his* loss had plunged her into a state of despair from which she knew she had never truly recovered. As the S.S. *Cuba* edged its way into the crescent of the harbour, she fought hard to banish her father from her thoughts, for she had no desire to temper the elation of her arrival with the sorrowful affliction of grief.

When she and her heavily perspiring husband finally arrived at their Castries guest house, they were met by an Englishwoman who appeared to be in charge, although she had some distant memory of the small property being owned by second or third cousins on her mother's side. Mrs. Ellis's face was heavily enameled, which she presumed made it difficult for the strange-looking lady to express any emotion other than mild discomfort, but they dutifully followed the proprietress up a narrow wooden staircase and listened to the woman's singsong voice as she apologetically recited the list of rules. Having run a finger along the top of the dresser to demonstrate the absence of dust, the woman untied a single key from a small assortment that she carried on a long ribbon around her neck and then handed it to Leslie, closed the door, and left the newly arrived couple in peace. She sat in silence for some moments on the side of the overly quilted twin bed before forcing herself to her feet. She glanced at her husband, who had slipped off his shoes and was spread-eagled across the coverlet, and then she decided to go out onto the balcony.

Down below, on a small outcrop of rocks overlooking the wide expanse of the harbour, she saw a young Negress standing by herself and pressing a headscarf to her hair as though worried that a sudden flurry might at any moment strip it from her. Her husband soon joined her on the balcony, but neither of them said anything as they peered down on the woman, who stared blankly at the sea. After a short interval, Leslie retreated back into their room, leaving her alone, and she in turn took up a seat on a small metal chair. Two hours later the bright afternoon glare began to fade and the day offered no resistance to the upsurge of night.

After much tossing and turning in the lumpy bed, she woke suddenly to a blade of light streaming into the room. It was still dark, however, and she realized that the intrusive glow was from a streetlamp that was situated just below their room. She had no inclination to disturb her husband, so she lay quietly and waited to be greeted by the noises of a West Indian day; to begin with she heard the rattling of carts in the street, then the shrieking of seagulls wheeling in the ill-defined border between sea and land, and then the more boisterous and intrusive noises of the cook beginning to busy herself in the small yard to the side of the establishment. The woman would no doubt be preparing breakfast for the two guests from England, who she had most likely been told would expect to be treated regally. A sluggish-looking Leslie opened his eyes as though unsure of where exactly he was, and she took this as her cue to leave the bed and put on her dressing gown. Since their arrival there had been no conversation of any substance between them, and it was difficult to determine if her husband was excited or disappointed. No doubt once he discovered his bearings he would have something to say, but in the meantime she was grateful that he appeared to be allowing her time to re-enter her world in peace. She stepped out onto the balcony and looked down at the beach, where she saw a man riding a horse at a full gallop along the line where the sea was breaking in a flat, hushed whisper. With each hoofbeat a small shower of brine exploded and animated the otherwise tranquil scene. She imagined the hunched rider being stirred by both the snorting and wheezing of the animal and the roar of the wind in his ears, and she felt sure that the thunder of each stride would be rattling his every bone, but from her own distant vantage point there was a mute silken grace to the movement of man and horse.

As it transpired, she spent the greater part of the day nursing Leslie, who directly after breakfast succumbed to diarrhea, which forced him to remain confined to their room. It had been clear to her that the bacon was overcooked, and she had avoided it, fearing a failed attempt by the cook to compensate for the lack of any cold storage, but Leslie had eaten a hearty helping. Whilst her husband tossed and turned, looking as though he might at any moment wilt in the heat and humidity, she was able to lightly doze in a wicker chair that was set in the shade away from the window and accustom herself to the heavy thickness of the air. By late afternoon Leslie had recovered sufficiently to be able to contemplate joining her for dinner, and she was relieved to see an untroubled ease to his gait as he made his way downstairs to the dining room. After dinner, they accepted Mrs. Ellis's offer to join her in the parlour and listen to Mr. Ellis playing the piano. As Mrs. Ellis introduced them to her mild-mannered husband, she instantly surmised that Mr. Ellis was the type of Englishman who in the privacy of his own home would habitually soak his feet in a basin of hot water and each night place his teeth in a glass. The man's dark eyebrows almost met, and his slightly slack-jawed mouth was disturbingly overcrowded with his ill-fitting dentures. The proprietress informed her guests that when they lived in Kent her husband used to provide the accompaniment to the silent pictures at the cinema, but tonight she and Mr. Tilden Smith would constitute his audience. Mr. Ellis proposed playing for them a selection of classical and popular favourites, although Mrs. Ellis quickly interrupted and warned them that her husband drew the line at German music, which had never had any place in his repertoire. Mrs. Ellis must have warmed to her guests, for before the onset of the recital the woman offered them a specially imported blend of fragrant tea and a plate of sliced fruitcake, all served on what was clearly her best china. An hour later Mr. Ellis concluded his presentation, but he remained seated at the piano, his dull-hooded eyes wide open as he continued to stare at the keys where his meaty fingers remained poised. It was then that she noticed that Mr. Ellis was wearing brown carpet slippers with ill-matching socks—one grey and one black—and in an instant she understood the Ellises' story to be one of difficulty and struggle.

Mr. Ellis continued to wait, but for what it was impossible for her to divine. Mrs. Ellis, on the other hand, seemed completely unperturbed by the melancholy stupor into which her husband appeared to have fallen, and she stood and in one fluid movement picked up the tray of tea and untouched cake. With this done, she shuffled her way out of the room and closed the door behind her. Shortly thereafter Mr. Ellis appeared to return to the world. Standing up from his piano stool, he padded his way to the drinks cabinet, inside of which was gathered a nest of small glasses and a bottle of sherry. He quietly poured two neat measures, which he handed to his guests, commenting that it helped with the cold on a dark night. With this done, he poured himself an allowance and then sat opposite them both, and it was possible for her to see that the man's eyes were now damp with emotion. As Mr. Ellis lifted the glass to his lips, she understood that he would say no more. A few minutes later, Mrs. Ellis re-entered the room and looked tenderly at her tranquil husband and simply said, "It's time, Alfred," at which point the man rose to his feet and diligently replaced his empty, but unwashed, glass in the cabinet. He then positioned himself by his wife's side, but he continued to look much affected, as though he had suffered some great loss. "Good night," said Mrs. Ellis, offering them both the briefest glimpse of a smile. "Perhaps you'd be so kind as to turn out the lights when you retire."

Once upstairs, she put on a cardigan and then opened the door to the balcony and took her glass of sherry with her out into the cool night air. The salty smell of the sea stung her nose with a sharpness she had not noticed during the daytime, but she decided to remain outside until her husband had fallen asleep. It occurred to her that Mr. Ellis most likely felt obliged to obey his wife, for it was probably Mrs. Ellis's money (a bequest perhaps?) that had enabled them to travel out to the West Indies. There was no doubt that it was her fierce energy that kept the hotel running smoothly, for Mr. Ellis appeared to be incapable of rising to meet such responsibilities. She conjectured that Mr. Ellis's dreams of a life in music, giving recitals and composing melodies, had been unhappily shipwrecked on the rocky shore of his wife's practical common sense. Over dinner the woman had, after all, shared a little of their history with her guests. ("Alfred's doctor insisted that he wouldn't last another winter in England, so I said, For heaven's sake, let's find some sun.") Out on the small balcony, a shiver ran through her as the wind rose, and she wondered if she had correctly intuited the source of the sadness that hovered over the lives of Mr. and Mrs. Ellis.

59

A Now Empty World

In the morning, she found herself wide awake and listening to the monotony of Leslie's light snoring while it was still dark outside. All night her memory had rushed crazily, and it was her mother who featured at every turn, until finally she looked into the woman's dim eyes and asked for forgiveness, but her mother seemed puzzled and assured her that she had done nothing for which she needed to be forgiven, and then she woke suddenly, as though a blanket had been torn away, and she blinked hard and eventually realized where she was. The prospect of a sleepy early-morning exchange with Leslie seemed too awkward to consider and so she dressed quietly and left their shared bedroom. She tiptoed down the stairs and stepped into her shoes at the front door, taking particular care not to disturb the small table which supported Mrs. Ellis's delicately balanced vase of poinsettias. Once outside, the cloying density of the night air and the strong chorus of palpitating insect life let her know that dawn remained some way off, but her mind was made up. She moved purposefully through the silent streets and in the direction of the small outcrop of rocks overlooking the harbour, where she intended to station herself so that, in an hour or two, as the listless waves continued to lap, she might witness the full glory of the sun rising over her now empty world.

60

A Dream

She perched awkwardly on the clump of damp rocks, and although she felt uncomfortable, she was determined to remain motionless and empty her troubled mind of her joyless life in England and, perhaps in this manner, make room for the present. However, as she waited patiently for evidence of the first light of dawn, she continued to be tormented by last night's dreams of her mother, and then she was alarmed to remember that, at some point before sitting bolt upright in bed, Lancey had made an uninvited and prolonged appearance in her overwrought imagination.

She dreamed that once she reached Charles Street she warily mounted the steps and rang the doorbell, whose resonant chimes sounded just as ominous as they had done a quarter of a century earlier. However, the apparition who opened the door was not familiar to her. Lancey was now white-haired, rheumy-eyed, and most shockingly, he was bent over and supporting himself by leaning heavily against a cane.

She had sent a message to Lancey from the hotel so he would know that she intended to call upon him, but when she asked at the concierge's desk if there was a letter for her, she was informed that there were no messages. Although initially puzzled, she eventually persuaded herself that the lack of a response meant that Lancey was happy for her to visit, even at such short notice, and so she set out for Mayfair. Lancey smiled and held on to the door, but she could see that pain was lodged just beneath the surface of his warm smile. Slowly he stepped to one side to let her pass and enter.

As she sat down on the drawing-room sofa, it was immediately clear to her that this large grand house was now far too much for Lancey to manage. The disarray and dust were unhealthy, and judging by the scattered debris, it appeared that Lancey spent the greater part of his time in this one cold room. Where was his butler? Where were his servants? On the mantlepiece sat a framed photograph of Julian, and Lancey's eyes followed hers to the portrait. "I imagine you heard?" he began. "We lost Cousin Julian during the war. Ypres. He fell along with most of the men under his command. Such a waste, but although I was devoted to him, I haven't forgotten that you two had your quarrels and you thought him a horrid person." Lancey continued and told her about his mother, who lived to be nearly eighty-five, and then he remembered himself and asked if she might like some tea, or perhaps something a little stronger. "I'm sure I've got a drop somewhere." She shook her head, and then it was her turn. There had been a husband, and time spent in France, and now she was back in London, where she had secured for herself a second husband, but she didn't say more than this, for she was not hankering to advertise her own situation. Truthfully, given the startling state of Lancey's health, she was now beginning to rue having called upon him. As the silence between them deepened, she sensed that Lancey was trying to decide whether to remain faithful to his preferred mode of polite reticence, or whether he should make the effort to speak from the heart. He looked up and met her eyes. "You do understand that we all make mistakes in life, don't you? As a result, I feel I must apologize for whatever hurt I might have caused you. My dear child, I felt trapped by circumstance, but why should this lessen your sense of injustice?" She was unsure if he expected her to answer, but she said nothing. Lancey's gaze fell to the floor, and she gaped at the bald spot on the top of his head and tried hard to reconcile herself to the fact that the shell of a person before her was the man she had loved. He coughed and stammered slightly, for he was clearly struggling to maintain the fluid grace of his speech. "Shall we dine together this evening? I can call on you at any time that is convenient. Shall we say eight o'clock?" Seeing the hopeful gleam in his eyes, she nodded and confirmed the name of her hotel. She then rose to her feet and watched as Lancey pushed forcefully against his cane and pressed himself upright. "Now then, you will require some time to rest and make yourself ready. I can call a taxicab for you, or better still, I can walk with you, as the exercise will most likely do me some good." She smiled at him, but declined his offer. "Thank you, I shall be fine."

Once she left Charles Street, she turned away from the direction of her hotel and set out towards Hyde Park, where she soon found an empty bench to sit on. A light breeze carried the voices of happy children up into the air and in her direction, but she tried to block them out. She wished to bestow the gift of contentment upon Lancey, some kind of closing of accounts that would allow him to stop worrying and go forward in peace, but she suspected that, having outlived his peers, the man was now dawdling in his mind and incapable of moving on. Sadly, she would now have to accustom herself to the fact that she had nothing further to offer him, and her heart sank, for she realized that it was foolish and selfish of her to have sought him out, and she was inundated with guilt. Her decision was lamentable, but inescapable, for it was now clear to her that this evening she should probably not leave the confines of her hotel room.

The following morning the front desk clerk telephoned her room. When she came down she discovered a dishevelled Lancey seated in the lobby in a dreary suit with his cane standing upright between his legs. He stood to greet her, and he raised his hat politely and asked if she felt inclined to take tea with him. Once they were seated in the dining room, she began to apologize, but he held up his hand. "Please, I'm conscious of the fact that I am hardly a feast for the eyes." Lancey reached into his inside pocket and pulled out a red velvet case which, when he finally fumbled it open, she could see contained a pearl necklace. "The necklace was my mother's. I would very much like you to have it." She thanked him, but made it plain that she couldn't possibly accept his benevolence. He smiled and lifted the long delicate object from its box, and then he placed it on the table in such a manner that it lay abandoned midway between them as though devoid of any value.

61

Why Don't They Like Us?

She watched Leslie steadily backing away from what remained of the Great House. He raised his camera to his face, then suddenly he lost his footing, and as he tumbled towards the dirt, he reached out an arm and braced himself against a fall. Righting himself, he dusted down his trousers and then found a flat rock upon which to stand, and again he raised his camera. The house was as Owen's letter had suggested she might find it—burned, but not quite to the ground. Charred beams remained where once there had been a roof, but the stone walls of the structure still allowed her to imagine the estate home that for her mother's family had been a country retreat for well over a century. Behind her husband, and brooding on the horizon, she could see the island of Martinique. It was a perfectly beautiful day, and with the sun at its highest point, no shadows were being cast.

This morning she made plans with the Paz Hotel for a car to take them to where the uphill track began. When they arrived at the clearing in the bush, they were met by an elderly Negro guide with two horses, who explained that the porters had already gone on ahead with the luncheon baskets, which contained everything that she and Leslie would require for a picnic. The woman behind the hotel desk had looked at her with incredulity when she announced that she intended to make this rigorous excursion, but the hotel employee knew that the estate was in her guest's family and so she refrained from offering an opinion. When their transport arrived at the Paz, Leslie eased himself into the backseat of the car next to her, and noticing that she was nervous, he instinctively reached over and took her hand. "You said you were happy there once, and so you'll be happy there again." She smiled without meeting his eyes, and then turned to look out of the window as the car engine coughed to life and they began to make their slow and dusty way through the still-cobbled streets of Roseau. This was only their third morning on the island and already she was doubting the wisdom of her decision to come home. The town needed a fresh coat of paint and the people appeared poor and slovenly. What troubled her the most, however, was the fact that the Negroes stared rudely at her and her husband when they walked together in the streets and she detected insolence in their faces. It would be hard to explain to Leslie the full extent of her disappointment, so she said nothing and simply tried to hold at bay the rising tide of resentment and embarrassment that seemed primed to engulf her.

By mid-morning even the horses were finding it diffi-cult to keep their footing on the narrow track. Leslie's mare was clearly the less robust of the two animals, and one foot was unshod, which caused the horse to occasionally stumble in an often alarming fashion. The intermittent rain only added to the misery of this steep ascent through dense, untamed foliage, which their barefoot guide had to regularly take his cutlass to. Thirty or so years ago she remembered making the journey by taking a precipitous mossy path which wound its way skywards beneath a sometime impenetrable thatch of overhanging trees. Light slanted down through the canopy and speckled the ground across which she and her siblings walked, and although these childhood journeys from Roseau to the Geneva estate were always a little arduous, they were also times of great joy and happiness, particularly for herself and Owen. What, she wondered as they continued to slip and slide, had happened to the stamped-in path? How could nature have triumphed so completely, and in such a short space of time?

"Mistress need to rest?"

The gap-toothed guide wiped some sweat from his brow with the tail of his soiled shirt, but she looked down at him and shook her head, insisting that they press on. As they did so, they approached a particularly wooded section of the meandering track where on the ground they were forced to negotiate huge gnarly tree roots, while overhead they were effectively roofed in by a dense forest. Entering a shaded region was like being doused by a waterfall, however, and she was happy for the welcome respite from the brutal heat.

"For Christ's sake, Leslie, put away the blasted camera. I can't bear to watch you taking any more photographs. And what exactly is it that you think you're capturing?"

She was sitting in a canvas chair that a porter had placed

beneath a pair of soaring palms that she remembered from her childhood. The guide and a second porter squatted some way off, preparing lunch, but she had long ago lost her appetite. A remorseful Leslie sat down in the chair next to her own.

"I'm sorry, I didn't mean to cause offence. I just thought that we should have some evidence of the place."

She said nothing, but used her arm to shade her eyes as Leslie removed his straw hat and began to fan his blotchy face.

"It's a damn fine view from up here, you can't argue with that." He pointed down into the valley below. "Are those the plantation works? Good Lord, you can see everything from up here."

Her mother used to boast that her family's Geneva estate covered nearly two thousand acres, and she would always insist that it was a place of great happiness for everybody. But if this was true, why had these ungrateful Negroes burned it down?

Leslie quickly lifted the binoculars from around his neck and stood and trained his gaze on a parrot that had alighted some distance off, but whose mournful call split the silence.

"My God, she's a beauty. Would you like to take a look?"

He began to strip the binoculars from his neck, but she held up her hand.

"Why don't they like us?"

"I'm sorry?"

She glowered at her husband, whose furrowed brow suggested that he had absolutely no idea of what she was talking about.

"It doesn't matter, Leslie."

She surveyed Martinique, which shimmered and seemed

to hover somewhat magically on the horizon. Above the island she could make out the ghostly outline of a rainbow, one foot of which was dipped into the sea, whose face was blemished by the dark shadows of languid clouds. Then she looked again at the burned-out, discarded ruin of her mother's family estate house. Indeed, once upon a time she had been happy here. And now this. As the Negro guide moved towards them with a cleaved coconut in each hand, she decided that she would go for a walk by herself and leave it to Leslie to explain that she no longer possessed an appetite for either coconut water or food.

62

Through the Saloon Doors

She sat on the side of the bed and continued to stare at her husband. Leslie was leaning against the wall to the side of the slightly ajar French windows, which gave out onto a small Juliet balcony, and he was looking down onto the inadequately illuminated streets of Roseau. The distant rumble of thunder heralded what was to come, but Leslie showed no inclination to close the windows and turn his attention to the bedroom, where the occasional beetle or moth was now making a practice of crashing into the naked lightbulb and creating a commotion out of all proportion to its size. An hour ago, to the dismay of her husband, she had finally settled Owen's affairs for him, and so, after the disappointment of the expedition to the Geneva estate, and the tension of this recent encounter with Owen's descendants, they were both now eager to leave Roseau. As a consequence, they had agreed that tonight would be their last evening in the capital before undertaking the journey to the north of the island, where they intended to spend the remainder of their time reading and relaxing in a small house that had been made available to them by friends of her mother's family.

She had asked Owen's daughter to meet her in the shabby and neglected bar of the Paz Hotel, which, when they arrived on the island, she had been reliably informed was these days considered a more acceptable option than the increasingly louche Cherry Lodge. A thin layer of dust coated the rows of sunlit bottles that decorated the shelves behind the bar. Leslie ordered a cold beer, while she asked for a rum and lime juice, and she watched closely to make sure that the young Negress mixed it with care. The bar was empty aside from a pair of rotund Syrian merchants in the far corner, whose cigarette tips glowed in the gloom, and then, safely tucked between forefinger and thumb, the red tips swooped as the men reached down to pick up their glasses of whisky. As she and Leslie carried their drinks to a table, she looked at the sad and fading photographs which decorated the walls, and the bunches of croton that had been stuffed into bowls that were randomly scattered on tabletops, and strangest of all, a bamboo birdcage but no bird, and she understood that this would be her one and only visit to this bar. They took up two seats beneath a nonchalantly turning fan, which gave off eddies of draughty air and immediately caused her to shiver. Before touching his beer, Leslie began to apply some colourless ointment to his lips, for the intrusive sun had caused them to begin cracking like paint and he had shared with her his worries that they might blister. Eventually the saloon-style doors slowly swung open and an attractive mulatto woman, followed by a bemused, fleshy teenage girl and a painfully thin young man, straggled their way into the bar. She smiled at them, but they seemed nervous, and so she raised a friendly hand and watched as they threaded their way towards her table. Once they stood before her, she was able to see that, although they possessed the nose and mouth of the Negro, their bright eyes and hair clearly belonged to her family. Leslie stood and offered his hand, which they each shook limply, and then he encouraged the family members to sit and he asked them what they would like to drink. The mulatto woman ignored the Englishman and addressed her relative. "Aunty, we taking soft," she whispered, apparently speaking for them all.

Finally the storm broke and the first torrents of rain began to pelt against the galvanized roof with double-barrelled accuracy, and this sudden downpour created a turbulence with which she was familiar. Her husband closed the French windows and came and sat on his bed and looked across at her.

"I'm sorry, Gwen, but it's difficult for me to watch people take advantage of you."

"Nobody took advantage of me. Owen will reimburse your money."

"But, Gwen, Owen has no money. And I simply don't understand how you can be so accommodating. After all, these people just sat there with their paws out as though you owed them something."

"We do owe them something."

"They are Owen's bastard issue, let *him* pay for them." He paused and crossed and then uncrossed his legs. "I'm sorry, but there's a distinct whiff of impropriety about this whole matter. Your brother should be man enough to take responsibility for the mistakes of his youth."

She scrutinized her husband and could see frustration giving way to anger, and so she reached out and placed a hand on his knee. She wanted Leslie to see her world, but it was already evident that the more her husband saw, the less he understood.

"Thank you," she said. Leslie looked quizzically at her. "For treating them with the greatest consideration."

"Is it the heat, Gwen, that causes this breakdown of order? Is this Owen's excuse?"

She said nothing as a pink-faced Leslie once again stood up and crossed to the window. Lost in his own thoughts, he stared out into the darkness as the thunderstorm reached its furious climax and a thousand gutters began to sputter thick cords of water down into the empty streets. She decided to begin preparing herself for bed, knowing full well that her stricken husband would make his own arrangements once the turmoil in his mind abated.

63

A View of the Empire at Sunset

"The way you were going on, anybody would think you'd won the bloody Victoria Cross."

Leslie put down his glass and stood up. As he turned to face her she could see that her ungenerous comment had struck home.

"I think it best that I go for a short walk."

Leslie picked up his straw hat, and for a moment her husband hesitated as though he might sit back down, but he decided to remain standing.

"Listen, Gwen, I know that today's events have upset you, but why take it out on me? Ever since we came to this place you've done little but snipe, and it's as though you're deliberately trying to make my life miserable."

She ignored him.

"Well, are you?"

Leaving Roseau for the north of the island and a few weeks' seclusion at this rundown estate house was supposed to offer them both the opportunity to read and relax and forget the various frustrations that had marred their disheartening stay in the capital. The additional bonus was that Leslie would no longer have to suffer the confusion of daily interaction with West Indian society, which he evidently found disenchanting and perplexing in equal part. The four-hour steamer journey from Roseau to Portsmouth had been difficult for them both, for they had been forced to share the unsophisticated accommodation aboard the small vessel with various animals and a dangerously excessive number of country Negroes. Thereafter, a car had transported them across the top of the island to the Atlantic coast, but the small estate house at Hampstead had been closed and shuttered for over a year and the servant had opened up the place only on the morning of their arrival. Nearly a week passed before the unpleasant smell and dampness left the premises, but this had entailed sleeping with the windows open and hoping that the ancient mosquito netting would prove to be a sufficiently effective deterrent which, predictably enough, it had not.

"Well," said an exasperated Leslie as he placed the straw hat on his head, "I do hope that you will be in better spirits when I return."

She watched her husband saunter his way around two large curved flowerpots, then step down off the veranda. She snatched up the bottle of cane rum and emptied the last drops into her tumbler, and then she hurled the heavy vessel in Leslie's direction and saw it flash by his head and crash into the bushes with an impatient thump, but they were both spared the drama of the bottle shattering. Her husband stopped as though gathering himself to turn and say something to her. "Go on, say it. You and your bloody senseless prudence." She stared as Leslie slowly plucked a handkerchief from the pocket of his flannels and painstakingly mopped his brow. Then he simply pushed the handkerchief back into his pocket and decided to continue to walk down the grassy hill towards the small strip of white sand beach.

When they received the second invitation to lunch, it was her husband who took the position that it would be rude to make up yet another excuse. He insisted that claiming to be fatigued was all well and good, but after two weeks in residence the Napiers would be cognizant of the fact that they were now rested and established on the estate. Leslie continued and reminded her that these neighbours were friends of her mother's family, and it was her mother's relatives who had kindly allowed them to make use of this Hampstead property, and so she reluctantly conceded. The Napiers sent their car and driver to collect their lunch guests, and after some twenty minutes of twisting and climbing, with the driver giving out occasional blasts of the horn to scatter the Negro children wandering by the roadside, and then pumping furiously on the brakes as they made sudden and treacherous descents, they were deposited at Pointe Baptiste and welcomed by their elegant hostess and her dapper husband.

The woman's hair was drawn back into a tight short ponytail, which suggested a severity that their hostess tried a little too hard to dispel with her overfriendly aspect. However, from the start this Mrs. Napier seemed interested only in Leslie, and once the woman discovered his connection to the London publishing world, she turned her whole body in Leslie's direction and fired off a volley of questions which seemed designed to offer him the opportunity of introducing her name into future exchanges with his colleagues. Or so it seemed to her as she tried to keep up with the gushing auto-biographical surge of this Mrs. Napier's prattle, while half-listening to the low drone of complaints that Mr. Napier seemed determined to share with her on the subject of garden management in the tropics. ("It's a devil of a task, but one mustn't shirk.") Lunch was edible, if simple, and comprised of yams, plantains, and unboned fish, followed by oranges and soursops, after which they retired to the veranda, where Mr. Napier, apparently sensing her discomfort with his conversation, seized her husband's attention and took it upon himself to mention his wartime service in the Royal Canadian Forces. She looked on as the strange man disappeared inside the house and emerged clutching a box of medals which he and Leslie began to finger like a pair of giddy schoolboys. This gave Mrs. Napier the opportunity to enlighten her female guest on developments on the island during the few years that she had been a resident, and share with her the many suggestions she had as to how things might well be improved if only these Dominican people would make the effort to find a way to work together.

She and her husband said little to each other as they were chauffeured back to Hampstead, aware that the driver worked for their hosts. But once the car backed its way out of the long driveway that was fringed on both sides by wild limes, she asked Leslie to send Fredrica, the servant, home for the day. Thereafter, she took up a seat on the veranda and stared intently out to sea. Her husband stepped out from the house with a bottle of rum and two glasses and sat down beside her. He poured the rum and handed her a glass.

"Well, my dear, at least that's done and out of the way. To be honest, I thought it was going to be more of an ordeal."

Leslie continued, and she listened as her husband praised the Napiers' hospitality, but she said nothing and poured herself another drink, and then another, and eventually Leslie stopped speaking. He turned to face her.

"Listen, Gwen, did I do or say something to offend you?"

As daylight started to ebb and the hummingbirds began to dart from one upturned bell to another in a beating hurry to drink the last beads of nectar before dark, she rose unsteadily from her chair and stumbled off in search of her husband. After a few minutes she discovered Leslie settled on a scrap of pasture that sat just above the modest expanse of beach. He was gazing at the Atlantic breakers, seemingly unconcerned that to his left three small goats that had been tethered by Fredrica's husband were busily chewing the wispy, poverty-stricken grass that had been distressed by drought and making their way ever closer towards him.

"Well, are you coming back to the house, or do you intend to sleep out here under the stars?" Leslie looked up, and she saw the sadness etched on her husband's face. "I'm sorry, Leslie, but these vile people won't do. They simply traipse around the empire talking about themselves. I know the type, but you don't. You're far too easily taken in by such idiots and their fictional stories of wartime heroics."

"That's enough, Gwen. You're being unfair."

"Am I? Unlike you I have no faith in the civilizing power of the English."

"Please, Gwen, no more."

"What the hell do you mean, 'no more'?" She stared angrily at him. "In a short while we'll return to Roseau and then depart for England and leave behind this place. Has it even occurred to you to ask yourself what this has all been about? For me, that is?" She waited. "Well, has this thought even crossed your mind?"

It was beginning to get dark now, and out at sea the wind was kicking up a fuss and causing the waves to curl and crash with increasing ferocity. They had no electricity at the house, and having dismissed the servant, they would have to light the lamps themselves. What *had* it all been about? They had visited places from her childhood. They had seen Owen's family. They had consulted with the staff at the hotel. They had travelled from one end of the island to the other. They had made small talk with the servant Fredrica and her husband. They had swum in the river by the semi-abandoned plantation works. At various times they had sat and looked at the French islands to both the north and the south. They had enjoyed freshly squeezed limes in their drinks. But never once had Leslie spoken to her about her home without some thinly veiled sense of disquiet on his part. Until today, that is. *I thought it was going to be more of an ordeal.* The Napiers were his type of people, cocooning themselves in smug shaded silence while their blissful days of blistering heat slid by, their peace only punctuated by imagined distant drumming or the whispered hush of trees as the wind suddenly rises, and come sunset, these people surface and begin to recite their litany of complaints about the difficulties of living "Behind God's Back," only bothering to display joyful animation when the subject of England is raised. "Tell me about everyone." Father was right, these people were not acceptable, and because she could see that they were now plentiful on her island *she* would have to go. She couldn't possibly stay. It would have to be

England again. But perhaps she ought to explain all of this to Leslie?

"Let's go back to the house, Gwen. Before night falls."

She stared at what remained of daylight fading on the restless ocean, and the failure of the whole venture threatened to overwhelm her, and so she closed her eyes against the futility of her situation. As she listened to the raucous and persistent engine of the sea she felt sorry for poor Leslie, anchored to her earth and floundering about in his ordered mind, and she understood that never before had the void between her world and his felt so vast.

64

Resting Place

By the time she reached the Anglican cemetery, morning light was beginning to bleed through the purple sky, although the outline of a slender crescent of moon was still visible. She saw nobody on the short walk from the Paz Hotel, except the occasional servant shuffling unhurriedly to work. Once she reached her destination, she noticed a mongrel bounding excitedly through the tombstones with a carefree glee illuminating its yellow eyes. She stood at the entrance gap, where she remembered there used to be a gate, and she could see that the ramshackle stone wall which surrounded the cemetery appeared to be tumbling down of its own accord. She knew that unless tropical cemeteries were maintained with great vigilance, such places had a tendency to quickly return to nature, and in Roseau only the much larger, and impeccably presented, Catholic cemetery seemed to be winning the fight. As the dog finally disappeared from view, and the sky began now to flood with light, she was able to make out some wilting flowers and curled wreaths, which announced a recent Anglican loss.

Entering the cemetery, she saw her father's weed-choked gravesite to her immediate left. On top of the slab an ancient-looking urn was crammed with brown, flowerless stems that she construed might snap with the lightest pinch of finger and thumb, and above both slab and urn a large stone Celtic Cross listed considerably off the vertical, but it was still possible for her to read the inscribed words, for they were emboldened with lead.

IN LOVING MEMORY
WILLIAM POTTS REES WILLIAMS
BORN IN CARNARVON, NORTH WALES
29TH SEPT. 1853
ENTERED INTO REST 19TH JUNE 1910
FOR 29 YEARS
MEDICAL OFFICER IN DOMINICA

She took a white cotton handkerchief from her sleeve and with one corner began to slowly clean each letter so that new life was affectionately rubbed into each word. Halfway through the task she became aware that she had an audience. The elderly Negro was barefoot and stood with a hand of ripe bananas balanced securely on his head. He had positioned himself some few yards away from her on the main pathway that cut through the heart of the cemetery and he stuttered slightly as he began to speak.

"Mistress, I place you. I believe you is the Williams girl from Cork Street?"

She stopped polishing the lead and looked up at the

grey-haired laggard, who was now grinning as though the fact that he had recognized her gave them both some special bond.

"And you are?"

He ignored her question and addressed the itch on the instep of one of his thickly calloused feet by scraping it against the dirt. Having solved the problem, he continued to beam as the sun began now to beat down on them both.

"Mistress, I can do that work for you."

She had forgotten to bring a hat and knew that the walk back to the hotel would be uncomfortable, but the sooner she finished her task, the sooner she would be able to leave her father in peace.

"Thank you, but I can manage quite well."

The Negro nodded, but continued to grin. As she once again rubbed a begrimed letter, she could feel the man watching her, but she was satisfied that he meant her no harm. If he maintained his distance she would, at the completion of her task, offer the Negro a handful of coins. Her father would, of course, have deemed it the right and proper thing to do.

65

Leaving

Just before the launch was due to leave Dominica, its captain sounded two loud whistles, which stopped traffic all along the bayfront. Throughout the length and breadth of the small capital people ceased what they were doing and listened to the sad wailing echo that hung in the air. Down by the pier, those who would remain raised their hands and squinted at friends and loved ones on deck who were leaning up against the railing and waving back their own farewells. Then, after a third and final blast of the whistle, the modest craft began to labour away from the island and inch its slow and circumspect passage past the flotilla of fishing boats beating a path home at dusk. Once clear of the small fleet, those on land could now see the launch beginning to move purposefully towards the horizon, where it would eventually slip out of sight and tumble down into a landless, watery world.

She was standing on deck when she heard the initial double blast of the whistle, and her heart quickened. But she understood that weeping for unrequited love is hopeless, for only one person suffers. She also understood that it is not enough to be recognized. The human soul demands more nourishment than mere recognition. As the launch picked up speed, she looked back at the vastness of the mountain range which hovered over the children's village that passed for a capital, and she realized that she was suffused with the kind of love that is impossible to explain to another person. Her island had both arranged and rearranged her, and she had no words. She dare not turn to face Leslie, who had informed her that he had spent the greater part of the early morning worrying about her absence, and at one point seriously considered informing the authorities. Now Leslie was standing tall by her side, and she could feel him leaning close to her and trying desperately to see whatever it was she was seeing. She turned and beheld him and smiled. She has been fortunate in dear Leslie, but pity would be an uncharitable gift. She took his hand and held it in one of her own, and then she turned back to her island and looked again at her mountains and rivers and quietly, without Leslie noticing, she broke off a piece of her heart and gently dropped it into the blue water.